D1172603

DECEPTION

BOOK II OF THE DARK MATTER TRILOGY

TERI TERRY

Published by Charlesbridge
85 Main Street, Watertown, MA 02472
(617) 926-0329 • www.charlesbridge.com

First published in 2018 by Orchard Books
An imprint of Hachette Children's Group
Part of The Watts Publishing Group Limited
Carmelite House
50 Victoria Embankment
London EC4Y 0DZ
An Hachette UK Company
www.hachette.co.uk
www.hachettechildrens.co.uk

Library of Congress Cataloging-in-Publication Data
Names: Terry, Teri, author.
Title: Deception / by Teri Terry.
Description: Watertown, MA: Charlesbridge, [2019] | Series: Dark matter trilogy; book 2 | "Orchard Books." | "First published in Great Britain in 2018 by The Watts Publishing Group"–Copyright page. |
Summary: "Believing that she is a carrier of the deadly disease they are calling the Aberdeen flu, Shay has surrendered herself to government armed forces and, along with other survivors, becomes an unwilling test subject in the effort to find a cure; but when the lab is attacked, she and a few of the others with the strongest supernatural abilities escape, and her boyfriend Kai is determined to find her, while ghostly Callie, the true carrier, will atone for her deception."–Provided by publisher.
Identifiers: LCCN 2018037920 (print) | LCCN 2018049079 (ebook) | ISBN 9781632898654 (ebook) | ISBN 9781623541064 (reinforced for library use)
Subjects: LCSH: Epidemics–Juvenile fiction. | Human experimentation in medicine–Juvenile fiction. | Carrier state (Communicable diseases)–Juvenile fiction. | Genetic engineering–Juvenile fiction. | Identity (Psychology)–Juvenile fiction. | Brothers and sisters–Juvenile fiction. | Science fiction. | Great Britain–Juvenile fiction. | CYAC: Science fiction. | Epidemics–Fiction. | Human experimentation in medicine–Fiction. | Diseases–Fiction. | Genetic engineering–Fiction. | Identity–Fiction. | Brothers and sisters–Fiction. | Great Britain–Fiction. | LCGFT: Science fiction.
Classification: LCC PZ7.T2815 (ebook) | LCC PZ7.T2815 De 2019 (print) | DDC 813.6 [Fic] –dc23
LC record available at https://lccn.loc.gov/2018037920

Printed in the United States
(hc) 10 9 8 7 6 5 4 3 2 1

Display type set in S&S Amberosa Sans by Gilang Purnama Jaya
Text type set in Stempel Garamond by Adobe
Printed by Berryville Graphics in Berryville, Virginia, USA
Production supervision by Brian G. Walker
Jacket and map art by Sarah Richards Taylor
Designed by Sarah Richards Taylor

The stages of deception–shock, outrage, examination, tolerance, and acceptance–inevitably lead to veneration. Deception can serve truth as well as truth can unseat deception . . . it's all a matter of perspective.

—Xander, *Multiverse Manifesto*

SCOTLAND
NEWCASTLE UPON TYNE
PENRITH
MIDDLEBROUGH
DARLINGTON
NORTH YORK MOORS
NORTH SEA
MATLOCK
CHESTER
ENGLAND
BIRMINGHAM
LONDON
CELTIC SEA

GREAT BRITAIN

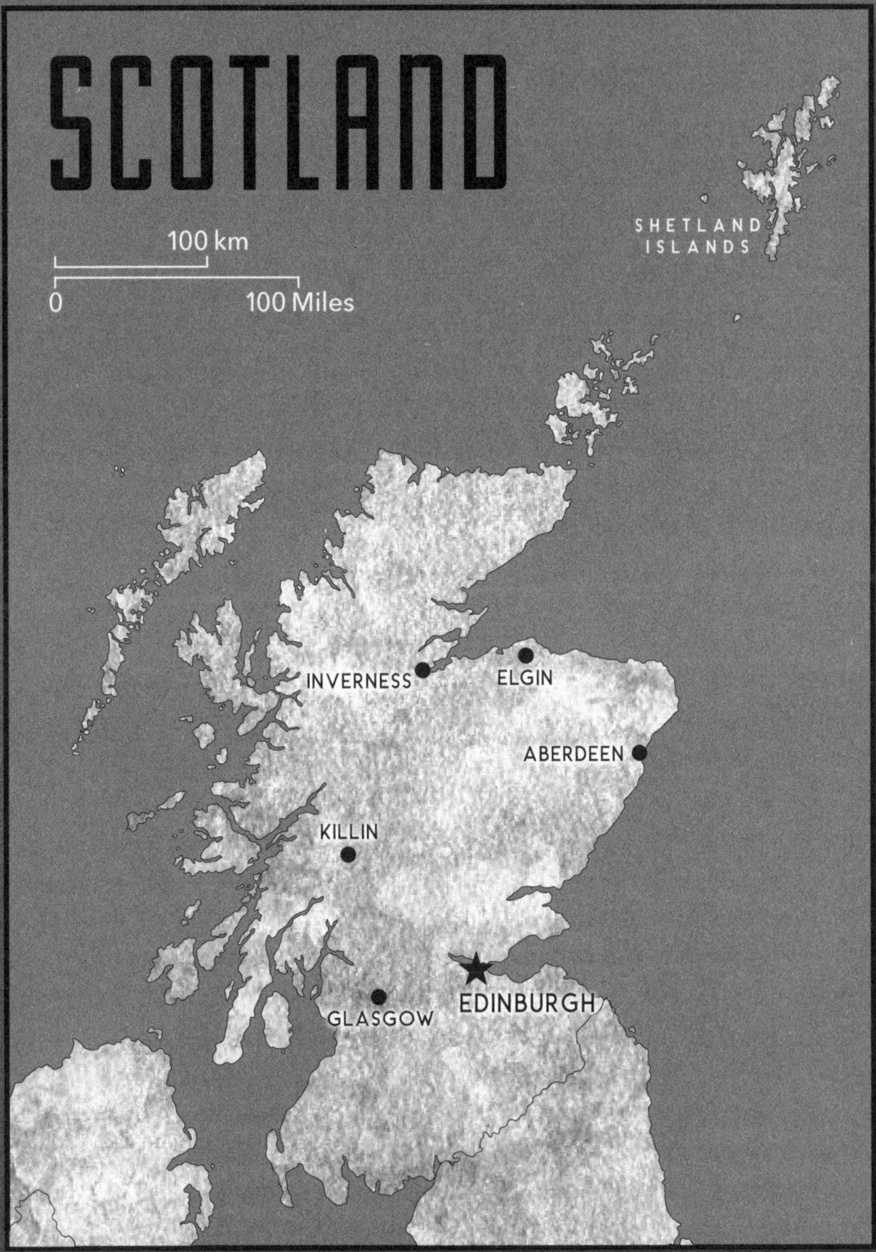

SCOTLAND

100 km
0
100 Miles

SHETLAND ISLANDS

INVERNESS
ELGIN
ABERDEEN
KILLIN
GLASGOW
EDINBURGH

100 km
100 Miles

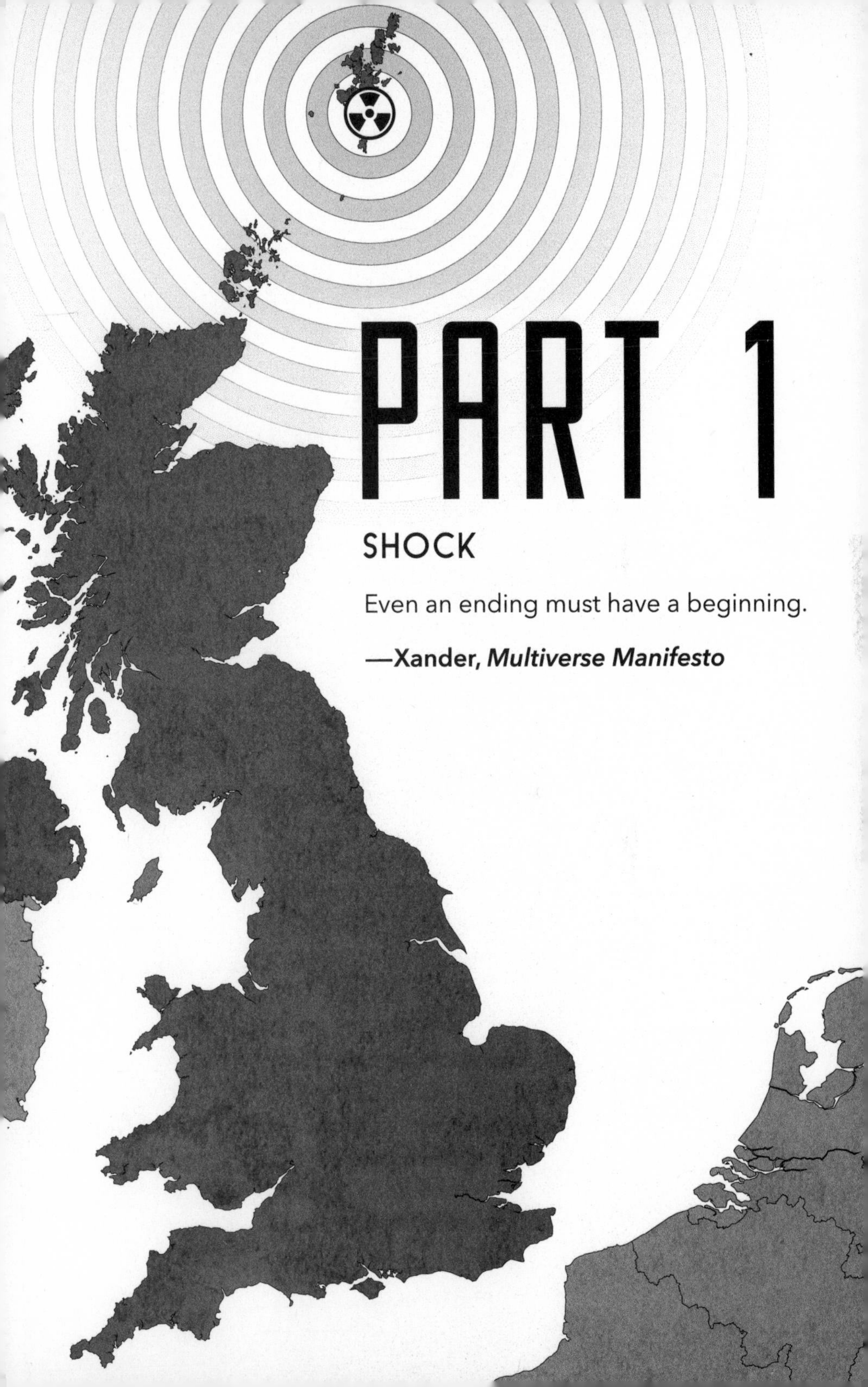

PART 1

SHOCK

Even an ending must have a beginning.

—Xander, *Multiverse Manifesto*

CHAPTER 1

CALLIE

I PANIC WHEN I RETURN to the house and my brother, Kai, isn't inside. Has he vanished while I was searching for Shay? Have they both left me behind?

But I soon find him behind the house, standing on the cliff and gazing at the sea. His arms are crossed, his body rigid. He stares at the waves breaking on the rocks far below, like he is thinking of joining them.

I'm afraid.

Don't leave me too, Kai. I need you. I say the words even though I know he can't hear me. Shay wasn't just Kai's girlfriend and my friend: she was also the only one who could see or hear me. Now that she's gone, I'm powerless to reach him.

I place myself between him and the cliff's edge. If I move close to him, I feel a resistance, the same as if I push against anything—a person, a rock, a door. They all feel the same to me. I stare at his eyes. They are hazel—almost green now in the sun—and are full of rage and pain. He is my brother, and there is nothing I can do to help him. Nothing I could do to stop him if he decided to step over the edge. I could go with him, fly down the cliff, watch his body smash on the rocks and break and bleed and die, but I would just go on and on.

It's hard to die when you're already dead.

But I'm hurting too. Shay left *both* of us. I want to tell him this, and the frustration of not being seen or heard makes me howl and wave my fists at the sea.

Kai looks toward me, his eyes startled. Did he hear something?

When I screamed in the underground institute at the techs who vacuumed up my ashes after Dr. 1 had me cured in fire, they jumped. Then later one of them whistled along when I sang. Maybe Kai *can* hear me, even if only a little?

Kai! I'm here! I shout the words out with all that I am.

He frowns, then shakes his head and turns and walks back to the house.

Maybe he can sense me, at least a little, but he doesn't believe it. At least I've interrupted whatever he was thinking as he stared at the rocks and the sea.

Inside, he paces back and forth. He reaches into his pocket and takes out a letter. It looks all crinkled, like he'd rolled it into a ball and then smoothed it out again. He looks at it, but moves it around too fast for me to see what it says.

He stuffs it back in his pocket and flops onto the sofa.

"Callie, are you there?"

I'm here, I'm here! I want to cry when I hear his voice, when I hear him say "Callie."

"Shay's left. She says she didn't take you with her, that you'd want to stay with me. That I should talk to you." He wraps his arms around himself like he's trying to hold something in.

"She's gone to turn herself in at the air force base, to tell them she's a carrier and that the epidemic started here in Shetland. In case . . . in case that goes wrong, she says we shouldn't follow. We should leave the island and go back to the mainland. Tell everyone we can about the origin and spread of the epidemic and don't let them cover it up.

"She says that I should tell you that she's *sorry*." His voice is bitter with anger. "Like being sorry makes it all right!" He raises his hand in a fist, but then his body seems to collapse in on itself. "Shay, how could you?" he whispers. He fights it, but his shoulders are shaking.

And . . . and . . . he's crying. Kai—my big brother—is *crying*?

This is so *wrong*. It makes me twist up inside like I'm about to cry too, but tears are something I don't have anymore. And even worse, there is a horrible feeling gnawing inside me.

It's my fault. Isn't it?

It's my fault Shay left. She thought she was contagious, that everyone—including her mother—caught *it* from her and got sick and died. I let her think this; I didn't tell her the truth.

I didn't tell her that it was *me* who was the carrier all along. It never occurred to her, what with me being dead: who ever heard of a contagious ghost? But all the major centers of the epidemic—from the beginning when it spread from Shetland to Aberdeen, then to Edinburgh, and then to Newcastle and beyond—were places I'd been. The disease always hit soon after I was there: it had to be me.

Later, when Shay got sick and survived, she could see and hear me. She was the only one who could after I was cured—apart from the dying. After that, the disease did follow wherever she went—but only because I was there too. She'd never even been to Aberdeen or Newcastle. She'd explained that away by saying there must have been other survivors in those places, but I never found any when I was there.

She would never have left Kai and me if I had told her the truth, but . . .

No!

It's not my fault; none of it. Everything goes back to Dr. 1. He's the one who did this to me. He's the doctor who gave me the illness in his lab underground—and when I survived and changed, he cured me in fire and turned me into whatever it is that I am now.

It's his fault.

Everything I've done from the beginning—getting Kai and Shay to come to this house on Shetland to find the source of the epidemic, and then not telling Shay that it's me who is the carrier, not her—was all to get at Dr. 1.

I wanted to go with Shay. Once she tells the government that Dr. 1 is the one who started the epidemic, they'll hunt him down. I want to be there when they find him. That's why I couldn't tell her the truth—she wouldn't have turned herself in if she'd known she wasn't the carrier.

But she left without me.

Why? Why didn't she take me with her?

Kai cries, and the rage and heat inside me strengthens, grows—a fury that could destroy and swallow the world.

Dr. 1 must pay for what he's done.

CHAPTER 2

SHAY

BEFORE I CAN FINALLY take off the biohazard suit that the soldiers made me wear, I'm locked in a small, sealed room. Even without the suit, the claustrophobic feeling of not being able to breathe fully is still there. One wall of the room is glass—very thick glass.

Dr. Morgan is on the other side of this transparent wall with two men—older ones, not the same ones who came out to get me earlier. All three are in uniform. They're talking, but I can't hear them.

I knock on the glass. They continue talking, but then a moment later Dr. Morgan reaches for some controls, and I can hear them clearly.

"Hello, Shay. Sorry about the barrier." She gestures at the wall between us. "Are you more comfortable without the suit?"

I shrug. "Sure. Yes."

She smiles, but there is an edge to it.

"Now, Shay, we've found out a few things about you." She looks at a tablet in her hands. "Such as . . . you are wanted in connection with a murder. Also, it says here that you were reported as immune?"

"I didn't kill anybody!" Then I realize that's not true: many, many people have died because of me, haven't they? I sigh and cross my arms. "I mean, I didn't shoot that boy they say I did."

She nods, a careful look on her face, disbelief in her aura.

No. *No way.* Are they not going to believe anything I say because I was framed by SAR?

I grip the edges of the table between me and the glass and lean forward. "Listen to me. You have to listen."

"We're listening," she says.

"I had the flu. I thought I was going to die. My mother did die." I push the pain away. "And we went back to Killin—"

"We? That'd be you and Kai Tanzer, currently also wanted after mysteriously going missing from a police cell in Inverness? Do you know where he is now?"

"No. Anyway, I said I was immune, like Kai. We helped at the hospital tent in Killin. Then this creepy lieutenant from SAR—"

"SAR?"

"Special Alternatives Regiment of the army."

She half raises an eyebrow, and I can see it: she's never heard of this regiment. How can that be? I know this is an air force base, not an army one, but I wouldn't have thought they were so separate that they didn't know the names of each other's regiments.

"Anyhow, this lieutenant—Kirkland-Smith, he said his name was—came looking for me and said he knew I was a survivor and that SAR was taking me away to help study the epidemic, but he was lying. They wanted to kill me."

"How did you know he was lying?"

"I just did."

"I see. Try this, Shay: I'll tell you two things—one a lie, and one the truth—and you tell me which is which."

"Seriously? Aren't there more important things to be—"

"Humor me. Please."

I stare back at her, then shrug my shoulders. I'll go along with anything if it'll help them believe me. "Okay, fine," I say.

"All right. My middle name is Hannah. My middle name is Helen." As she speaks, I study her aura—the waves of color that surround her, that are unique to her—as it changes with her thoughts and feelings. When she says "Helen," there are ripples of silver blue, and I feel the truth within them. When she says "Hannah," her aura is disturbed, with slashes of mustard and green—it's a lie.

"You lied about Hannah; your middle name is Helen."

"That's just a fifty-fifty guess," one of the men says. They've been silent until now. "Try again," he says, and gives me a list of ten possible middle names for himself.

I roll my eyes. "Your middle name is Monteroy. Congratulations on middle-name weirdness. Can we carry on now?"

He nods.

"Impressive," Dr. Morgan says. "Okay, so let's just assume you knew this lieutenant was lying. And then?"

"I ran away. They shot at me and hit me in the ear."

"That wasn't that long ago. I didn't notice any injury."

I shrug. "I healed it."

"Really."

"Oh, for . . . Look." I bite my lip, hard. A trickle of blood runs down my face, and the pain helps me to focus, to keep my temper.

"See? I'm bleeding." And then I close my eyes and *reach* for the pain, reach inside me: to the blood and tissue and their components, down to a cellular level, then molecular, and atomic. Atoms are made up of particles: particles that can behave as waves—waves that can be influenced and changed. I heal my lip and wipe off the blood from before. The cut is gone. "And now I'm not."

Dr. Morgan frowns. "I don't know what trick that is, but—"

"It's not a trick. It's part of being a survivor."

Her aura shifts; she's pleased. She's pleased I confirmed this?

"All right, then," she says, "let's say you are a survivor. Now let's get back to this boy you shot—"

"I didn't shoot anybody! A soldier from SAR shot at me, and Duncan pushed me out of the way and saved my life. The *soldier* shot Duncan."

"Really?" She doesn't believe me. If she doesn't believe that, how will she believe anything else?

After everything I've been through, after having to leave Kai—I push that pain away too, to save it for later—could it come down to this? That they won't believe me? I focus on Dr. Morgan; disbelief shimmers through her aura.

And on top of everything else, I'm tired, hungry, and getting more and more angry with these word games. "Now you three are going to sit there and listen. Not another word, all right?" Tendrils of my anger whip out and find the part of their auras that allows their free will to speak, to form words, to stand up—to do anything, really—and I hold it fast. *All* they can do is listen.

And I tell them *everything*. About SAR kidnapping Kai to try to trap me; about how I rescued him; about how we got away. That I came to Shetland to trace the cause of the epidemic. About the boat trip across to the island and the plague ship. About Dr. 1 and the research institute underground and what he was doing there with a particle accelerator: making and extracting quantum particles of some kind and using them as a biological weapon. He tested whatever he created on subjects and killed people. That it got out, and this is how the epidemic started. And then I tell them everywhere I've been and when, as the epidemic followed me across the country about a day behind. I leave out that Callie and Kai came here with me, but I tell them everything else.

When I finally stop talking, I'm exhausted—both from reliving the tale and from the effort of influencing all three of them at once. I release them.

"What did you do to us?" Dr. Morgan asks, her eyes round.

"You wouldn't listen. I made you listen."

There is fear on their faces, clear enough without even looking at their auras. They get up and almost run out a door on their side of the glass.

At least they listened.

Uneasy, I wrap my arms around myself. Maybe that display wasn't such a good idea. Maybe I'd have been better off keeping the things

I can do to myself. But I didn't *plan* to do that. I was angry, and it just sort of happened.

Too late to second-guess it now.

Someone comes to the door just as I'm falling asleep in the chair. He's in a full biohazard suit and goes through the double airlock into my small room.

"Hi, Shay. I'm here to help you put on your suit."

"And then what?"

"We're flying you to England, to talk to some experts there about the Aberdeen flu."

The knots inside me loosen. Did they believe at least part of what I said?

I get up, and he holds out the suit; I step into it. Again I have to fight the automatic urge to push it away, to stop his hands doing up the seals.

"I'll just adjust the ventilation," he says, and does something to the top of the suit before snapping it closed over my head. I'm so distracted by not wanting to be closed up inside of this thing that by the time I notice the deception in his aura, it's too late.

There's a funny taste and smell inside my suit. My head spins.

"What . . . what have you . . . done?" I manage to whisper the words, but the world is lurching—I'm falling. Like he was expecting this, he's there, ready, and I feel his hands through the suit catching me.

Everything goes black.

CHAPTER 3

CALLIE

THE NEXT MORNING Kai has Shay's letter out again, but this time he uses it to copy the username and password to log on to a website. It's JIT, the one set up by Shay's best friend, Iona, who blogs about all kinds of weird stuff that she thinks may be news. Shay said that Iona wants to be a journalist and that JIT stands for journalist-in-training.

At the top of the blog list is a draft post, the sort you can only see by logging in; it won't be public on the internet. Its title is "Shay??"

He clicks on it.

Iona: Shay, answer me! Don't do this—it's too dangerous. And how can you be sure you're a carrier? Shay?

Jealousy surges through me. Shay said she was my friend, but she left without me; she left without even saying goodbye. But she told Iona everything, didn't she?

Kai sighs and clicks "edit."

Kai: Iona—this is Kai. It's too late. She's gone.

He saves it. Waits a moment. Is Iona online? He hits "refresh," and a new edit appears.

Iona: No no no. Is she all right? How could you let her go?

Kai: I didn't let her do anything. She left when I was asleep. Left me a letter with the login for JIT. Told me not to follow her, to go back to mainland Scotland and spread the word about the cause of the epidemic.

He hits "refresh" again. And again. Finally, a response.

Iona: She makes sense. But . . .

Kai: Maybe. I don't care if it makes sense. It's wrong.

Iona: What are you going to do?

Kai: I'm going to go to the air force base. I've thought all night, and I have to find out if she's all right or I'll go insane. I wanted to tell you so somebody knew, in case . . . well. You know.

Iona: Okay, I understand. Get in touch when you can. Be careful.

Kai washes quickly, dresses. Eats some crackers and canned fruit out of the cupboards. There's not much left here; he'll have to leave soon no matter what, as there will be nothing to eat.

Yesterday's sunshine is gone. Dark clouds scuttle across the sky, and it's drizzling. As he walks across this untouched part of the island, then over the sand to the burned wasteland that is most of the rest of it, the rain comes down harder. He keeps walking.

I'm scared. What will they do to him when he gets there?

What did they do to Shay?

Maybe when I was searching the island for her, I couldn't sense her because . . . because . . . I was too late. Maybe they shot her like that SAR lieutenant tried to do before.

The air force base is miles away. By the time we get there, Kai is soaked. The base is quiet; there aren't any people moving around like there were when I came here the day before to look for Shay.

Kai walks up to the gate. That's odd: there isn't anyone on guard duty like there was yesterday either. Kai peers through, looks around, then opens the gate.

He walks across the road to the first temporary building.

He knocks, opens the door. "Hello?" he calls out. There's no answer. It's as if they've all left, or—

I stop when it hits me.

Yesterday I searched the whole base for Shay, didn't I? There were people everywhere then, people I went up close to. I was so focused on trying to find Shay that I didn't even think about what I was doing or what might happen to them.

Kai continues on to another, larger building. When I follow, that is when I start to hear it: the pain.

It is here.

He hesitates, like he can hear it too. Then he goes in.

This is where everyone is. There are the cries and the silences—the dying and the dead, and I'm full of horror. *I did this.* I've done it before, many times, many places, but that was before I had worked it out—before I knew that I was the carrier. That I was the one who made people suffer and die.

Kai, horror in the set of his face, hesitates by the door. Some of the ill are with it enough to notice he is there, to turn and stare.

"Leave," one says in a weak voice. "Before you catch it."

Kai walks over to the man's camp bed and kneels down.

"I'm immune. I can't catch it."

"Lucky you."

"Maybe you can help me, though. Someone I know—a girl, Shay McAllister—came here, and—"

"That bitch," the man says, and Kai recoils. "She did this to us. All of us. They put her in a suit, but it mustn't have been soon enough to stop it spreading." His face screws up with pain, then clears. He stares at me. "Who are you?"

I'm Callie. Tell Kai I'm here!

His eyes move from me to Kai and back again. "Callie says she's here."

Kai is shocked. "You can see her?"

It's because you're dying.

"Yes. Callie says it's because I'm dying. What a surprise."

"Where is Shay?" Kai says. "What have you done to her?"

"Nothing. But if I'd only known, I would have shot her myself. They flew her off Shetland before this hit."

"Where did they take her?"

"I don't know—I heard it was to some secret air force base out of the quarantine zone. Wherever it is, they're in trouble."

The whole time that he talks to Kai, he stares at me. "What are you?" he finally says, still staring.

I stare back at him and move closer. He's on the very edge of death now.

Don't talk about Shay like that. I'm your worst nightmare, not her. I spread the disease that is killing you.

I see the understanding register in his eyes just as the blood starts to come out of them. And then he's still. Dead. After what he said about Shay, I don't even care.

Kai looks around the room, shakes his head. Walks for the door, fast, as if he wants to run away from what he has seen and heard.

"Come on, Callie," he says. "There's nothing we can do to help them now. At least we know Shay isn't here anymore and we can leave Shetland."

Anywhere is good, so long as it is off this island. I *hate* being here. But if we leave, will what happened to me here always stick to me like filth, inside, wherever I go? Filth that spreads out and causes suffering all around me?

"So, we have to go back over the sea," Kai says. "Just like Shay told us to do." He swears under his breath and starts striding out, putting distance between us and the dead and the dying.

Kai pauses on the top of the hill, turns, and looks back. "Did they really catch that from her?" His face is pale.

"Oh, Shay," he murmurs under his breath. "What now?"

CHAPTER 4

SHAY

THERE IS SOMETHING MORE than the nothing that came before it. Some awareness, some sense of my body, that I'm breathing deep and even, and I'm completely, deliciously relaxed. I push these sensations away; I don't want them. I want to go back to floating in nothingness. In *nothing*, there is no pain, no loss, no decisions to make or actions to carry out. I want to stay there.

There is a dim sound: a click.

I swallow. My mouth is dry, tastes funny, and—

Awareness floods back. Was I drugged? Where am I? I struggle to move, to open my eyes, but even my eyelids are heavy.

Instead, I *reach* out to what is around me without using my ordinary senses.

Nothing.

Nothing? How can there be no life of any sort around me?

Panic gives me the energy to open my eyes, to stir. I swallow again and cough.

I'm in a small room on a narrow bed. There's a toilet in the corner, a sink, a blanket over me. And that is it.

There is *nothing* I can reach: no humans or animals or insects, not even a solitary spider.

I struggle to sit up. My head is pounding, and I'm thirsty. There's a plastic cup on the side of the sink. I reach out, turn on the tap, and fill it. My hands are a little shaky and water slops as I drink, leaving a cold trail down my front.

I reach down to brush at the water I spilled on myself, and there is a further shock: I'm wearing some sort of shapeless gown, like from a hospital, and nothing else. Someone took off my clothes and put me in this while I was unconscious?

My skin is crawling. I feel sick. I wrap my arms around myself, but that isn't enough. I grab the blanket and wrap that around me too.

I have this creepy-crawly sensation like there is someone watching me, even though I can't sense anyone there. My eyes hunt around, and every wall looks even, solid—the ceiling and floor too.

That's when I realize there are no windows or doors; at least, none that I can see. There must be: how else did I get in here?

That weird feeling of being watched is still on my skin, as if eyes leave fingerprints I can feel. Could there be a hidden watcher?

I swallow again.

"Hello?" I say tentatively. My voice feels rusty, like I haven't used it for a while.

I try again, and this time it is stronger: "Hello? Is there anybody there?"

My voice seems to echo off the bare walls, ceiling, and floor before bouncing back to my ears.

No one answers. Can't anyone hear me?

Panic is rising up inside, waves that build and build, and I'm shaking. Where am I? I don't want to be here.

"Let me out of here! Let me out!"

I say it loud, and louder again, until I'm screaming.

CHAPTER 5

CALLIE

KAI'S HANDS ARE SHAKING as he types a message on JIT for Iona.

Kai: Everyone I saw at the air force base had the flu or was already dead. They think they caught it from Shay. One of them told me she was flown off Shetland last night before they started getting sick.

He hits "save" and has a long drink from a bottle of red wine that he found in the back of a cupboard.

Iona: So . . . she was right? She's definitely a carrier?

Kai: It looks that way. Her reasoning before was sound too. I just didn't want to believe it.

Iona: Me neither. Any idea where they may have taken her?

Kai: The one I spoke to said it was to a secret air force base outside the quarantine zone, but he didn't know where it was. It could be anywhere.

Iona: Okay. I'll do some research, see if I can narrow that down a little. What are you going to do now?

Kai has another drink from the bottle.

Kai: Leave Shetland, like Shay said. I have to try to find her. And the doctor who is responsible for all of this.

Iona: How will you get back here?

Kai: The people on the boat that brought us said to return to the cave they hide in during the day and wait for a ride back. But that boat didn't make it: they all died of the flu.

Iona: I know. Shay told me.

Kai: But I'm sure they said there's more than one boat that goes there, so I'll go and wait, see if one shows up. I don't know what else to try.

Iona: Okay. If that doesn't work, let me know; I'll see if I can find out anything about other ways off Shetland. But there's just one problem.

Kai: Only one?

Iona: I was going to suggest destroying the laptop you are using, or throwing it in the sea–to make sure that if the owner returns, they can't trace what you've done on it and track us down. But you can't do that if you might need to use it again.

Iona starts giving Kai detailed instructions for erasing history off the computer once they're finished, and I drift away.

My original excitement that Kai knew for sure I'm with him has faded. He still can't hear me, and he seems to have forgotten to talk to me since we left the air force base, even though that guy told him I was there.

I go outside. The sun is low in the sky, though it isn't dark, not really. Shay said this far north in the summer, it doesn't get dark—just dim. The summer dim, she called it.

The rain has stopped—not that I care—and I stand on the cliff where I found Kai yesterday. I can't feel the wind, but I can see it is there in the fierce shaking of the long grass, the white froth of the angry sea below.

On impulse I dive off the cliff, down, down, down . . .

Then I stop and hang in midair, just where the waves break on the rocks. Spray flies all around me.

In the thin light, I can see my hands if I hold them up: an outline of darkness. Water splashes through them as if they're not there, and I can't even feel it.

I'm weighed down with not being able to touch, to feel. I drop lower and slide into the water. Rocks under the waves stretch out from the cliff, and they stop me from going down farther; the water doesn't. It should be cold, but there is no feeling of that either.

If I could dive off a cliff like Kai could and have everything just *stop*—would I?

Darkness. Death. That's all I am. I could stay here alone forever and who would care? Kai only knew I was here because Shay told him; if I left now, he wouldn't even know the difference.

Without Shay there to tell her, my mum didn't know I was there either. I had to leave her to go with Kai. The loss is an ache that stretches on and on.

And my father? I can't even remember him. I know his name, from things Shay and Kai said—Dr. Alex Cross. He was Kai's stepfather, and Kai hates him. Kai thinks he had something to do with what happened to me, though Shay and my mum didn't seem to agree. But what does that matter if I don't even remember anything about him?

I have nothing.

But there is one thing *more* that I am; something that I know will pull me away from this place and off the island. It still feels hot inside me even though the cold of this water and the warmth of the sun are things I can't feel anymore.

Hot, red, and strong:

Anger.

There is a distant crash up above.

Kai?

Panic has me blur back up to the top of the cliff and into the house. He stands there in the front room, red spreading on the light carpet, splashed across the wall, but he's all right—it isn't blood. It's wine. Broken glass is scattered from one side of the room to the other. He must have thrown what was left of that bottle of wine against the wall with a lot of force to make as much mess as this.

His fists are clenched, and even though he can't feel me, I stand next to him, hold my fists next to his.

He can't hear me, he can't see me, but we are in this together.

Anger isn't a big enough word to cover how Dr. 1 makes me feel. He made this illness that changed Shay and me; he cured me too—burned me in fire to make me what I am now.

Together, Kai and I will find him and make him suffer.

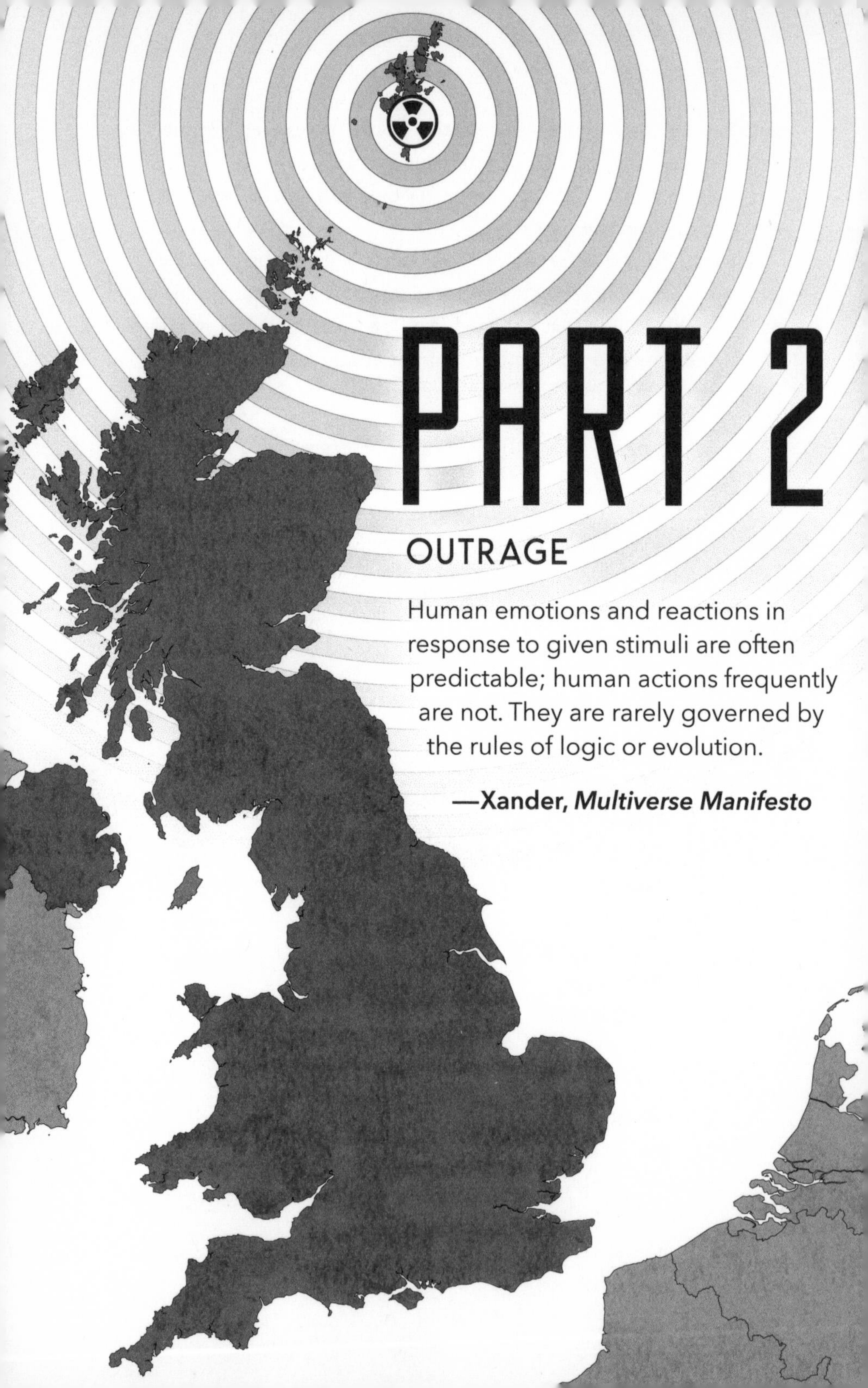

PART 2

OUTRAGE

Human emotions and reactions in response to given stimuli are often predictable; human actions frequently are not. They are rarely governed by the rules of logic or evolution.

—Xander, *Multiverse Manifesto*

CHAPTER 1

KAI

IT IS BETTER TO MOVE. The rain is good too—being cold and wet gives me something else to feel.

The tight feeling across my chest is still there, but when I'm walking fast like I am now, I have to keep breathing to keep moving; my heart must keep beating.

I won't fail again. *I can't.*

Shay, I will find you.

And then? What then?

Then can wait. Find her—find her first.

My feet falter when I reach the grassy place above the cliffs where Shay fell asleep against my shoulder in the sun after we climbed up from the beach.

I can feel her body, warm and curled against mine, and smell her hair, still damp from the waterfall—she was just here.

Move. Keep moving.

I start to climb straight down the cliff, not the easier way we came up. The rain has stopped now, but my foot slips on wet rock.

My hands and feet scrabble against rock, and one hand slams into a crevice. There is sharp pain in my palm, but I hold on. My feet search side to side, find a toehold so I can ease weight off my hand. And there's an *almost sound*, like an echo of a shout in my mind, like I thought I heard on that cliff behind the house yesterday.

"Is that you, Callie?" I say. "Don't worry, I'm all right."

I take more care, reach the bottom, then inspect my hand. Just a cut in the fleshy part—a little blood. It's nothing.

Though if Mum were here, she'd be grabbing disinfectant and a bandage. Then I'm remembering cutting myself on Callie's broken glass teddy bear in her room, and Mum cleaning and bandaging it. She said she wished all my hurts were so easy to fix. But they just get worse and worse, don't they?

The tide is farther out than it was when the rowboat left Shay and me here, but the sea isn't as calm. Should I wait to see if it improves? I stare at the water. Keep moving, I decide.

I take off my T-shirt and jeans—wrap them in plastic and put them inside my backpack with the last of the food and bottled water I could find at the house.

One foot in the water, I curse under my breath—it's so bloody cold. Quick in is best, isn't it? I take a few steps to deeper water and dive in.

The shock chokes my breath for real now, and it's hard to reach out with my arms and swim when it is telling me to get out, to wrap something around myself and get warm.

I swim, hard, to try to get some warmth into arms and legs that feel clumsy and numb. The cove is soon behind me and the rocks cleared; the water is getting deeper. Now it's much rougher. The cave is along the coast to the left, but when I try to head in that direction the current fights against me, pushing me across to the right. Instead, I head farther out to sea, away from the island—just edging to the left gradually in ever-rougher water.

Each stroke is getting harder.

Spots dance in my vision.

Exhausted, I close my eyes to rest for a moment, floating, letting the swirling cold water take me where it will. My thoughts are jumpy and scattered. Shay and Mum and Callie's faces flit in and out, and . . .

No!

I jump, open my eyes. That was less of an echo and more of a shout.

"Right, Callie. On we go." I make myself start swimming harder across to the left. The undertow is less now that I'm farther out, and I overshoot the cave on purpose, then start to cut back in to the island. The current strengthens and drags me to the right once again as I swim for the shore.

Gradually the sea quiets. In the shadow of cliffs, I swim for the dark gap in the rocks.

CHAPTER 2

CALLIE

KAI PULLS HIMSELF UP on a rock near the entrance of the cave, breathing heavily, not moving.

I feel like I'm breathing as hard, my heart thumping as fast. He kept going farther out, then just *stopped*—floating in the water, eyes shut, being dragged by the sea away from the island.

He definitely heard me that time. When I screamed at him to swim to the shore, he actually jumped. Then I was really scared: people only hear me if they're about to die. How close was he to giving up?

I'm so focused on Kai, on watching the movement of his chest as he breathes, that at first I don't see it.

Farther inside the cave behind us.

It's a boat. It's nothing like the one we came here in, not at all. It's white, sleek, and pretty, while the other one was rough and heavy. The sails are down now, but that is what it is: a sailboat.

It's quiet. Is anyone there?

Kai is stirring behind me now.

He sits up on the rock, still breathing hard, and his eyes must have adjusted to the darkness by now. He sees it, he must see it. He turns toward it. His eyes widen.

The water inside the cave is almost still. Kai slips back into it and swims the few strokes to where the boat is tied. He clambers onto the rocks next to it.

"Hello?" he says.

There is no sound.

He's shivering even more violently now, goose bumps standing up on his arms and legs. He takes off the backpack and gets his clothes out, then struggles to pull them on as they stick to his wet skin.

"Hello?" he says again, then covers his nose and mouth with his hand like something smells bad.

I slip into the boat.

It doesn't take long to find them.

Three red-haired children. A woman with long red hair, lying next to them. Their eyes are open, staring; dark, dried blood around them. They've been dead a while.

And sitting next to them? A man. Alive. He would be tall if stretched out, but he is folded in on himself on the deck. His arms are wrapped around his knees, and he's humming quietly, eyes closed, his body rocking back and forth.

Can you hear me? I try. No flicker of response, so either he's ignoring me or he's not dying himself.

Kai climbs up the short ladder by the rocks and looks into the boat. His white face goes even paler.

CHAPTER 3

KAI

I CLEAR MY THROAT. “Hello. Can I come aboard?”

No answer. The only sounds are the gentle lapping of the water and bird calls, muted, from outside the cave. And the tuneless humming from the man who ignores me. Eyes closed, he rocks slightly back and forth next to what must be his family—they were his family. I try to avert my eyes, but they are drawn again and again.

I’ve seen the dead—bodies of all ages, shapes, and sizes that I carried to the pyres, first in Newcastle, then in Killin. I could close myself off to what they were and do what had to be done, but they always came back to haunt me at odd moments—lurking in corners of my mind, appearing in my dreams late at night.

But not like this. He’s arranged them together at his feet, on the deck, and they’ve been there for some time. There is decay, and the particular horrifying smell of rotting flesh, and my senses are imprinted with things I know will stay inside in places I don’t want to visit but will again and again.

This boat is a mausoleum, and I want to back away.

But I can't leave him.

He hasn't gotten sick in however long they've been like this; he must be immune like I am. To leave him would be for him to starve and die slowly, alone with their ghosts.

I climb into the boat. Stepping away from them and focusing on him, I keep my eyes on his thin shoulders, dark hair. His head is turned down.

"What's your name?" I say.

He doesn't look up. There's no answer, but there is a small break in his humming. It resumes again.

"I'm Kai."

This time his head moves a little. His eyes flick up to me, then slide away.

I maneuver myself to sit down next to him and lean against the railing, with him between them and me. "Were they your family? I'm sorry."

No response. He hums a little louder, as if trying to block me out.

"Do you need a drink?" I get a water bottle from my pack, hold it out, and then touch the man's shoulder. He flinches and looks up.

"Here." I hold the water bottle by his mouth and angle it back a little so it splashes his lips. He licks his lips, tilts his head back, and I hold up the bottle so he can have a proper drink. He swallows, coughs, and then turns his head away from the bottle.

"This is wrong," he whispers. "I'm waiting to die. That won't help."

"You're not sick, though, are you?" He shakes his head slightly. "You must be immune like me."

No answer. His arms are wrapped back around his knees, his body still rocking.

I lean back against the side of the boat.

There is nothing I can do to help him, nothing I can even imagine about the pain he is in right now. And then my blood is rushing, my muscles clenching, and I'm *angry*, full of red-rage fury—at what has happened to this man's family, to Callie, to so many people; all the bodies I carried to the pyres. Back in England and the rest of Scotland, it's probably even worse now.

And somebody did this.

It's not an accident of nature, some flu mutation or new virus caught from a mosquito or a monkey in a forest—somebody *made* this happen.

I swear loudly.

He turns, looks at me. His humming stops.

I do it again, even louder, and slam my hand down hard on the deck. "It's wrong that this happened to your family. To you. To me. To the world! It's not fair!"

"It's my fault," he says. "Sally wanted to leave ages ago." His voice is hoarse, and I hold out the water bottle. This time he takes it in his hands, has a long drink, and then gives it back. "I wouldn't go, kept thinking things would get sorted out, that they'd find a cure. That we'd be all right. Then when she finally talked me around, it was too late. The kids started to get sick before we were even halfway here."

"But what are you going to do about it?"

"Do about it? What do you mean?"

"Listen to me."

He shakes his head, puts his arms back around his knees, rocking. Humming.

But I tell him: about Shay, that she is a survivor, and why we came to Shetland. Where the illness started: underground in a lab. That someone did it *on purpose*, and that the army is involved somehow—that it's *their* fault, not his. That Shay turned herself in to the air force when she realized she was a carrier. That now we need to leave this island, go back to mainland Scotland, and make sure those responsible are held accountable.

He doesn't look at me the whole time I'm talking. He stays as he is, as if he's pretending I'm not here, he's not here, nothing exists.

When I'm finished, there is silence for a while, a long while.

Then he stops rocking.

He doesn't look up. He says something, but it is muffled against his knees, not loud enough to hear.

"What's that?"

He turns back toward me. His face is still pale, but where all was dull in his eyes before, now there is a trace of a spark, of anger—of fire.

"Bobby. My name is Bobby." He holds out a hand, and I grasp it, hold it tight.

Bobby leans forward against me and cries.

CHAPTER 4

CALLIE

THERE'S A SMALL LIFEBOAT, and that's where they put Bobby's family. Kai tries to help, but Bobby insists on doing it himself and fusses over how to have them—the smallest child, a boy, on his mother, the two girls on either side. Their favorite toys with them. When he tucks a soft blanket all around them with trembling hands, there is such care on his face, even when he soaks it with gasoline. Bobby's eyes are dry now, as if the tears before were all he had left, but it is all over Kai's face that he's struggling not to break down.

Near dusk Bobby uses the engine to maneuver the sailboat out of the cave and away from the island, with the lifeboat towed behind. The sea swells are bigger than they were earlier; the wind has picked up. When they judge they've gone far enough away from the shore, Bobby pulls the lifeboat up to the sailboat.

Now he needs help. He can't bring himself to do it.

Kai uses matches to light the torch they made.

He holds it aloft, then throws it onto the lifeboat. When they're sure it has caught, they release the boat and push it away with an oar.

Flames dance into the sky.

Later, Bobby shouts instructions at Kai and between the two of them—Bobby knowing what to do, and Kai having the strength to do it—they somehow get the sails up. The wind is steady and the stars in the sky are clear as we sail through the night and all the next day for Scotland.

CHAPTER 5

KAI

THE ST. ANDREWS MARINA is deserted when Bobby bumps us up gently against the pier. I clamber along the side of the sailboat, unwrap the ropes, and sling them over the pilings.

We'd thought about what to say if challenged by the coast guard or anyone at the marina, but it seems authorities only care if you're trying to leave. No one wants to come here unless they belong.

Now that we've docked, Bobby doesn't seem to want to leave his boat. He goes below, and after a while, I follow. He's in the cabin, touching things, picking them up and putting them down again.

He turns and sees me. "Wish I'd burned the lot," he mutters.

"We wouldn't be here if you had."

He draws in a shuddering breath. "No. And so I have to go on." He opens a drawer, takes out some keys, and gestures toward the ladder. "Come on."

We climb off the boat and walk along the pier to the harbor. Bobby doesn't look back.

Apart from the sounds of the sea and some seagulls, everything is quiet, still. There are no people anywhere.

There's a parking lot behind the jetty, and we go there. "Here," he says, pointing at a four-wheel drive, and he hits the key fob in his hand. The lights flash and it beeps. We get in; he starts it. He shakes his head. "Seems so weird that this is still here. That I can just get in and start the car that we left behind."

"How long has it been?"

"I lost count of the days, but not many. Though it is a lifetime—four lifetimes—ago. Over in a minute."

I don't say anything. There is nothing I can say.

We drive along a deserted road: deserted, as in no one else is driving along it, but every now and then a car is empty and abandoned, and Bobby has to maneuver around it. The traffic lights are dead—there's no power? Everywhere we look is dark, silent.

We get to a junction, and Bobby starts to take the left turn. He stops, hesitates, then reverses a little and turns right. "Change of plan," he says. "We're going to the pub."

"The pub?"

"Tonight is their wake. Tomorrow will come soon enough."

He pulls in front of a big, old country pub. It's cold, dark. The sun is almost gone now. We get out and walk to the door. It's locked. I peer through the window but can't see anything in the dim shadows.

Bobby picks up a brick that was on the ground, the sort probably used to prop the door open on a fine day. He shrugs and knocks on the door. "It seems wrong not to knock," he says. But then he uses the brick to smash a window.

I help him kick out the panes of glass, and we climb in. It's almost dark outside now and even darker inside, and we stand, waiting, while our eyes adjust.

"There are tea lights. They used them at dinner." Bobby feels his way through a door to tables; we gather a few together. Matches he finds in a drawer behind a desk. He lights a match, and the thin flame wavers as his hand shakes. I guide it to a candle, and the wick catches.

"Sit," I say, and push Bobby onto a bar stool. I go behind the bar. "What'll it be?"

Bobby tells their stories over a few pints of beer. His hands and voice are steadier now as he lights four candles. One for Sally, who changed his life forever when he met her, here, by this bar a dozen years ago. One for their first daughter, Erin, the daydreamer—so like her mother. One for Maddy, who was never still or quiet and loved to run. And one for Jackson, so small they were only just starting to know who he was.

And I don't know how he can do this. How he can sit and talk and not *scream with rage*. I want to shake him, to make him find the anger that will help keep him going.

The way mine does me.

CHAPTER 6

CALLIE

KAI'S SLEEP IS TROUBLED. He's caught in a dream—not a good one; he must be. He twists and shudders, and I wish I could wake him.

If I could sleep, what dreams would I have? I shrug. Nightmares couldn't be much worse than here and now.

I leave Kai at Bobby's house. I can't see the sun yet, but the sky is starting to lighten.

The signs say this place is St. Andrews. Bobby's house is a grand one, and there was another car at the house—a sporty red one—and he's got that sailboat too. He's got all the nice things and had the matching family and vacations along with it. Their faces smile in frames on the walls—in swimsuits on sandy beaches and in ski gear in the snow.

It doesn't care who you are, though, does it? Rich, poor; young, old; loved, hated—where you are from or the color of your skin—it just doesn't care.

The whole town is empty and dark. No power, no sound—no people sounds, that is. There are birds and the surf and some barking dogs running loose here and there, and that is it.

The only people I find are the silent ones; the dead.

Mostly they're at home, tucked into bed or on their sofas, together or alone. Some have been dead longer than others. No one is collecting them, taking them to pyres to burn. They're just left to rot where they died.

Not as many people as you'd think for the number of houses, though. Did some get away?

And where are the immune, like Kai and Bobby? I'm curious and look closer, everywhere I can, but no one stirs. In a place this size, there should be some immune. Something like five percent of people are immune—isn't that what the scientists say?

Where have they all gone?

CHAPTER 7

KAI

I'M RUNNING. AS FAR AND AS FAST AS I CAN, *but it's never fast enough. I can still hear Shay: she's crying out for me to help her. She's inside me, outside me, coming from every direction. The pain and fear in her voice tear into my gut so that it is all I can do to not scream.*

But that's not the worst.

I'm not running to Shay—I'm running away from her.

Soaked in sweat, I push the blankets off. The curtains are open and the sun is beaming in through the window—the light must have woken me. I'm glad.

My heart is pounding, and I'm exhausted, as if I really had been running all night. I pull myself up, go to the window, and stare out without seeing.

The dream won't leave me. I can still hear Shay, as if she were here, pleading with me to help her inside my head. And I feel sick with it. *She* left; she tricked me and she left. I didn't make her go.

But it was my job to keep her safe, and she's not safe, is she? I feel like I've failed her, like I did in my dream by running away.

Where is she? There's a sense of panic inside. I was too late with Callie; I have to find Shay before it's too late to help her too.

There are sounds down below: Bobby must be up. Last night I'd driven us back here to his house, helped him inside. He didn't want to go upstairs and instead made for the sofa; he told me where to find the guest room.

I go downstairs and find Bobby in the garage. He's pulling a box down from a shelf.

He glances over as he opens the box.

"Sleep okay?"

"Not really."

"Dreams?"

I nod.

He pulls some sort of camp stove out of the box, and it clangs loudly against the metal shelf.

He winces, puts it down, and rubs his head. "Too many beers. But at least I slept like the dead." He says it like he wants to go back there for real and forever this time.

"We need a plan," I say. "Or, at least, I need one."

"Yes. But first I need some tea."

I take the stove and follow him back into the house and to the kitchen. It smells, and it's bad—the fridge and freezer are full of spoiled food. How long has the power been off? We rummage through cupboards and find some canned beans, crackers, tea, and shelf-stable milk.

We go outside. He lights the stove, goes back into the kitchen, and returns with a pot of water, mugs, and a battery-operated radio.

He hands it to me. "Give that a try while I get domestic."

I turn it on and it crackles with static. Battery is low. I hit the presets, one after another; crackle, static. Nothing.

I look up at Bobby. I'm somehow shocked, despite everything, that radio is off the air.

"Creepy," Bobby says. "The presets were all local and music stations. Try to find something else?"

I go through the tuner slowly. He's put the beans on and handed me a cup of tea when the static finally makes way for a clear voice: bingo.

It's steady, calm, modulated—a woman's voice, a BBC reporter whose voice I recognize but can't name. But this is no normal news report, and it's a moment before the words register enough to make sense:

. . . contact with others. If you become ill, stay where you are. Do not seek medical aid. The cause of the epidemic is unknown, and there is no treatment. If you try to leave the quarantine zone, lethal force may be used to stop you.

If you are immune, report to the authorities at the current quarantine zone boundaries for testing and mandatory work assignment.

All survivors must be reported to the army at once. They pose a risk to public health.

This message will now repeat.

This is an automated message for residents of Scotland and northern England. All of Scotland north of Glasgow is quarantined. To the south of Glasgow, the quarantine zone stretches east from the M74 and A74 down to Penrith. The boundary then follows the A66 to Darlington and Middlesbrough.

Avoid contact with others. If you become ill, stay where you are. Do not seek medical aid. The cause of the epidemic is unknown, and there is no treatment. If you try to leave the quarantine zone, lethal force may be used—

Bobby reaches out a shaking hand and turns it off.

His eyes reach mine. "Bloody hell," he says.

"Does that mean . . . is everyone in all those places . . . " I can't finish the sentence out loud. *Are they all dead?*

"Sounds that way. So, what do we do now?"

"Tell the truth. Make sure everybody—"

"Everybody who's left."

"Yes. Make sure they know what causes the illness. That recording says it isn't known. Shay risked her life to tell the authorities; what if that message hasn't been passed along?"

"Maybe the message was recorded before they learned this?"

"I don't think so. They obviously know survivors are carriers now—they're a risk to public health, it said. She went to tell them both of these things."

"What now?" Bobby asks.

"I need access to the internet. Which means power."

"We could head for the border of the quarantine zone, as we were instructed—Glasgow, maybe?"

"Yes. I was told Shay had been taken out of the quarantine zone; I need to leave it to start looking for her."

"So that's where we'll go."

"That's where *I'll* go. There's more I haven't told you. You need to know everything before you decide what you want to do."

"Tell me."

So I tell Bobby about the Special Alternatives Regiment, SAR; about how they tried to kill Shay and took me as a hostage. How we were both wanted in connection with a murder and fled a quarantine zone illegally.

He stares back; nods. "So it seems to me that before we head for Glasgow, you need a new identity. And there's something that I need to do too."

Bobby packs some things—a few clothes, favorite photos, and a tablet and phone in case we find a network anywhere. We take his sports car, as it has more gas, and stop at his sister's house.

She, her husband, and their son are all at home, forever. Still. Quiet.

We make a pyre for them in their backyard.

What will happen in all the places like this inside the quarantine zone? Are they being left to the dead and their ghosts? What of their bodies—of decay and disease that will follow with no one here to do what must be done?

After that grim task, I become Bobby's nephew: John MacIver. His clothes fit me, near enough. He was a year younger—seventeen—and he'd never had a driver's license or passport, so hopefully there are no images of him anywhere official. Maybe everything will be in so much turmoil that no one will notice there is nothing of Scotland in the way I speak.

CHAPTER 8

CALLIE

WE DRIVE THROUGH THE SCOTTISH COUNTRYSIDE on a beautiful summer's day. There's no traffic; none that moves, anyway, and Bobby drives fast—way faster than the speed limit. Sometimes he has to brake hard and maneuver around cars and trucks that have been abandoned along the road, either with or without silent occupants. Once Kai even has to get out and push a body aside from a driver's seat, then drive the car out of the way so we can continue.

Despite these things, I feel better than I have for a while. The sunshine is part of it; getting farther from Shetland and what happened there is another. Road signs count down the miles to Glasgow, and the closer we get to leaving the quarantine zone, the closer we may be to finding Shay.

Then Bobby brakes hard again and slows down.

Wow.

There's a roadblock ahead of us; the city is near. But that isn't where my *wow* comes from. The roadblock stretches on and on—to both sides as far as you can see—becoming not so much a roadblock as a fence, a barrier.

And here, finally, are people. There are buildings to one side of the road, smoke rising lazily behind, and on the other, a fenced tent city. Faces—bare, no biohazard suits—peer through a chain-link fence twice as high as they are tall. There's barbed wire along the top of it.

Along the roadblock and outside the fences, there are some people wearing biohazard suits, but there's no mistaking that there are uniforms inside them. Army personnel are everywhere—with guns.

One gestures at us to stop, and Bobby pulls in. "Best let me do the talking," he says to Kai.

Bobby opens the window. "We're immune," he says.

"We'll be the judge of that. Get out of the car, slowly. Hands where we can see them."

Guns are trained on Kai and Bobby as they do what they were told; fingers are on the triggers. Not just those of the two closest to us, but others on the perimeter, watching from a distance.

"Take a left." They gesture. The tent city is to the right; to the left are buildings and what looks like . . . a roadside service plaza? In front of it are more army, more guns.

"What's going on? We're immune; the recording on the radio said to—"

"Be quiet. You have to be tested. Everything will be fine if you really are immune."

Kai and Bobby exchange a glance, then walk across to the building and go in. It actually *is* a service plaza. But inside, chairs and tables have been ripped out to make an open space; food outlets are shut, and behind barricades there is a load of medical-looking equipment. There are a few technicians, without biohazard suits, and they have some sort of funny mark on their left hands.

And there are more suited guards—not just standing there idly like guards usually do, but tense with weapons ready.

"Sit," one of them says, and gestures to a row of chairs. Two others—a man and a girl about ten years old—are there already. Kai and Bobby sit next to them.

There are odd clunky noises coming from behind a partition, then silence. A few muffled voices, then a door opens.

A technician stands there. "Next!" she says.

The girl stands up at her dad's urging, fear all over her face.

The technician's face softens. "This won't hurt, I promise," she says. "It's just a scan."

The girl steps forward with the technician. They disappear through the door. A minute or so later there's equipment whirring, clunking noises again for a few minutes. Muffled voices, another door opens and closes.

The technician reappears. "Next!" she says.

The man gets up. Curious, I go with him as he follows the tech. "What are you scanning for?" the man asks.

The tech doesn't answer. "Just cooperate. They're trigger-happy." There are more armed guards in here too—one with a gun trained on the man.

"Lie down here. The platform will move you along; the machine is a little noisy. Stay still and it'll be over quicker."

He lies down where he's told. The platform whirs to life, moving him into some big tube thing. I've been in something like this in that place underground; it was some test or scan or something, and it freaked me out being trapped in the small space inside it. They had to strap me down; when that didn't keep me still enough, they injected me with something that knocked me out.

There's some loud whirring and banging sort of noises as the whole thing moves around the man. He stays still, like he was told. I watch over the technician's shoulder behind another partition. She's looking at a screen with numbers and lines on graphs.

I glide back around for a closer look at the machine, then along the platform inside of it. There's something about it that makes me think of the worm—that massive metal thing underground in Shetland. The humming inside the worm somehow drew me to race along its surface, and I'm drawn to this now in the same way. But this is much smaller, and—

Beep-beep. Beep-beep. Beep-beep . . .

Is that an alarm?

The machine stops and the platform slides out. Two guards are here now; they're grabbing the man, pulling him away, and twisting his arms behind his back.

"Wait; I don't understand," the technician says. "The reading was way, way too high. Maybe it's a malfunction? Let's scan him again."

The soldiers ignore her. The man is still struggling, yelling; one of them hits him in the head with his gun. Blood trickles down his head and drips onto the floor, and he stops struggling.

The soldiers drag the man out the door, through the waiting area.

"What's going on?" Bobby demands. He starts to get up, but then another guard moves closer to him and Kai and points his gun in their faces.

"Stay where you are!" the guard says.

The man is dragged out of the building, gone from sight.

"Where are you taking him?" Kai asks.

"Quiet!"

The door opens over his shoulder; it's the same technician, a bit paler now. "Next," she says.

"You!" A gun is gestured at Kai, and he starts to get to his feet.

I'm scared. Did the machine malfunction, like the tech said? What will happen if it does it again?

Wait a minute. The alarm only went off when I was there, when I was looking inside the machine. Maybe, somehow, it was me being there that set it off?

I feel sick. The guards hit that man on the head; they dragged him away. What will they do to him?

I shrink as far away from Kai as I can get and still hear what is happening. Kai gets on the platform like he's told. The machine whirs and makes its odd noises.

There's a pause, and I'm scared, waiting for the alarm, but all there is is silence.

When Kai emerges through the door, I rush to him, give him a hug he can't feel.

"Go through there," the tech tells him—and points at a door on the other side of the room.

He goes through, me alongside him, into an office. There is a woman at a desk, a computer and papers in front of her.

"Have a seat," she says, and gestures at chairs opposite the desk. "What's your name?"

Kai almost forgets and starts to say his real name, then turns it into a cough. "John MacIver," he says.

"Are you on your own here today?"

He shakes his head. "My uncle is with me; he was next."

"Okay, we'll wait a moment."

Bobby comes through the door a minute or two later.

She asks questions and enters names, addresses, dates of birth, and occupations on the computer screen. Kai's is given as a student; Bobby is a golf pro. I didn't know he did that.

"What's happening?" Bobby asks. "Are we getting out of the quarantine zone now?"

"There's just one last stage of processing." She pushes a buzzer on her desk and another door opens. Two suited soldiers stand there.

"Follow us," one of them says.

Kai and Bobby are taken to another door inside the service plaza—to what used to be a newsstand?—and told they must go in, that if they're still alive in twenty-four hours they'll be let out.

As soon as the door opens, a boy and girl rush toward it, but the guards push them back. One of them is the girl who was ahead of Kai, Bobby, and the man who got dragged out.

The door swings shut and clicks locked.

The two children aren't the only other ones inside. There are men, women, children—forty or so. Some standing, some sitting, arms around themselves, faces blank, eyes wide. Others lie on the floor.

"Where's our daddy?" the girl says to Bobby and Kai. "You were after him. Why isn't he here?"

Hysteria is in her voice, each word louder than the last until she ends almost in a scream. Everyone is looking over now—looking at the two children with fear and loathing.

"Your father must have failed the scan," a woman says, her voice accusing. "He faked being immune, but they caught him!"

"No, no; that's not true!" the girl says. "We're all immune! Only our mum . . ." Her voice breaks. "Daddy didn't get sick like she did."

People are angry, scared, glaring at the children. Bobby stares them down. "You should be ashamed of yourselves! They're just a couple of kids!"

He turns and kneels next to them. "I'm sorry, but we don't know where your dad is. They took him away."

Another woman looks over listlessly from where she lies on the floor. "When I arrived here this morning, someone didn't pass," she says. "He was dragged out before I went in. They took him to the pyre with the dead, tied him up, and threw him on the fire."

I stare at her in horror. Did she have to tell them *that*? The children are really wailing now, and I want to join them. Their mum, already dead; now their dad . . . was it really my fault?

"They wouldn't do that to somebody just for not passing some scan," Kai says. "No way, it can't be."

"He was pretending to be immune, that's why," the first woman says.

"He was a survivor; he must have been," someone else whispers, between spasms of pain. "I thought I was immune, but I was wrong. He was next to me when we were waiting; he made me sick."

Bobby huddles together with the two children as they cry, trying to comfort them, and Kai stands there next to them with a helpless look on his face. He doesn't know what to do; neither do I.

Like the one who spoke before, there are a few other people who are sick, crying, lying on the floor on mattresses. They have *it*.

There is a girl on the ground who is close to death. She looks about thirteen or fourteen, a little older than me.

Hi, I say.

Her eyes widen so much they look as though they could pop out of her head, but she doesn't scream. Good.

"Hi," she whispers back. She looks at me nervously, licks her lips. "What are you?"

I'm a ghost. Could you give my brother a message for me? Without, you know, making a big deal about it that everyone can hear.

She shrugs. "Not doing much else," she whispers. "Who is he?"

Kai. He's one of the ones that just came in—the younger one.

She waves until she catches Kai's eye, then beckons him over. "Kai?" she says.

He's startled. "How do you know my name?" he says.

"Your sister told me. She wants me to tell you something."

He kneels down next to her. "What's your name?"

"Jody."

"Hi, Jody." He takes her hand, holds it. "Okay, what does she have to say?"

Tell him: I'll find Shay. Wherever she is, I'll find her.

Jody repeats what I said.

"Thank you," Kai says. "Thanks to both of you."

Jody clings to his hand. "Don't go. I'm scared. Am I going to end up like her?" she says, and stares at me as if that would be worse than dying. She might be right.

But do I look that scary?

"I don't think so," Kai answers. "She seems to be a one-off."

He's right. Just me, myself, and I.

"If I die, will I be with my mum?"

"Yes. I'm sure of it," Kai says.

She nods and blinks. There is blood in her eyes. They lose focus, and then she's gone.

The evening passes slowly. A few times the door is opened, and either a few new arrivals trickle in or names are called and some who have made it twenty-four hours leave. Bodies, like Jody's, are removed. Boxes of food and water arrive.

There's a TV up on a wall with endless cartoons, and wails of protest when someone switches it over for the news bulletin.

A reporter in a studio tells us that the new quarantine zone measures appear to be working.

New measures: fences, guards, scanners, and a sickening smack to the head with a gun when an alarm goes off. And then what: the flames of the pyre?

Even worse, it's clear from what is said that they still don't know what causes *it*. Does that mean they're not even bothering to look for Dr. 1?

They say the quarantine zone boundaries are holding. They think they can just lock everyone inside them and wait it out.

But I'm here now. They're wrong.

Maybe if it spreads beyond the zones, that will make them try harder to work out what causes it, and to find Dr. 1.

CHAPTER 9

KAI

THE DOOR OPENS AND IT'S FINALLY OUR TURN: the twenty-four hours are up. A guard calls out our names from his list, and those of the two children too—Adriana and Jacob.

We get to our feet and walk to the door. To . . . freedom?

No. At least, not yet.

Bobby wants to argue with what comes next.

"Seriously? It's bad enough for us, but you're going to tattoo *children*?"

"It's been too easy for people to steal or fake immune passes. It has to be something that can't be faked."

"They can't copy the tattoo?"

"No. It's a special ink that only we have access to that shows up a certain way on a hand scan. Look, you can refuse, but then you'll never be let out of the quarantine zone."

"We're going to get a tattoo?" Jacob is excited. "Can I get one of a *dinosaur*?"

But his sister is horrified. "They don't have the stick-on kind; real tattoos are done with *needles.*" His face falls.

"I'll go first, and you'll see it's not so bad," I say.

The four of us are ushered into a room together, and the guy inside there sighs when he sees the children.

He's not your typical government worker type—he has long hair and vivid, colorful tattoos up and down his arms.

"Me first," I say, and sit on the chair when he points.

"Keep still and it'll be over quicker."

Small needles; ink in a little jar. The needles pierce the skin, tiny little stabs; in, out, in, out. His hands are quick and sure. The ink seems to have no color at all in the jar; it develops under the skin to a silvery gray that soon starts to look like a capital letter *I*.

And I have to fight to keep still. Not because it hurts—it does a little, but I can ignore that—but because here I am, eighteen, having my first ever tattoo, and I didn't decide to have it. I might never have made that decision, but if I had, it wouldn't have been some lame *I* for *immune* in God-knows-what weird chemical government ink. And I can't make a fuss because of Adriana and Jacob, who watch with wide eyes.

"Does it hurt?" Adriana says.

"It's not a big hurt, just a little one," I say. "You'll be fine." Just then a jab hits a sensitive spot, and I struggle not to wince.

I glance up at Bobby. He's a bit pale and very studiously not watching.

Adriana goes next. She tries to be brave but there are tears in her eyes, and I hold her other hand. Jacob is worse. He howls and has to be held down.

Bobby faints.

CHAPTER 10

CALLIE

I'M FASCINATED WITH THE NEEDLES and watch as they go in, out, in, out.

The man is very quick doing one on Bobby. He says that with a fainter it's best to do it before they wake up. Who would have guessed that after everything Bobby's been through, tiny needles would make him pass out?

After it's done, Bobby starts to come to and Kai helps him up. He seems confused about where he is and then looks wide-eyed with panic when he remembers.

"No, I really can't have a tattoo," Bobby says. "I've got a phobia of needles."

"It's too late, you've got one," Kai says.

Bobby almost passes out again, but Kai helps him out of the room and into the sunshine, and he starts to breathe easier again.

The four of them are directed across the road to a registration desk, where a man notes their names and ages.

"Can't we go to Glasgow now?" Kai asks, impatient.

"You can leave the zone and enter the Glasgow area if you have a place to stay there—friends or family—that we can verify. Otherwise we have to find a sponsor or a job for you."

"How long does that take?" Bobby asks.

"There are jobs available for fit adults. Just a day or two."

"What about Adriana and Jacob?"

He looks at the paperwork. "They are unaccompanied minors, so we need to find suitable foster homes. These are, well, stretched at the moment. We've been trying to increase capacity, but the thing is, even though we know these kids are immune, families are afraid to open their doors to them. Just in case."

"Stretched. How stretched? How long will it take to get them into a foster home?"

"Weeks, maybe months." He shrugs. "Really, we don't know how long it'll be."

"Can't they come with me?"

"Not unless you're a blood relative, or a registered foster parent."

"And in the meantime?"

He gestures across at the tent city we saw when we arrived. "Accommodation will be found here."

They are led toward it. Faces are pressed against the chain-link fence, eyes watching. Children and teenagers, mostly. Some elderly people—no jobs for them? A woman on crutches. A man in a wheelchair. There are tents in a muddy field behind them.

"How many unaccompanied minors have you got?" Bobby asks.

"At last count? In the region of three hundred."

The gate is opened and locked with a clang behind Kai, Bobby, Adriana, and Jacob. A frazzled woman is handling things inside.

"John and Bobby, I see you'll be temporary for work placement—take tent fifty-two. You'll find it in supplies." She gestures to a tent along the side of the fence behind her. "Adriana can stay in tent thirty-eight with some of the other girls, and Jacob in sixty-one with the boys," she says.

"Can't we stay together?" Bobby asks.

"No. There aren't any family tents left, and anyhow, you're not family, are you?" She hands each of them a sleeping bag, a water bottle, and a wrapped sandwich. "You've missed dinner. Breakfast bell rings at eight."

They find Adriana's tent, thirty-eight, first. It's wall-to-wall dirty sleeping bags on a damp floor. Girls stare back at them, quiet, still. There is the stink of latrines dug in ditches behind the tent.

"No way," Bobby mutters. "I don't care what they say, you're staying with us. Let's find tent fifty-two."

They go to the supply tent, and their tent is handed over not assembled.

They head as far away from the latrine pits as they can, and others must have had the same idea: it gets more and more crowded and muddy. They find a patch of ground that might be big enough.

Kai and Bobby wrestle to get the tent up; it's small.

Bobby peers in. "It'll be tops and tails, just like I did with my three when the power was out and they wanted to sleep with us."

They start sorting out the sleeping bags, but I've had enough of this place.

I zoom up over the fence around the mud and the tents, out to where the barricade begins—the line that separates the quarantine zone from the rest.

It looks like the barricade stretches forever in both directions—as far as I can see—and I'm curious how far it goes on.

I zoom along the top of it to the left—fast and then faster, so the fence and ground blur below me.

And it does go on and on all the way to the sea. It's not the same everywhere. In some places it's barely a fence at all, but in those places there are guards with guns in their hands.

And at regular intervals there are signs on the fence, big and stark:

YOU CANNOT LEAVE THE QUARANTINE ZONE. LETHAL FORCE WILL BE USED TO STOP YOU IF YOU TRY.

Unless you are immune.

Or unless you are me.

CHAPTER 11

KAI

THE STARS ARE OUT, BUT WHERE WE ARE, it's hard not to focus on the chain link of the high fence, to feel closed in, instead of focusing on the distance of the sky.

"They're both finally asleep," Bobby says, slipping out of the tent to sit next to me.

The shock of the last days is heavy on his face, and I feel it on my own. I can't believe this is happening, here, in Scotland—in the UK. Those tents with children all sandwiched in filthy sleeping bags on the ground. No one to look after them properly or look out for them, and the people in charge are just going to leave them here until they can convince somebody out of the zone to step up and take them in.

"Time to talk?" I say, my voice low, and he nods.

"They keep asking for their dad," Bobby says. "What has happened to him? Why?"

"Do you think, what that woman said—about being tied up and thrown on the pyre—could they really have done that?"

Neither of us can answer that question, and there is another question I can't say out loud that is raised by the first: if the authorities are burning survivors, are they creating more Callies? She was a survivor until she was cured in fire. Callie might know if there are others like her around, but I have no way to ask her.

"And that scan he failed," Bobby says. "What were they scanning for?"

"I've been wondering about that too. I'd assumed at first that the scan was meant to check that we were immune somehow. But then why did they lock us up for a day to make sure we weren't infected? They must have come up with a way to scan for survivors. It's the only answer that fits."

"That seems to be what the others thought. But Adriana and Jacob said their dad never had it, so he couldn't be a survivor—but he failed the scan. I'm sure they're not lying."

"Maybe they didn't know—he could have hidden it from them."

"How could a scan identify survivors?"

I lower my voice even further. "Maybe the authorities *do* know the cause now but aren't letting on. You know how I told you that we learned on Shetland that the illness is caused by antimatter? Maybe survivors still have some of that inside of them and that's why they're contagious. Then the scan could be for antimatter or something weird like that."

"Could be. But on the news we watched in that isolation room, they said they still haven't confirmed the cause of the epidemic."

"Maybe they're lying. But why?"

Behind us Adriana whimpers in her sleep; Bobby leans back into the open tent. He strokes her hair and she settles. His face is full of pain as he looks at this young girl—she must remind him of what he has lost.

And what of her father—what have they done to him? Would they really throw him on a fire, still alive?

Like Callie.

I've been trying not to think about something by keeping my mind occupied with anything else, but it isn't working. I shudder inside, struggling to keep it from my face. If they brought Shay out of the quarantine zone when survivors are treated like *that* for trying to leave it—what would they have done to her?

No matter how hopeless it is, I have to try to find her. Callie said she'd help, but what good will that do? If Callie finds Shay, she won't be able to tell me where she is unless there is someone dying at hand to relay the message.

And Bobby may be sitting next to me now, but I know he is more with those two behind us than he can be with anyone else.

"I need to get out of the zone as soon as I can," I say. "To tell people about the cause of the epidemic and look for Shay. But you aren't coming with me, are you?"

He looks relieved to hear me say the words. "No, Kai. I need to stay here. You go and save the world. It is enough for me if I can save two kids, maybe more."

"It's okay. I understand." And I do, but I still wish he were coming with me.

"You'll be all right," he says, as if he could hear the thought I never said. "All the things you and that girl have done already . . . well. There's just no stopping you, is there?"

"Yeah. Sure."

"But first up," he says, and holds up his tablet, "I'm going to wander about tonight and tomorrow and take some photos. Then you take this with you. Show people what is happening here, and maybe it will help."

CHAPTER 12

CALLIE

AFTER THE WORST-LOOKING WATERY PORRIDGE in the history of the *world* is ladled into their bowls, Kai and Bobby are called to report to the gate with their possessions.

They go up together, but when they reach the gate, Bobby doubles over and clutches his chest. "I've got chest pains," he says to the woman there.

"Sorry. You can't go, then. I'll put you on the medical list to see a doctor, but it will be a while. It's a long list."

She hands Kai some papers and a card. "John, show these to the guards at the gate and catch the bus into the city. On the card here is the address of a hostel where you've got a room; the bus will stop there. You get tomorrow to settle in, and then report to work crew thirteen, as detailed, the next morning."

Time to say goodbye.

Kai nods at Bobby, holds out his hand. They start to shake, but then Bobby pulls him in close, gives him an awkward hug. "I hope you find her," he says, his voice low. "Take care."

"Thanks. You too."

"This may help." He holds out a wad of cash, hidden between his hands, and Kai starts to protest. "Don't argue! Just take it. I've got more, and bank cards too—if they still work anywhere. You don't, *John.*" Slight stress on the name.

Kai stuffs it in his pack and puts it back on his shoulder. He walks to the barricade, papers in hand.

A guard checks them, nods, and radios the guards at the gate. Kai walks toward them and then goes through. And just like that, he is out of the quarantine zone.

The guards on the perimeter of the zone all wear biohazard suits. Those who come through this gate, like Kai just did, don't have suits: they're immune. They're safe.

But once we move away from there, farther from the zone boundary, that will change. Not everyone outside the zone is immune, but they won't wear suits: *it* hasn't made it there yet, has it?

But things are about to change. All the fences and guards in the world can't stop me.

CHAPTER 13

KAI

THE BUS IS THERE LIKE SHE SAID IT WOULD BE. It's a minibus, actually, about half full when I get on. We wait and wait, parked in the sun, until more people come through the gates and get on, and then finally it pulls up the road and into the city.

I've been to Glasgow before, and once we're away from the fences, everything looks so *ordinary*.

We rattle along down streets I don't know, heading to a scruffy part of town. The bus stops a few times before the driver calls out the name of my hostel.

I get off the bus in front of a three-story building of crumbling concrete, overflowing trashcans at the front.

The door is propped open.

Inside is an open office of sorts with a desk. A woman sits there. There is a lounge area past her with sprawling sofas that have seen better days.

"Hello," she says, and smiles—a proper, friendly, welcoming smile. "Are you moving in?"

I smile back, relieved someone seems happy to see me. "I think so," I say, and give her my papers.

She has a look. "All right then, John. You're in room five, second floor, bed four. Here's a towel and"—she turns around and digs in a cupboard—"a blanket. Sheets. Information about the place is in this leaflet." She hands me everything. "What have they got you doing?" She looks at my papers again and makes a sympathetic face. "Crew thirteen: that's barriers."

"What does that mean?"

"Hard labor, shoring up sections of the quarantine zone barrier. But you don't have to report until the day after tomorrow."

So one free day and then a work assignment. I've got other ideas about what I'm here for, but this is a place to start.

I head up the stairs. There are rooms with six beds each. I find mine and glance at the leaflet. There are meal times, a Wi-Fi code, and a phone we can use.

What now?

The place seems to be empty; everyone must be at work—hard labor or whatever else. I need to get online with the tablet Bobby gave me; I could use the Wi-Fi here, but after being locked up the last few days, I'm restless and don't want to stay where I've been told.

As I head back down the stairs, my hand itches. The fresh *I* tattooed in my skin marks me forever as immune: no pass required. Unless I lose my hand, it will always be there.

I walk around the streets until I find a café with Wi-Fi and use some of Bobby's cash for coffee and sandwiches.

News sites first. The zones are still holding; there is optimism that the epidemic will be contained with the new measures in place. Do those cozy people outside the zones have any idea what is happening on the other side of the fences?

They will soon.

There is nothing I can find on the cause of the epidemic—*nothing*. Studies are continuing and there is hope of progress. There are all the empty sorts of promises with no meaning that politicians always make.

There's fear swirling in my gut that the reason they don't know is because Shay never got through to anyone important enough to tell them; that despite what I was told at the air force base, she never even made it off Shetland.

She could be captured. Shot. Burned on a pyre. All the possibilities are in my mind—her screams in my ears, the rising smoke making me sick . . .

And then what? Would she become like Callie, unheard and unseen, maybe forever?

I push it away with a force of will. I don't *know* this to be true and until I do . . . *NO*.

Anyhow, the government *must* know at least part of it, right? Those scans they were doing prove it. They couldn't somehow scan for survivors unless they know what it is they're dealing with. So they must know at least *something* about the cause, but they're staying silent.

If this is some huge cover-up, what will they do to people who know the truth?

This knowledge I have—that Shay has—could be dangerous. The word needs to get out, but we've got to be careful how we do it.

Once enough of us know the truth, what can they really do about it? That is the best way to make Shay safe—spread the news around.

Iona next. I log on to her website, JIT, with the passwords I memorized from Shay's note. It's evening; I hope she's there now.

I start a new post as a draft so it won't be visible online. For the title, I type in: "Glasgow is nice this time of year."

She answers right away.

Iona: You're okay?

Kai: Yes. Long story for another time, but I'm in Glasgow. All okay with you?

Iona: We're still clear. Feeling cut off from civilization and bored as hell. Power is out, but we've got generators. Thank God the broadband still works or I'd really go crazy.

Kai: I've got a story for you.

I outline the conditions of the reception center by the quarantine zone boundaries.

Iona: Seriously? Hundreds of kids are just being left out there indefinitely?

Kai: Yes. Hang on, I'll attach photos.

I load them up and zap them across.

Iona: I'll get that out everywhere I can.

Kai: Thanks. Next up: I've been searching but couldn't find anything re the cause of the epidemic online just now. Is there any news on that that you know of?

Iona: Survivors are known to be carriers. Nothing else. I've been trying to look into it and tell people about it, but many of my networks have been shut down; either people have lost power, or . . . well. I don't like to think about it.

Kai: Do you have any idea where Shay may have been taken?

Iona: I've been researching air force bases or places they are said to be, but I haven't found anything definite. There are rumors that there's a secret location where survivors are being studied. I'm trying to trace the location but keep hitting walls. And also it's said there's some kind of test now so they can detect survivors.

Kai: There was a scan as part of the screening to get out of the QZ. We figured out it must be a scan for survivors somehow, so that confirms what we thought. Someone failed it and was dragged off.

Iona: Interesting.

Kai: Especially for him and his two children.

Iona: Sorry. Some other news . . .

Kai: Yes?

Iona: I contacted your mother like you asked. Set up a separate email address that bounces around so it shouldn't be traceable. So I couldn't really tell her who I was, but I said what you told me to: about the cause, that we needed help to get the word out.

Kai: And?

Iona: She must have thought I was some kind of nutcase. She didn't believe me; at least, I don't think she did.

Kai: Unless she's being monitored, and so she's being careful.

Iona: Maybe, but I don't think so. She doesn't know who I am, after all. Why would she believe a random weird emailer?

Kai: I'll have to call her.

Iona: If she really is being monitored, calling her could be dangerous. Be careful.

There's a phone downstairs in the hostel. Another extension upstairs. Downstairs is the TV room, pool table, a desk, and an office and dining room. It's busy now; people are back from whatever fun they've been assigned to.

Upstairs is quieter and looks like a better bet for not being overheard. There's a small communal area with couches. With bedrooms leading off of it, people come and go. Iona said to be careful, and she's right. If the authorities are looking for me in connection with that false murder accusation against Shay, it's reasonable to assume they'll be keeping an eye on Mum in case I contact her, and they may be monitoring her phone. It's hard to believe they'd go to those lengths, but just in case my call is traced back to here, I don't want to be seen on the phone. I wait, impatient, until the room is finally empty and dial.

It rings too many times, but then, just before the message should kick in, there is a click and a breathless "Hello?" A voice I'd know anywhere.

"Hi, Mum, it's me."

"You're all right, thank God! Where are you?"

"Best not to say. Listen, you know Shay was a survivor. She surrendered at an air force base in Shetland. Where would they have taken her?"

"She did?" Surprise in her voice. "I haven't heard this."

"But you've been studying survivors, haven't you? Because it is known that they are carriers?"

"No. Well, it has been established that they're carriers, but not scientifically—just anecdotally."

"So there's no actual proof?"

"Well, not in a rigorous way. They still haven't identified the agent that causes the illness."

"Listen to me; I can't talk for long. There was an underground lab on Shetland doing shady research with a particle accelerator, and what they were making got out. It might have been secret weapons research masquerading as finding a cure for cancer, or maybe they really were trying to cure cancer. Either way, the agent they were using got out, it's killing people, and—"

"Kai, I've heard this theory before. It's nonsense to think that would work, and, even if it could, that it would be covered up like this. I don't believe it. The best brains in the world are doing what they can to work this out; leave it to them."

"They're wrong. You're wrong. Question things, damn it!"

"Even if Shay was taken somewhere, what good would finding out where she was taken *do*, Kai? You can't be together; she's a carrier. Come home."

There is a brief silence; things both of us aren't saying.

"I'll try to get back in touch when I can," I finally say.

"Please come home. I'll get a good lawyer; you'll be fine. They want me to continue this work. They'll take care of you too."

I rub my hand where it itches. "Have you got an immune tattoo?" I ask.

Hesitation. "Yes."

My mother's clever hands, one marred like mine.

There are footsteps on the stairs. I hang up the phone and jump into a chair with Bobby's tablet in my hands. A guy and a girl come in, nod at me, and walk through, then go into a room.

I don't think they saw me move from the phone; they didn't react if they did. That was close.

So. Mum doesn't believe what she's been told, by both Iona and me. This must mean that the cause of the epidemic hasn't been passed on through government channels; this is bad.

She wouldn't lie to me; she might evade, but not out-and-out lie.

So it isn't just the general public being kept in the dark—it is the scientists and doctors who are trying to deal with the epidemic too. But how *can* they if they aren't given all the facts?

Or maybe they're like Mum: she wouldn't believe the facts, not even when I was the one telling her.

The dinner bell rings downstairs, but after eating at the café earlier, I'm not hungry. I wander up the next flight of stairs. Past the landing is a door that leads out to a balcony. I sit on a metal chair under the stars, find the code I noted earlier, and check to see if the Wi-Fi will work out here. It does.

If Iona hasn't been able to find out where survivors are being taken, then I have no chance, do I? But I have to try.

I open a search engine, enter *air force bases*, and go to the official government website. A huge list comes up. They're literally *everywhere*. But a secret place wouldn't be listed here, would it? Not unless they're hiding something inside of something else.

Next I search for *secret air force bases*. Pages of nonsense scroll past on the screen—paranoid ramblings of strange people. This is Iona's hunting ground; if she hasn't found anything, I'm not likely to.

Finally I do one more search—the one I've been leaving for last, afraid of what I might find: *Aberdeen flu survivors*.

Nothing comes up that I want to see.

There's a government website where you can report anyone suspected of being a survivor. You're told not to approach them; they're dangerous.

Shay, dangerous? Her eyes, the way they, I don't know, tilt when she is interested in something. That way she has of laughing, low, in the back of her throat—so sexy. I don't think she even knows. She's fine and delicate and strong at the same time—and infuriating. How can she be *dangerous*?

Yet I know some of the things she's done. To that soldier who was going to shoot her—she did something to him with her mind, and he fell over as if his heart had stopped. So she *is* dangerous—to someone who is trying to kill her, at least.

But that isn't the way they mean—they mean that survivors carry the epidemic, don't they? Or maybe that isn't all there is to it. Maybe it's the other stuff she can do as well that they're afraid of.

I sigh. Mum was right about one thing, though: even if I find Shay, what can I do? She *can't* be let out. People would die.

But I still have to find her.

I have to know that she is all right—the other options I can't contemplate, can't deal with. Even though she tricked me, and there is a well of hurt and fury inside about *how* she did it, by taking me up to bed. And now I'm thinking of her kisses on my skin, her hands in my hair, and my blood is rushing . . .

Stop this. Focus.

I make my way through the links from my search. There's a website where sightings of survivors can be reported; another one listing known survivors on the run. There's one particularly organized-looking group called Vigil asking for leads. It looks like anybody can say somebody is a survivor, and then that person is hated, hunted. There's a report on a news website that makes my gut twist—a suspected survivor was chased into a barn, and the barn was locked and then set ablaze.

There's so much hysteria around survivors, and it's the *tone* of it all that is really disturbing. As if people who survive horrible illness then deliberately set out to make others sick. As if they're evil—like demons. Or witches.

I make myself keep going through the links—despite the ever-increasing sick feeling rising inside—just in case there might be something, anything, that could be a clue to where Shay has been taken.

In the middle of a page is a link to a video streaming site. It's a channel called "It's all lies."

I hesitate, then click on the link.

The view wobbles and blurs; a hand reaches toward me, and it steadies.

"You have to listen to me."

It's a voice of steel and desperation that somehow doesn't match the speaker—blonde, pale blonde, almost white hair, fair skin. She looks Scandinavian—Danish, maybe, with that impossibly healthy look they can have—but her accent is from London.

"Survivors aren't carriers. They're lying; everyone is lying. Stop believing the lies. I'm a survivor. I got sick in northern England but didn't die. I've been back in London for weeks, close to countless people who can't possibly all be immune, and none of them have caught it—not one.

"It's all lies. Don't believe the lies."

CHAPTER 14

CALLIE

I'M SOON BORED WATCHING KAI read stuff on the internet, and I wander around the building and then head down to the street.

It's early evening now, and it's quiet. Most things are closed, except an old and worn-looking pub and a corner shop. Drinkers sit in the pub, people buy trinkets in the shop, and everywhere I look there are no biohazard suits.

I try to remember to not get too close to anyone.

Two black vans pull in a few doors down from the hostel where Kai is staying. They're full of people in uniforms of some sort—they're wearing dark, nondescript clothes, but you can tell what they are by the look of them and how they move. They get out.

And then they walk toward the hostel.

Why are they here?

Worried, I follow them to listen.

They go in the front door. One of them flashes ID at the woman at the desk.

"Where is the telephone residents use?" he asks her.

"Just here," she says, and points at a telephone on the wall. "And there is another extension upstairs."

"There was a call made from here"—he glances at his watch—"twenty-three minutes ago. I want to know who made it."

Is that when Kai called Mum?

She shrugs. "I haven't been keeping track."

Are they after Kai? Not being able to speak is making me *crazy*. I can't warn him; I can't do anything.

They spread out and start to check out everyone on this floor—basically they just look at them. That means they know who they are looking for, doesn't it?

A few of them stay here by the door, and the rest go up the stairs to the next level.

They go into all the rooms one by one, first just checking faces like they did downstairs. Then they start to ask if anyone has been seen using the phone half an hour ago. Everyone says the same thing: none of them saw it being used. The uniforms are impatient, annoyed; they think someone is lying.

They start to walk up the next flight of stairs, then toward the door that leads to the balcony where Kai is. I have to do *something*, anything, to stop them and warn him.

There is only one thing I can do.

Who is in charge of the uniforms? It's easy to tell. He hangs back, gestures at the others where to go.

Today isn't his day.

I fill myself with hot fury, rage: it's always there, just simmering underneath, so it only takes seconds to find it and ignite.

I throw myself at him.

He screams as he erupts into fire from inside out. His companions—including the ones heading for Kai's balcony—run toward him, then back away.

No one is looking up the stairs when Kai peeks through a doorway and then shuts the door.

CHAPTER 15

KAI

I LEAN ON THE OTHER SIDE OF THE DOOR.

The horrible screaming; the smell of the smoke still caught in my throat—like a barbecue but sweeter, and worse, and wrong, as if someone were making a pyre inside the building.

There are voices shouting below. A fire alarm starts screeching out a high-pitched warning.

My stomach is heaving, and I struggle to control it, to leave that part of what I saw behind and focus on the rest of it. The men down there now—whatever happened to one of them—are trouble. Are they army or police? They weren't in uniform, but they all had an army haircut and wore similar plain, dark clothes.

Why are they here? A cold feeling in the pit of my stomach replaces the nausea. I called Mum, what—half an hour ago? And here they are. Did they trace the call and come looking for me? Even though I'd thought it was possible, I'm still shocked to find out it may be true. And that they got here so fast.

I peer carefully over the side of the balcony. It's dark, but I can just make out two men down below to my right watching the back door; one has something rectangular in his hand—a radio, a phone? Despite what is happening inside, they've kept their position.

When the ones downstairs remember why they're here, they're sure to come and check this door too. I move one of the chairs on the balcony carefully, quietly, and wedge it under the door handle. That won't slow them down for long.

What now?

There's another balcony below this one. If I climb down to it on the left side, the balcony should block the view of the two men below, and they shouldn't be able to hear me with the fire alarm still wailing away.

If I don't fall. If there aren't more of them down there, watching the other side from the shadows . . .

The door rattles behind me—someone is trying to open it.

I tuck the tablet into the back of my jeans, ease myself up onto the railing, swing my feet over, and climb down the side. Something—a pebble?—is dislodged and clatters down the side between alarm wails, and I'm sure they'll hear it.

I'm hanging there, about to swing my feet onto the balcony below, when I hear the chair crash and give way above me. At almost the same moment, the back door opens below. There are voices and the sounds of people spilling outside.

I swing and drop to the balcony under this one just as sirens sound loudly in the night air. I duck down against the building. There are more sirens in the distance now, police and ambulance.

The two who were watching the door below are still there, but they've moved away from the door. They're hanging back, looking at everyone who is coming out because of the fire alarm.

There are footsteps on the balcony above now; if they peer over, they'll see me. If I jump down, the two down there will see me. I try the door to the inside from the balcony; it's locked.

The sirens are closer now; then there are flashing lights as police cars and ambulances pull in.

Above me the footsteps retreat to the door; it opens and closes. The two down below disappear up the lane.

They're not police, then, are they? Not if they're avoiding the emergency workers.

This balcony is only one flight up from the ground. I swing myself over the edge and drop.

I hit the ground, hard, the shock running up my feet and legs, and I crouch on the ground a moment.

"Are you all right?" A hand helps me up. It's a policewoman.

"Fine, yeah. Just wanted to get out of there." I shudder, remembering the screams and the smell from that man—from his flesh, burning—and this time don't fight it. I'm sick on the ground.

"Whoa, that's gross," someone says—one of the guys from the hostel who's standing around out back.

"Is it true?" another one asks. "Did somebody actually just burst into flames for no reason? Did you see?"

Without any other reason to explain barfing on the pavement, I nod yes.

"They're taking statements from witnesses out front," the policewoman says.

"Give me a sec. I think I'm going to be sick again." She walks away in a hurry.

"Are you all right?" A girl passes me some tissues out of her handbag, and I wipe my face.

"Thanks. I'm fine."

"He really just suddenly burned up," she says. "So freaky."

"You saw it too? Who were those guys anyhow?"

She shrugs. "They were asking who'd been using the phone. Did you see anyone? We saw you were there when we came through."

I look at her again—was she the girl who'd walked through with a boy just after I'd used the phone? I didn't think they'd seen me move.

"No, no one used the phone when I was there."

"Or maybe it was you, John, and you're the one they're after." She smiles. Is it to show she's not serious? How does she know my name? She must have asked about the new guy at the reception desk, and that much curiosity makes me nervous. "Anyhow, you're safe now; they all left quickly as soon as they heard the sirens. Weird, huh? I thought *they* were police."

"No idea what that's about," I say, but I've never been a good liar.

The policewoman who helped me up before gestures for me to come over.

"Gotta go."

I walk to where they are taking statements. I can feel that girl's eyes on my back: what are the chances of her not repeating what she just said to me?

Not much. Maybe not to authority, but if she talks, it could travel easily enough.

I've got to get out of here.

I wait until the policewoman is speaking to someone else and has turned away, then slip to the other edge of the milling crowd and walk quickly up the road.

Once I'm out of sight, I go faster and turn a few corners quickly in case anybody tries to follow.

What now?

Before I was interrupted by all that weirdness—could that man really just have spontaneously combusted?—I was watching that video I'd found, over and over again.

It's itching at me; I want to go back online. With all the things I have to think about, the one thing stuck in my mind is that blonde girl . . . *It's all lies,* she said.

I force myself to wait until I'm a fair distance away from the hostel before trying to find some Wi-Fi. Finally, I find a small pub down a side street and slip in the door. "Have you got Wi-Fi?" I ask the guy behind the bar.

"For customers."

Stomach too sour to think of drink, I order a barely edible hamburger and log on.

But I can't find her channel. I'm baffled and go through history, click on the link—it's gone.

Has it been taken down?

I do another general search: *survivors, Aberdeen flu, lies.*

And one comes up, called "It's still all lies." Could this be it?

I click on it, and there she is.

"Hi, me again. I'm still a survivor. If what I'm saying isn't true, why are my posts taken down as fast as I can put them up? Why would anyone bother unless they don't want people to know the truth?

"Look, I'll prove it. I'll show you.

"Now watch." She smiles and slips a scarf around her hair.

The camera—a phone camera, most likely—moves as she walks down a street.

People are walking around her in every direction, and I recognize where she is: Piccadilly Circus. It's not as busy as that part of London would usually be—it's usually swarming with tourists in the summer—and many people are wearing masks like you sometimes see in footage of places like Japan, the sort they wear when someone has a cold. Not that that sort of mask would stop the epidemic, but London is still clear, isn't it?

She steps into a doorway, and the screen focuses on her face again.

"Did you see where I am? And all those people I walked so close to?" she says, voice low. "I'm a survivor. If survivors were contagious, they could all be infected right now. They could be dead in a day.

"But they won't be, and that is because it's a pack of lies.

"Why is the government lying about this? I don't know. Maybe they've got something to hide."

I look again and again, but there are no more installments. And soon the one I'd just watched vanishes.

I'm afraid to let myself hope that she could be telling the truth.

Maybe Iona knows something about her? I have to tell her what happened tonight too.

I log on to JIT and start a new draft post, titled "Are you there?"

I hit refresh again and again. The guy at the bar is looking at the plate I pushed away ages ago; maybe I need to have something else to keep using their Wi-Fi undisturbed. I order a soft drink.

The screen updates, at last.

Iona: I am now. What's up?

Kai: I called my mother and twenty minutes or so later had to slip away from a bunch of pseudo-police.

Iona: OMG. You're all right?

Kai: Yes, but more down to luck—and someone else's lack of it—than anything else.

Iona: I've got some news. There have been more rumors surfacing of a facility where survivors are being held. I don't know if it is or isn't true; it's all reactionary—as in, let's find it and burn it down.

Kai: Any idea where?

Iona: England, by the sounds of things. I'm working on narrowing it down.

Kai: There's something else I want to ask you about. Have you heard or seen a vlog, initially called "It's all lies"?

Iona: Do you mean that girl in London? There's been panic over there, but consensus is she's never had the flu—that she is attention-seeking or unstable, and it's made up. And how would she have gotten out of the quarantine zone without being screened anyhow?

Kai: It has been done before. Shay and I sneaked out of the zone when we left Killin, after all. But there's more. When I was talking to Mum, she said that survivors being carriers hasn't really been proven. That the evidence is all anecdotal.

Iona: I'm sorry to say this, but you may be clutching at straws. What Shay said about where you've been and the flu following was pretty convincing, anecdotal or not.

Kai: I know.

I type the words, but I can't stop thinking of that girl—the sincerity in her voice. It felt so real. Could she really be making it up? But she'd sound sincere if she's unbalanced and believes what she is saying. I shake my head.

Iona: What now for you?

Kai: Good question.

Iona: Do you need somewhere to go while you work things out?

There's a friend who lives not far from Glasgow—in Paisley. Hang on, I'll see if he answers a message.

I wait, sip at my soft drink.

Iona: Yep, you can stay there. I trust him completely.

She gives me the details.

We say our goodbyes, and I shut down the tablet, yawning. What do I do for tonight? It's too late to try to get to Iona's friend—it's too far to walk, and the trains will have stopped for the night.

Those men—police but not police, or whatever they were—would they have put the word out about me? Am I wanted in Glasgow? If they go back and talk to that girl—well, they'll put it together fast enough. I definitely can't go back there.

I walk up to the bar. "Is there a hotel or B&B around here?"

He looks me up and down. "You got cash?"

"Yeah."

"There's a room over the bar. You want to see it?"

I nod and follow him up the stairs. It's small and noisy from the bar below, but it looks clean.

"Cash up front," he says, and doesn't ask my name.

I bolt the door behind him. Despite the racket downstairs, I'm asleep in seconds.

The next morning I'm on the Wi-Fi again before I even search for coffee. I find her on yet another channel.

Her smile fills the screen, then she backs the camera away.

"Hi, it's me again. People are asking questions about me online; some are saying I'm either lying or crazy and never had the flu.

"So. This is me." She holds up an ID card: *Freja Eriksen* is printed on it. She's a little younger and in a school uniform—it's a school ID. She looks bored, like the smile isn't in her eyes. She looks more alive on her channel in London.

"I boarded at Durham School in Durham. The entire place was wiped out by the Aberdeen flu, apart from a few who were immune, and then there was me: I'm a survivor. Find the immune from school and ask them; they know that I was sick.

"Ciao for now."

I search for information on her school but don't find anything about the flu—the school website was last updated weeks ago. But the school is definitely inside the quarantine zone.

I head out, walking, not sure what to do. I should go to Iona's friend's place, I guess, but Iona said the rumors point to England, didn't she? Not west of Glasgow.

I can't stop myself from stepping into every café with Wi-Fi as I go. I'm glued to the internet, to finding Freja's posts before they get deleted.

Every hour or so another one appears. She's mocking the authorities—they can't keep up with her. They'll get to her eventually to shut her up, won't they?

Now she's by St. Paul's Cathedral in another disguise. She suddenly pockets her phone without turning it off; the view is of fabric and thin light moving through it, and police sirens sound nearby.

I almost hold my breath for the next installment, and check again and again. It's a few hours before I finally find her, and relief rushes through me to see her standing on the Millennium Bridge. She got away. Then that is replaced by disbelief that she'd stand in the middle of a bridge and stream this live: what if they rush to both ends of the bridge? She'd be trapped.

Then her face focuses in, and she whispers: "After nearly getting picked up at St. Paul's, I'm putting this up after I've left."

I breathe easier again.

She even makes the TV news on my café wall. There's panic spreading in London, but so far *it* still isn't there. She's wanted for questioning by the police, her image up on the screen, but there aren't any reports of the flu from places she's been.

This girl, this Freja, can't be a survivor; she *can't*—where are all the cases of flu if she is?

Could Shay have gotten things so wrong?

But what about how everyone got sick and died at the Shetland air force base after Shay went there? What other explanation could there possibly be for that?

It can't be true; I can't make it so just because I want it to be.

But doubt gnaws inside, finds places and pain, and—*no,* I can't discount this. If there is any doubt at all about Shay being a carrier, I have to find out.

I have to know the truth.

What do I do now?

I can't be John anymore; it's too risky—they might link that name to the phone call to Mum. I can't be Kai either. I want to find Shay, but I can't even begin to guess where to look for her.

It goes over and over again in my head, and I can't let it go: *What if we've got it all wrong?* What if Shay was never a carrier in the first place?

I can't believe it. Everything she worked out made sense. But I can't let it alone either.

Mum said the evidence was only anecdotal. Without knowing the cause of the illness, it couldn't be anything else—they couldn't prove how it was transmitted without knowing how it was caused in the first place.

What if this Freja is right and everyone else is wrong?

There's only one way to find out if she's telling the truth: I've got to find her. I know enough about what being a survivor is from Shay. I'll see for myself and judge whether Freja is or isn't. Anyhow, Iona said the place survivors have been taken is probably in England. Freja is in London; at least if I go to look for her, I'll be heading in the right direction.

And then it hits me: there is one way to know for sure. If Freja can see and hear Callie, she must be a survivor.

I have to find her.

In a quiet corner of a park, I sit on a bench and hope no one can hear me. But if anyone does, they'll just think I'm a bit odd and talking to myself, won't they?

"Callie, are you there?" I say, voice low. "We're going to London to find Freja. When we get there, I can work out where she's been last from her video messages, but then I need your help. I need you to find her and tell her where I am, so she can come to me."

CHAPTER 16

CALLIE

I STARE BACK AT KAI.

What do I do?

If Freja is a survivor, will she be able to hear and see me like Shay could? Kai seems to assume she will, but I don't know if he's right—Shay is the only survivor I've ever known.

It'd be amazing to be heard again! I wouldn't be so alone.

But I'd have to be careful, very careful. I'd have to hide that I'm the carrier down deep inside, where she'd never spot it.

CHAPTER 17

KAI

HOW DO I GET TO LONDON?

I can't travel as Kai or John.

To be fair, I don't know if the authorities *are* actively looking for me or if it is just whoever it was that searched the hostel. They ran when the police came, after all. But anyway, I can't risk using either name. I've got cash—thanks again, Bobby—but it will only go so far.

Instead of heading for Iona's friend, I get on a bus that goes in the direction of the M74. From there I'll hitch all the way to London if I have to.

CHAPTER 18

CALLIE

KAI'S HAD HIS THUMB OUT FOR A WHILE NOW. What would Mum say if she could see him? Of course, she doesn't know I'm here. If anyone tries anything with Kai—well, they'll wish they hadn't, once I've made them burn.

Cars and trucks zoom past. Finally a truck slows, then stops up ahead.

Kai jogs up to where it's pulled in.

The trucker leans across and opens the passenger-side door. "Where you heading?"

"London, or that direction, anyhow."

"Get in."

Kai climbs in, and the truck pulls back out onto the frontage road. Soon we're on the highway. The driver introduces himself as Mork—that's his handle, he says, for the radio, and everyone calls him that. He's a talker. That must be why he stopped and picked up Kai, to have someone to listen. Within fifty miles Mork has told Kai all about his three daughters and six grandkids, what the government has done wrong for the last twenty years, and his theory of the Aberdeen flu being caused by an invading race of aliens. Then his radio crackles.

Mork turns a dial and it gets louder. "Attention, all. There are suspected cases of Aberdeen flu in Glasgow, and all roads in and out of the city are being sealed off."

He whistles. "That was lucky. We just made it out, didn't we?"

"I thought the zones were holding?"

"They were for a while. Anyhow, I've got one of these," Mork says, and holds out his hand—an *I* for immune is tattooed on it. "They'd have let me out eventually, but it might have taken a while."

Kai holds up his hand, shows his identical tattoo.

"Worth gold, that is."

"How so?"

"Truckers are disappearing; no one wants to risk travel in case the zone boundaries shift and trap them. If you're immune, you can get in and out of the zones, and with so few who can, we get paid like crazy in bonuses."

So it sounds like *it* has breached the zone and gone into Glasgow. Of course it has—I was there.

I tried to keep away from people when we first left the zone; I really did. I don't want to make people sick—not unless they deserve it. But then those uniforms came for Kai, and I had no choice: I had to listen in to find out what they were doing; I had to act to save him. The only way to do that was to get up close. Since then I've stayed by Kai's side, afraid to let him out of my sight in case anyone else is after him.

And now we're going to London.

It's a city; it'll be crowded with people, won't it? So many people. I'm sunk down on the floor of the truck, hiding—even though no one can see me.

I'm disaster. Death. If people knew, they'd hate me, wouldn't they?

I hate me.

Kai hopes we'll find Freja, that she'll prove that survivors aren't carriers. How long will it be until somebody makes the connection and realizes it's me?

Then Kai will hate me. If we find Shay, she'll hate me too.

It's not fair!

I didn't ask to be like this; it's all Dr. 1's fault. I have to stay strong, stay focused: find Dr. 1 and make him suffer. If Kai finds Freja and I can talk to her, then I can make sure he remembers that this is what we must do. Then I'll make sure we leave London as fast as we can, before either of them notices the epidemic is following us again—following *me*.

I slide off of the floor of the cab and back onto the seat next to Kai, watching the countryside zip past as Mork prattles on about alien abduction.

I slip my hand over Kai's. Me and my big brother: we're in this together.

CHAPTER 19

KAI

WE DON'T STOP FOR AGES in case the zones are extended. When Mork finally pulls into a café on the M6, I'm starving.

"I'll buy you some lunch?" I offer, knowing I should but wondering how long the money Bobby gave me will last.

We load our trays up, I pay, and we sit down. The food is so good even Mork stops talking for a while.

And there is Wi-Fi. Iona and her friend must be thinking the worst about what has happened to me. I log on, but can't stop myself from first searching for the latest version of "It's all lies."

Freja's face fills the screen.

"Yes, I'm still on the loose, and London is still clear." Behind her is Westminster Abbey. She grins at the camera.

Mork looks over my shoulder. "What a stunner. Is that why you're heading for London?"

"Yes." And it is, of course—not the way he means, but it is.

"Pie is on me," Mork says. While he goes to get it, I log on to JIT.

What I see there makes my full stomach twist, and I feel sick.

There's a new post, a title only with no content: JIT is compromised.

And that's it; everything else has been deleted. It was posted hours ago. What's happened?

Is Iona all right? Her friend? Has being in touch with me done this? I'm aware that Mork has returned with two plates of pie and has polished his off, and I'm still just staring at the screen.

"If you're not eating that pie, then I will," he says. I push the plate over to him. "Is something wrong?" he asks.

"I'm just worried about some friends in Scotland," I answer truthfully.

"Things are getting worse," he says, and nods to the TV screen I haven't been watching. Aberdeen flu has been confirmed to be in Glasgow now. The quarantine zones are being repositioned. "We better get going before the roads go even crazier. Everyone'll be heading south now, scared the zone will race past them."

Mork was right. It starts as heavy traffic at a good pace, but bit by bit we're going slower and slower until we're crawling.

He's on his radio, then swears. "They've put a block up ahead at Birmingham, turning people around who haven't got a good reason to go farther south."

"Who decides?"

"Bah. Army, most likely."

"I reckon I could walk to London faster than this," I say nervously. I'm wondering if I should get out in case it *is* army and they are looking for me.

"There's a priority lane set up—transport qualifies. We'll get around it."

We crawl toward Birmingham. Mork is chattering on about the pros and cons of the EU now, but his voice has become a drone that doesn't register. What do I do? Stay in the truck and risk it? Get out? But then how do I get to London?

I'm undecided and stay where I am, my tension increasing, as we inch toward the checkpoint. As we get closer, I strain to see what is happening, who is there.

I breathe easier as we approach. Not army after all; it looks like ordinary police.

Of course I'm probably wanted by them too.

But Mork was right: in a truck with transport papers, they barely bother to glance at our immune tattoos before waving us on. I allow myself to relax as the checkpoint is left behind us.

"Traffic should be all right now," Mork says, and he's right again: it gradually thins out to a fraction of what it would normally be, with everyone held up behind us at the checkpoint. We race toward London.

CHAPTER 20

CALLIE

KAI WALKS UP THE ROAD, Mork giving a *toot-toot* behind. Kai waves with one hand, doesn't turn around.

Mork's last words as Kai climbed out of the cab of the truck were "Don't do anything I wouldn't do," and his laugh had to do with the blonde girl he saw on the screen. That might be something Kai has difficulty with, but not the way Mork means. Trouble seems to follow close to Kai's footsteps, much like I do. Maybe we're the same thing.

Have I ever been to London before? I don't remember anything about where we are; we could be anywhere as we walk up streets with parked cars, shops, cafés, and bars. There's nothing of the London I've seen on TV.

The sun is setting and still Kai trudges up the road. His face is drawn, and I wish I could tell him I'm here, that I'm looking out for him.

Finally he slows and hesitates outside a pub. He pulls the door open and goes in.

CHAPTER 21

KAI

I CHECK THERE IS WI-FI before ordering something to drink, suddenly parched.

I'm even more desperate to log on to JIT again to check—maybe I imagined that post title before. Maybe everything is okay?

But I know I didn't.

I remember Iona's mobile number from when she was helping me find Shay in Killin, and I want to call her. But if her website is compromised, could they be monitoring her phone?

If she's still all right, calling her might be the thing that gets her into serious trouble.

But maybe there is another way.

I look around the room. A few drinkers sit in groups here and there, and one woman, forty or so, is at the bar, alone, making serious inroads into a very large glass of wine. A nearly empty bottle is beside her.

I walk over to her and smile. "Listen, could you do me a favor?"

She looks at me suspiciously. "Could you call a number and ask for somebody, and then hang up if she answers?"

"Why?"

"I'll buy you a drink." I give what I hope is a winning smile.

"You're checking up on your girlfriend, aren't you, and don't want her to know."

"You've got me. Will you do it?"

"Oh sure, make it a large one and then why not. Name and number?"

"Iona," I say, then tell her the digits as she hits the keys on her phone.

It must be ringing. Is there no answer? How many rings is that?

But then she nods at me. "Hello? Can I speak to Iona?" she says. And then she hangs up.

"She answered?"

"She did."

"How did she sound?"

She shrugs. "We didn't have that much of a chat." She raises an eyebrow. "You know something, trust is very important in a relationship."

"I know. You're right. And . . . ?"

"She just said, this is Iona. She sounded normal apart from being Scottish. That's all I can report, unless you want me to call her again and ask for more information?"

"No, no thanks. That's good."

So JIT is compromised, but Iona is still answering her phone. Either they're watching her or they're not, but in any case, hopefully she's all right and will stay that way. I can't think of any way to tell her I'm okay without putting her into even more trouble if she is being monitored—but maybe, just maybe, she'll work out that was from me.

Sorry, Iona.

I buy the woman at the bar her large glass of wine and hope for her sake that random hung-up calls aren't being traced. And that if they are, her wine goggles are on enough that she won't remember what I look like. Then I leave the bar, just in case.

CHAPTER 22

CALLIE

AFTER A LONG, RAMBLING WALK, Kai finds another pub with Wi-Fi, one with a room upstairs. This one looks even dodgier than the one in Glasgow: what would Mum think of Kai staying in places like this?

Once he locks himself into his room, he's on Bobby's tablet again searching for Freja. He finds her at last under another post: "Lies, lies, lies."

But this time when she stares back from the screen, she looks a mess, like she hasn't slept.

"I don't know how much longer I can keep this up. Think I might have to skip town. But here is a last look at London for you." She moves a little and then you see she is on a bridge with the big wheel of the London Eye lit up behind her. It's dusk, so it was maybe a few hours ago.

The screen goes dark.

Kai closes the tablet, sits back, and ruffles his hair.

"Callie? Are you there? Listen up. I won't be able to find Freja on my own. I need your help. I'll stay here until the morning. See if you can trace her from where she was last and try to convince her to come to me. If that doesn't work, then ask her to email me." He repeats an email address several times for me to remember, saying it is one he set up earlier for this purpose.

"I'll set an alarm to check it every hour."

Sure, Kai. I'll just dash off around London, where I've never been before, find the London Eye, and then find somebody I don't know, based on where she was hours ago. No problem.

Well, if I can't do it, then who can?

Though maybe showing me a map would have been useful.

I head out and roam up and down dark streets until I find a busier road. There are people walking around, and I try to keep my distance. Some are wearing masks.

There's a bus stop, and inside a bus shelter is a map.

I stare at it but still have no idea where I am. None of the street names or anything on the map is familiar. I could wander around for hours like this and find nothing.

Instead, I zoom up into the night sky, higher and higher, until the city is laid out below me. That's better.

Freja was on a bridge—there was a river. That'd be the Thames, right? Below me a dark shape of water snakes around. It doesn't flow very straight. I follow it along until there it is, lit up like a big wheel of fire: the London Eye.

It can't be too busy with tourists, what with the country being quarantined, but it's still turning at night. People still sit in the pods and take photos and look at the view. How late does it run?

There are a lot of police around, though. Are they looking for Freja?

Where could she be? Somebody must be helping her, hiding her. At least they have been, but the way she said she might have to skip town, maybe not anymore.

With Shay, if she was anywhere near me I could sense her, but I knew Shay.

Can I sense another survivor's mind in the same way?

Like when I was hunting for Shay on the island, in Shetland, I start at the London Eye and cast out in ever-widening circles—listening, feeling, calling out her name. Would Freja have to answer for me to find her? I don't know. I don't know if she can even hear me.

Once I think I sense somebody and drop down low only to find a cat. I sit next to it on top of a stone wall. It hisses, tail fluffed out, and slinks away.

This isn't working. What else can I do?

I go back to where I started. The London Eye isn't running anymore. It's late, but there are still people walking around everywhere.

I go close enough to listen in on snatches of conversations around me for anything useful, but all I get are people planning drinks, deciding where to go, a few kissing. Everyone seems sort of manic—a bit hyped up and crazy. Like they think the end of the world is on its way, and they are determined to have some fun first.

Maybe it is.

But there is nothing to help me find Freja.

How about the police? I could listen in and follow them. Maybe they have an idea where she is?

There are still loads of them in the area. I watch them: they're not walking around randomly. They're checking every face, every corner; going into businesses that are open and doing the same.

Are they searching for Freja? She's not going to be around here still, is she?

I didn't really search this area close to the Eye properly; I figured even on foot she'd have been miles away by now.

They don't seem to think so, though, so maybe they know something I don't.

I sit on the top of the London Eye and cast out, for something, anything.

There is a place not far away, by the river, where something sort of vibrates; there is some concentration of feeling. It's probably another cat.

I probe and prod to try to localize it better, and then—it's gone. That's odd. I focus in on the place I thought it came from. There are some boats tied to a pier on the river, and I go to the pier. I cast my senses around: no cats hiss back, but was there *something*—some flicker of energy?

I go to the boat I think it came from and stand on the deck.

Hello, Freja? Are you there? I want to help you. Please answer me.

Nothing.

At least, there is no answer, no presence I can feel now, but did I hear something—a slight noise—behind me?

It's probably a rat.

I'm getting creeped out now, and I don't know why. Even the world's biggest killer zombie rat couldn't do anything to me, could it? But I'm scared. If I had skin, it would be crawling. There's something terrifying on this boat, I'm sure of it, and I'm about to fly up into the sky to get away from it when . . . I feel a slight nudge. Something—someone—is making me scared, to make me go away.

I give a push back. *That's enough of that fooling around now, Freja.*

There's a sense of puzzlement, uncertainty.

Fine, she says—not out loud, but in my head. A bit of tarp on the deck moves and she peeks out.

CHAPTER 23

KAI

BZZZ, BZZZ.

I struggle to push sleep away, and turn off the alarm. I switch the tablet back on again; still no email.

It's been four hours since Callie left.

At least, it's been four hours since I thought she was here and listening to me, and then went off. Maybe she's found something more interesting to do by now, and I was just talking to myself.

I'm feeling anxious and wired now, and more and more awake. I do a search, just in case, for any new versions of Freja's channel: nothing.

I told Callie I'd be here until morning, but I can't stay still, inside, waiting; not anymore. I have to move.

I find some paper and a pen in a drawer and write a note: *I'll be back.* And then head out into the night.

I start walking, eventually find a night bus heading in the right direction, and get on.

CHAPTER 24

CALLIE

"WHOA. WHAT THE HELL ARE YOU?" Freja says it out loud, forgetting to be quiet.

I was a survivor, like you.

"What happened?"

She's radiating a mixture of curiosity and horror.

It's kind of a long story. How about we concentrate on getting you away from here and the police first?

"Sure. Now why didn't I think of that?" she says, and there's some pain mixed in with her thoughts.

What's wrong?

"I massively sprained my ankle." She holds her foot out, and it really is impressively swollen.

So fix it.

She laughs. "How?"

You're a survivor; you can do that sort of thing. Like this.

I try to show her in my mind what I'd felt Shay do when she healed herself—*reaching* in instead of out, finding waves of healing inside.

"Wow. That'll work?"

It should.

"Okay, I'll try." Her pale gray eyes swirl into darkness and like with Shay before, I can half sense what she is trying to do. She seems to get lost inside herself, and I have to make myself be patient, to not interrupt.

Finally her eyes and thoughts return to normal, and she stands tentatively. Then hops on her previously sprained foot.

"That's a helluva trick, thank you! And goodbye."

Where are you going to go?

She shrugs like she's not bothered, but she's hiding fear. "I'll work something out."

There are police everywhere. I describe the scene above.

She swears.

Let me help you.

"Why?"

Again, it's a long story.

"I'm not going anywhere with you without some idea what the hell is going on and why you're here. Whatever you are."

Okay. My brother's girlfriend is a survivor; she turned herself in to the air force and told them that she's a carrier.

She snorts. "Idiot."

Well, she was sure she was right, and I guess it seemed like a good idea at the time. And now Kai—that's my brother—needs to find her. But then he saw your stuff online that survivors aren't carriers and wants to know if it's true.

"It is. And . . . ?"

He'd like it if you could help him with all that.

"What's in it for me?"

I sigh. *Has anyone ever told you that you're, like,* really *annoying?*

"Yes." She laughs inside again, but it's bravado—is that the right word? She's scared, but she's even more scared to accept help from anybody.

Well, for a start I can look and see where the police are so you don't walk into any of them by mistake.

"That could be useful."

Kai is somewhat good at beating people up when they deserve it.

"Also potentially useful."

Plus, we want to get the word out, like you do—tell everybody the truth about survivors.

She's silent a moment. Then nods. "Okay, let's say you've convinced me, at least for now. Let's get out of here."

We can either go to Kai or I've got an email address for him, and he can meet us somewhere.

"I haven't got a phone; I dumped the last one I used in the river. I'm pretty sure they'd have been tracking it by now."

Okay, sounds like it's just you and me that need to figure this out. Wait here: I'll check what's going on.

I flit up into the night. I wouldn't have thought it possible, but it looks like there are even *more* police in the area now. They seem to be searching in a circle that is getting smaller as they go, so they're getting closer to each other—and we're right in the middle of them all. Maybe, like me, they started farther away, thinking she'd be long gone, but then when they couldn't find her they started to pull back in.

And now a few of them are approaching the end of the pier where Freja's boat is tied.

I go back to Freja.

We're in some trouble. I tell her what I saw.

"I think we're going to have to play dominos."

What do you mean?

"If we run into one of them, hit him hard so he crashes into the other one, then run."

Sure. Easy. Though maybe we should try to avoid that. It might be noisy, and more police may come.

"Spoil my fun, why don't you?"

Let me check where they are now, I say, and once I have, I rush back. *Two policemen are on this pier, between us and the shore. One is going on boats and checking them one at a time; the other is staying on the pier and keeping watch. He's scanning back and forth, but slowly. So when I say "Now," climb out of the boat fast and then duck down.*

"Okay, sounds like a plan."

I watch the policeman closely. He scans this way, then turns. *Go now!*

Freja climbs quickly out of the boat, then ducks down in the darkness.

This might be easier if you can see too, I say, and then show her what I can see in her mind.

She's startled. *Cool trick,* she says, in her thoughts this time instead of out loud.

The officer is looking this way again. When his head turns away, she scuttles up to the shadow of the next boat.

But at some point we're going to have to get past them—how do we do that? she says.

I give a mental shrug.

We go up to another boat, then another.

They're very close now.

She's uncertain what to do; she wants to run very fast and hope they can't catch her.

No! Shrink down when they go past you.

I'm not invisible.

Think yourself invisible, I say, and I show her something I've seen Shay do.

You can't see me, nothing here, you can't see me, nothing here . . . She visualizes empty deck and repeats it over and over again.

The other policeman climbs off the boat he was checking, nods to his companion. The two of them step forward; one step, then another.

You can't see me, nothing here, you can't see me, nothing here . . .

They walk right past us.

They're checking the boat Freja was hiding in now; I tell her to wait to move until they're farther along.

Again, I project the images to her.

When the officer on the deck is looking the other way, she goes a few steps forward, then freezes. Repeats.

This is actually working! she thinks.

Yes.

We're nearly at the end of the pier when a bright light shines in our eyes.

CHAPTER 25

KAI

THERE ARE POLICE EVERYWHERE, heading for the river. Have they got Freja?

Somehow I don't think so. They look far too intent to have caught anyone yet; more likely they're on the chase.

There's a bright light shining down below, near the water.

"Get down and put your hands up," someone shouts.

But there are other dark figures—they're not with the police?—creeping down the slope.

A gunshot rings out, loud in the night.

Seconds later a girl runs off the pier and straight for me, fair hair shimmering in the dim light. She grabs my hand.

"Kai?" she says.

"Freja?"

"Run!"

We bolt up the road.

"This way," she gasps, again and again dodging between and around cars, hiding, then jumping out again, just managing to evade the police who are swarming around the area.

Who was shot? Who did it?

But there is no breath for speaking. It's all for running.

CHAPTER 26

CALLIE

MILES LATER THEY SLOW DOWN TO A WALK. They're on back streets, far from where they started. It's quiet.

They wander into a cemetery and find a bench; I tell Freja I'll keep watch, and I shield my thoughts. I'm nervous, jumpy. There were so many people last night that I couldn't help but get close to them to help Freja and Kai get away. *It* will be in London soon; we need to leave.

They sit there next to each other, not saying anything, watching the sun come up. Are they both too exhausted to speak?

Finally, Freja stirs and breaks the silence.

"What now?" she says.

"Good question," Kai says. "How about we go back to the beginning? I'm Kai."

"Hi, Kai, I'm Freja. Pleased to meet you," she says, and shakes his hand as if they were at a garden party. "Your sister, Callie, I met earlier."

"Can you tell me what happened just before we ran? Somebody shot somebody, but who?"

"It wasn't me. I haven't got a gun. Callie found me, and we were actually doing a very good job of getting away from the police without firearms or other deadly means."

"And then?"

"There was another policeman at the end of the pier who we didn't spot."

Sorry about that.

"Callie's apologizing, but she had been pretty busy keeping tabs on the others." She pauses, swallows. "So, they had me: there was nothing I could do. But then—somebody shot the policeman right in front of us."

There is such horror in her words, on her face, but if that hadn't happened, I would have made him burn. Watching him scream as he went up in flames might have been worse for Freja. I try to hide that thought where she won't see it, but she's focusing too intently on Kai to notice anyhow.

"But who pulled the trigger?" Kai asks.

"We don't know who they were or why they did it, but Callie said a woman and a man in dark clothes were hiding down at the side of the pier, and the woman stood up and just shot him."

"What did they look like? Did they look like army?"

No. He had long hair, and she wasn't the type either.

Freja relays what I said.

"It's hard not to be glad I got away, but how . . ." She shudders. "Who could it have been?"

"I saw a few dark figures creeping down the slope; it must have been them. They obviously weren't with the police, since they shot one of them. Going by Callie's description, they're unlikely to be army either. And they killed somebody so you could get away."

That's not all they were doing.

"What's that, Callie?" Freja says.

They were trying to chase you too, when you ran away; it wasn't just the police. And they seemed to be tracking where the police would be; they were good at avoiding them.

Freja repeats what I said, then shakes her head. "If it wasn't for them, I wouldn't have gotten away. But why did she do it? What do they want? Even if it was just to help me, I don't want anything to do with someone who shoots people like that."

We need to get out of London. The police are after you; they probably think you shot that policeman too.

Freja relays what I said, then frowns. "*We* need to get out of London? I don't know about any *we*." She turns to Kai. "Callie's told me a little of why you were trying to find me, but I want to hear it from you."

"To start with, I want to thank you."

"What for?"

"For proving something I never dared hope could be true. Survivors aren't carriers."

"You believe me?"

"Of course. Not just anyone can hear and see Callie. It proves you're a survivor. And you've been all over London, and where's the outbreak? Nowhere."

There are tears in Freja's eyes, but she blinks them back. "Now we just have to convince the rest of the world."

"Yes. That's the first priority."

"Even over finding your girlfriend?"

He hesitates.

"Save the world, then save the girl," he says, and I'm sure he's not lying, not exactly—he means what he says. Maybe because he knows Shay will never be safe otherwise? But I bet that if she were standing there, and he could save her but only if he turned his back on all the rest, he'd do it. "You said on your channel that you were going to leave London. Where were you planning to go?"

She sighs. "There is a group of survivors who contacted me because of my channel and want me to join them. But I'm not really sure I want to."

"Why?"

"I don't think they know what they're doing. Are they just hiding? Are they going to try to *do* something, like I was? They say they want the truth to get out about survivors, but all they seem to actually be doing is hiding." She shrugs, and there is a sense of distaste and unease inside her.

She doesn't like the thought of being part of a group that decides what all of them will do. She likes to make decisions for herself, alone.

Too right, Freja says to me, catching my thoughts.

"Maybe we should check them out," Kai says. "Perhaps they need somebody to tell them what to do."

"Are you volunteering?"

"Me? Ha! No, I was thinking of you. I have a feeling you can be bossy."

She snorts. "Only when people aren't doing what they should."

"It makes sense, don't you think? To find them and see what they're about—see if we can help each other. Got any other ideas?"

She shakes her head. "I suppose not. I'm not convinced, but you're right: we should check them out."

"We?"

"For now, yes. But there is a problem. I promised I wouldn't tell anybody where this group can be found, so how can I tell you?"

"Did you promise you wouldn't *show* anybody?"

"I suppose not."

She's uncomfortable, though. She wasn't supposed to tell anybody anything about them at all, was she?

Shush, you, she says to me.

"So you can take me there. Is it a deal?" Kai holds out his hand, but there is somebody they've forgotten who is part of this, and I'm tired of being unheard.

Wait a minute. There's something I want too.

Freja tells him what I said.

"What is it, Callie?" Kai says.

Dr. 1: the one who started it all. We have to find him.

Freja repeats what I said, then frowns. "I don't understand. Who is Dr. 1?"

"He's the doctor responsible for the epidemic," Kai answers. "It was engineered in a lab, and it escaped."

Freja's shock is extreme. "*What?* Are you serious?"

"I'm afraid so." And Kai tells her all about Shetland and what happened there, with me chipping in bits alongside.

"So Callie wants to find this Dr. 1. And then what? What happens to him if you find him?"

Neither of us answers her. I hide my thoughts, deep down, so she won't see them: I'll make him ill and watch him die. But maybe I'll let Kai have a go at him first—see if we can learn anything useful.

But I'm sure Freja can guess that whatever happens to him, it'll be nothing good. Is she about to argue, with this thing she seems to have against violence, like shooting that policeman so she could get away? Even if it is somebody who is responsible for so much death?

But Kai shakes his head before she can say anything. "It has to be part of the pact between the three of us; Callie wants to find him, and so do I. He may know a way to stop the epidemic," he adds, almost as an afterthought. Kai holds out his hand. "Is it a deal?"

Freja hesitates. Then she puts her hand in his, and I put mine on both of theirs. We all shake hands together.

"It's a deal," she says. "We're like the Three Musketeers."

"They don't know who they've messed with!" Kai says and stands, one hand on his hip behind, the other waving around a pretend sword. Freja clutches her chest, pretends to be stabbed, and falls to the ground.

All for one and one for all.

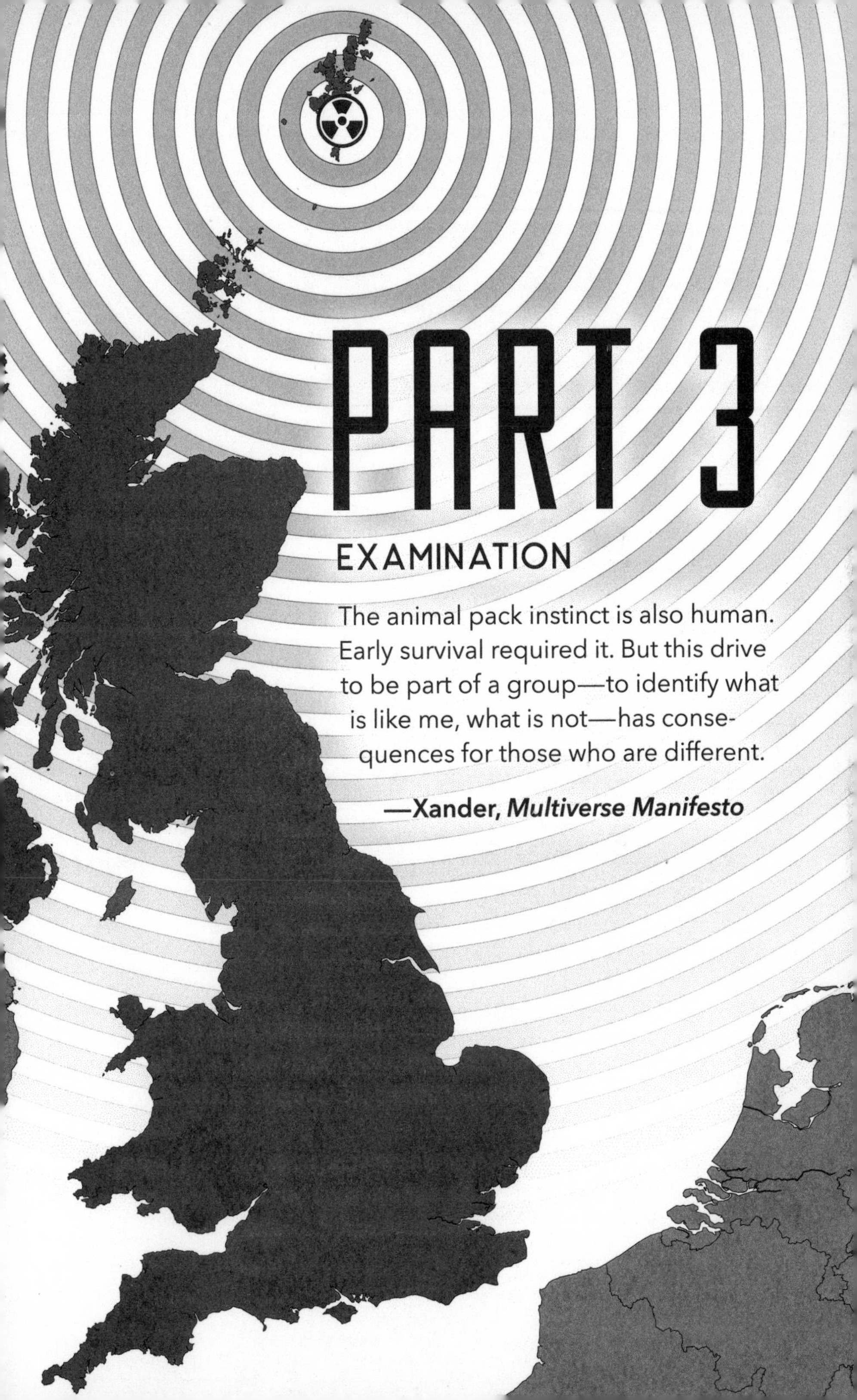

PART 3

EXAMINATION

The animal pack instinct is also human. Early survival required it. But this drive to be part of a group—to identify what is like me, what is not—has consequences for those who are different.

—**Xander, *Multiverse Manifesto***

CHAPTER 1

TIME HAS GOTTEN LOST. The usual reference points for it are gone. Sometimes I'm awake, sometimes asleep. Sometimes neither, but in a drugged state where there are no dreams—just vague memories of pain when I finally come to again, alone.

There is no sun, no moon; no night or day.

No life to reach to; nothing to feel or touch or taste.

Always alone.

CHAPTER 2

THEN, ONE DAY, I HEAR A VOICE.

I just listen to the sound it makes at first, without focusing on the words, and only realize they have meaning when they repeat: "Good morning, Shay."

It's a man's voice. It has a certain, I don't know, *quality* to it: something warm and familiar, yet alien at the same time.

I sit up. I'm in my usual place—small room, no doors, no windows—and in my usual haute-couture outfit: hospital gown. But something is different. My head feels clearer, and some clothes are folded neatly on the end of the bed.

"Good morning," I say, and I'm as surprised to hear my voice as I was his. "Is it morning?"

"It is, and a sunny one."

As he speaks this time I *reach* for his voice, but I can't *feel* his presence—only hear his words.

"Get dressed and we'll have a chat."

I hesitate.

"No one is watching."

Then how did he know I hesitated?

I change into the clothes awkwardly under the sheet on my bed. Underwear, jeans, and a plain T-shirt, but they fit more or less, and they feel *wonderful.*

Now what?

As if in answer to my silent question, one of the walls starts to move. There's a door? Despite hunting again and again in odd lucid moments, I could never find it—the walls around me always felt completely smooth.

Now I just push it open and step through.

There's a short hall, and I walk to the end, then go through another door. And there he is.

My eyes open wide. "It's *you!*" I say, words that are half question, half exclamation. Before me stands Dr. Alex Cross—Kai's stepfather, at least until his mum divorced the guy, and Callie's dad. And my dad too. Not that he knows anything about me being his daughter.

He smiles warmly and holds out a hand. "Hi, Shay. I'm very happy to see you again," he says.

And without knowing how he fits into all of this or whether I should believe him or why he is here, my hand reaches out and is in his, holding on to it—physical contact with another human, for the first time in how long? His eyes are searching mine and I turn away, let go.

"Dr. Cross—" I say.

"Call me Alex."

"Okay, Alex. So . . ."

"So what the hell is going on, and why am I here?"

"Pretty much, yeah. I figured you must have died in Edinburgh."

"Alas, no—it turns out I'm immune." He holds up his left hand and there, on the back of it, is a faint silvery *I*.

"Lucky."

"Indeed. Come, have a seat, and I'll tell you what I can."

That's when I see there's a small table and two chairs in the corner of the room. We go there and sit down.

"You know I was a professor in physics?"

My thoughts are slow and muddy, but I remember—the model of the atom in his office. The particles it contained that were outside the standard model. "Yes. No matter what they've done to me here, my brain still seems to be working."

"Glad to hear it. They've asked me to get involved in . . . ah . . . studying you. I was appalled when I got here to learn how they've been treating you, keeping you and the others in isolation from each other."

"The others?"

"The other survivors. There are currently twenty-three of you in this facility, gathered from all over the country."

"I'm not the only one?"

"No, and you'll get to meet them all soon. And things are going to be different from now on—better. I promise you that."

Kai wouldn't believe his promises, and I'm not sure I should either. But here I am, out of my room, not in a hospital gown, talking to somebody besides myself—so no matter what I may or may not think of the choice of conversationalist, it's already a vast improvement.

Later I'm in an internal courtyard, blinking in the sun. The courtyard is surrounded on all sides by this building—there's no way out—but at least there is actual fresh air. Insects. A few plants in pots in the corners. Since becoming a survivor I'd begun to take for granted the constant presence of other life around me—the way I can feel the aura of living things, and how I can *reach* out and join with them. The complete absence of other life forms in that sterile place has almost been harder to take than not having any people around me.

A bird flies by overhead, and without even thinking about it, I *reach* out to her.

I *feel* the bird as she soars higher in the sky. My mind touches hers and I join her in flight as she drifts lazily in a warm updraft, high above me. From her eyes' view, I'm shocked how little there is to see of this place. Our buildings are camouflaged, built into the landscape; without her sharp eyes, I doubt I'd see it at all.

A bleak, open terrain of rocky hills and moorland. No roads or other buildings are in sight.

I'm torn from her and brought back to myself by the sounds of a door. One by one, others emerge like I did—like bears out of hibernation—male and female, all ages from my sixteen up to seventy or so, and a few younger ones too. We're all shapes, sizes, races, as if someone picked out a random population sample of the UK and plunked us here. There is nothing we have in common apart from one overriding, all-encompassing fact: we're survivors. And as each one steps outside, they blink and squint against the sun like I did: how long has it been since we've felt its rays on our skin?

We say hello, introduce ourselves, but names are forgotten almost as soon as they're said. Conversations start and stutter, trail off. Unused to this much human contact, it feels odd and unnatural, but that isn't the real reason; at least, not for me. There's just so much *energy* emanating from everyone. The waves of sound and color in each person's aura—or Vox, as Dr. 1 called it—are all blinding and different; they crowd into each other, and it's too much to take in. It's like nothing I've seen before—survivors' auras are more vibrant, beautiful, and just plain *loud* than anyone else's.

But that's not all. There is so much feeling. It starts low, like our emotions have had to wake up as much as our bodies did, but it is growing, swelling.

Confusion.

Fear.

Anger.

But most of all, *pain*—not the physical sort, but that which comes from what we have lost; *who* we have lost.

As I become more aware, it is as if my mother is dying next to me all over again. As if I'm saying goodbye to Kai as he sleeps, right now; looking at his face for the last time. His eyes are closed, never to open and see me again.

It's a massive understatement to say that the physical pain from being sick was pretty bad, but *nothing* could be worse than this.

We're drowning in a tidal wave of pain that pushes us apart and keeps us silent.

CHAPTER 3

AFTER A WHILE, A WOMAN APPEARS. She's not a survivor—her aura is damped down, muted, in comparison to ours. Her knuckles are clenched white around a clipboard clutched to her chest. There is a faint silvery *I* tattooed on her hand, like Alex had: she's immune too.

"Hi, everyone. If you could follow me? I'll show you to your rooms."

"You're *not* putting us back there," a man says, and there is horror and threat all through his aura; he's poised to do *something*—whether fight or flight, I can't tell, and I don't think he knows either.

But she shakes her head no and he relaxes slightly. "You're not going back to the hospital, where you were before."

The youngest of our group, a girl of eight or nine, goes up to her. "Will it be nice where we're going?" Her eyes are big and round.

The woman softens. "It is, I promise. Come and see."

We follow her across the courtyard to a door; through it is what she calls the dormitory wing. Each bedroom sleeps three or four in single beds and has its own bathroom, and it *is* nice. Ish. Plain, but better than all right when you consider where we've been. And down at the end of the hall is a big TV room and a dining hall. Dinner is in an hour, she says.

Room assignments have been worked out. I find a door with three names—Beatriz, Amaranth, and *Sharona*—and I wince.

A tall girl perhaps a few years older than me is there already when I walk in.

"Don't say anything; let me guess," she says. "Beatriz?"

I shake my head. "Sharona. But *please* don't call me that. I'm Shay."

"I'm Ami—with an *i*, please—and I will if you will. Who is Beatriz?"

"Me," a small voice says, and in the doorway stands the child who spoke before.

We're told to go to the TV room before dinner, but the TV is switched off. I'm hoping Dr. Cross—Alex—will come. I'm anguished when I realize I didn't ask him the one question I should have: if he has any news of Kai. Did he get off Shetland? Is he okay?

Instead, there is another woman in a white coat.

She smiles. She's nervous too, but hides it better than the other woman did earlier.

"Good evening. I'm Dr. Smith and I'm a psychiatrist. I want to tell you a little about what is happening, both here and in the outside world, and then answer any questions you may have."

A psychiatrist? Named Dr. Smith. Sure, that's her name: her aura says otherwise.

"But first of all I thought it would be helpful if we each introduce ourselves, say where we're from and a little about ourselves."

I exchange glances with Ami-with-an-i. What is this, some sort of group therapy session?

"I'll start," Dr. Smith says. "I'm from London"—no kidding, we got that from the accent—"and I went to Oxford." I'd expect nothing less. "I have come here to help with your rehabilitation, and—"

"Wait a minute. Where is *here*? Where are we?" The question is asked by a tall boy with glasses—probably Ami's age or a little older.

"We are in a secure air force facility. Now, who would—"

"And where is this facility?" he persists.

She smiles. "Sorry, what is your name?"

"Spike."

"I'm sorry, Spike; I can't tell you. That information is classified."
She's hiding something; it's all through her aura. What is it?

Spike is locked in a kind of staring contest with her, and someone has to back him up.

"How can it be classified from *us*, when we're actually here?" I say.

"I don't have clearance to answer that question, but I'll see if I can get it for you. All right?"

"For now," Spike says, and he looks at me. He raises an eyebrow and seems to be asking me a question without words, but I don't know what it is.

What? I say silently, directing it at him but not sure if he'll hear my thought this way.

He smiles as if he were waiting for me to speak to him like this. *She doesn't know where we are any more than we do,* he says, answering back the same way.

No. Really? I look back at her and probe around her aura: he's right. It isn't the place she is hiding, but her lack of knowledge of it.

I wonder if she was brought here unconscious too?

Either that or blindfolded.

He grins. *Next question?*

"Dr. Smith," he says, "what do you mean by our *rehabilitation*?"

"We'll explain more about that another day."

"You said you were going to answer our questions," I say. "You haven't so far."

Bravo, Spike says.

"What was being done to us in that hospital, or whatever it was?" Spike says. "I've got holes in my memory—like I was drugged the whole time. But the bits I remember aren't good."

"Were we being drugged and experimented on without our permission?" I say. "Isn't that illegal?"

Her smile is still there but more and more strained. "We'll get to the answers to your questions, but not all at once. There are a few very important things I have to tell you now, and it's crucial for your safety that you all listen very carefully."

She looks around the room at each of us in turn. "You must all know by now that, as survivors of the flu, you are carriers of this dreadful epidemic. Other than to the very few, like me, who are immune, you pose a grave potential threat to everyone on the planet. Despite this, we've been persuaded by one of our colleagues to bring you all out here together like this to see if we can help you. But if anything goes wrong, the consequences could be severe. So there is a condition. Anyone who breaches the condition will be returned to solitary confinement in a hospital room, where we can look after you but also be sure you won't be a danger to anyone else."

Everyone is listening and silent now.

"Some of you have been documented as having certain . . . abilities," she says. "This is part of what we want to learn more about, together. But if anybody uses these abilities to attempt to bend the will of others or to try to leave this facility, I'm sorry, but for the safety of all of us—and everyone outside of these walls too—that person will be returned to the hospital wing. Now, are there any questions?"

I glance around. Some of us clearly know exactly what she is talking about—Spike and Beatriz are among them—while others, like Ami, have no idea. But all remain silent.

She smiles. "Good. Now, let's go on with introducing ourselves and learning a little about each other. Who'd like to go first?"

Nobody, as it turns out, so she starts on one side of the room. It's halting to begin with, but soon it is like everyone is telling things, personal things, that on another day they might keep to themselves. As if we are all raw and still unable to process what is happening and unable to block anything out.

Elena's children and grandchildren: all dead.

David's parents and cousins and brothers died too. When he didn't, he was chased by a mob and only escaped by jumping from a bridge.

Ali's family—all gone.

Our stories are all variations on the same theme: We were ill. Our families and friends died. We woke up one day and found ourselves here.

And then it is little Beatriz's turn. She's calm, composed. Her voice is steady when she tells us her parents, brother, and two sisters all died from the flu around her. That she was alone with their bodies for days before she was found, half starving, and brought here.

After that our questions don't seem that important anymore.

Later we have dinner in the dining hall next to the TV room. Today has been too much—*way* too much—and I'm desperate to be alone, or as alone as I can get with two roommates. It's all I can do to finish dinner and stumble back to our room with Ami and Beatriz.

I'm tired, but there is so much to think about, to process, and I know I have to do this before I can switch off enough to relax and rest. My last conscious thought is: *I'll never get to sleep . . .*

CHAPTER 4

SOMEWHERE A BELL IS RINGING, over and over. I open my eyes just as the lights in our room come on. Finally the bell stops, but the lights are still on.

Ami swears creatively. I throw a pillow at her and then gesture at Beatriz: eight-year-old ears shouldn't be exposed to that.

"What's that?" Beatriz points at the door. In front of it on the floor is a white sheet of paper.

I get up, yawning, and pick it up. "Ah, now let's see: it's our schedule for the day. It starts with six a.m. alarm and lights. Yep, think we got that part already."

"Six a.m. is *not* morning!" Ami says. She pulls a pillow over her head.

"What next?" Beatriz asks.

"Showers, then seven a.m. breakfast. Then at eight a.m., it's games!"

"What sort of games?" Beatriz says.

"I don't know. But apparently we're going to play games while a few of us at a time have individual sessions and tests or something."

"Sounds just like school," Beatriz says.

Pretty much.

"Dibs last shower," Ami says from under her pillow.

When we get to the dining hall—a little late, dragging a protesting Ami along with us—Spike waves, and we go to sit with him.

"Sleep okay?" he asks me, out loud.

"Strangely, I did." I frown. Despite being in a fog of exhaustion, once I'd dragged myself to bed I'd been sure I would lie awake all night with everything there was to think about. But once I closed my eyes, I was gone.

He raises an eyebrow again, like he did yesterday, like he wants to talk silently.

Yes?

I think we were drugged. Must have been in our dinner. I was hoping we could talk afterward, but we all had dinner and then . . . bam. No one could stay awake.

My eyes widen. I was so tired myself I didn't notice what the story was with everyone else. *Why would they do that?*

Why do they do anything? We need to work this out.

I nod, thinking for a while. *We're getting taken for individual sessions this morning. Maybe . . .*

What?

Good cop, bad cop. One of us slams the questions; the other goes softly, softly. Then we compare notes after.

He nods. *Good idea. But you'd better go for softly, I'm terrible at that.*

Ami snaps her fingers in front of my eyes. "What's with you, zombie girl? I thought I was the one who was half-asleep."

After breakfast another schedule is posted up in the TV room. There are two lists—Dr. Smith and Dr. Jones. Sure. On Dr. Smith's list, Spike is first, and I'm second.

That can't be random, he thinks, *that the two who questioned things last night are first up with her.*

His thoughts trail off as he disappears behind a door with Dr. Smith.

Board games with an intense eight-year-old and a bored nineteen-year-old are not my idea of fun. Time ticks slowly by as Ami tries the buy-everything Monopoly strategy and Beatriz remains unmoved by the thrill of property ownership.

Finally Spike returns: he was in there for a while. They're already behind schedule—I was supposed to go in twenty minutes ago.

Poor woman is having a difficult morning, he thinks, as I pass him on the way to the door.

"Sharona? Good morning," Dr. Smith says. There are spots of bright pink in her cheeks.

I smile as sweetly and hesitantly as I can. *I'm a lost girl, I need help, I'm a lost girl, I need help,* I think at her.

"I'm sorry if I was rude last night," I say. "I'm just so scared about what is going to happen to us."

"Oh, my dear, don't be scared. I'm here to help you."

I make my eyes round.

I'm a lost girl, I need help, I'm a lost girl, I need help . . .

"And I couldn't sleep last night."

"You couldn't?"

Her degree of surprise is beyond anything reasonable: I'm sure lots of people wouldn't be able to sleep after what we went through yesterday. Spike must be right—they may have let us out of our solitary hospital cells, but somehow they're still controlling us with drugs. I stuff down the anger, hide it for later.

"I couldn't sleep at first. But then I slept really soundly, which is weird. I usually can't sleep in new places."

She smiles. "Hopefully that means you are settling in well."

"And not knowing where we are is just so . . . *weird.*" I sigh and look down through my lashes. I wish I'd gotten the role of bad cop; I'm being so sweet and helpless I'm making myself want to vomit.

I look up at Dr. Smith again. "And we've been here for ages, haven't we? What's going on out there? I'm from London originally; are my friends in London still safe?"

"Yes. The quarantine zone boundaries are holding; they'll be fine." She's sincere. That much she knows.

"But you know where we are now, don't you? You know that we're safe here?"

"You're safe and sound, I promise."

"Will I ever be able to see my friends in London again?"

"I don't know, Sharona."

"Call me Shay."

She smiles, like being given my nickname is a treat. "Shay, then. We're hoping we'll find a way to . . . decontaminate you, and then you may be able to leave this place and go back to your lives as much as you can."

Decontaminate? They think we're contaminated? I'm forgetting to radiate sweet; now I'm just shocked.

She must read my face. "Don't worry, Shay. No matter what—you're safe here. Now, how about we start with a few simple psychological tests?"

She shows me some blots of ink on paper and asks me what they look like. Then tries the I-say-one-word-and-you-say-whatever-pops-into-your-head malarkey.

And then finishing sentences.

"Try this one, Shay. The thing I want most in the world is . . ."

"Mum and Kai back."

She smiles sympathetically.

"I'm really good at . . ."

"Science. Puzzles. Finding missing pieces, working things out."

"I'm really bad at . . ."

"Housework. Remembering where I put things."

She nods intently and records what I say. "We're nearly done for today; I just have one more question to ask you. Since you were ill and then recovered, what has changed?" She says the words in an offhand way, like this is a throwaway at the end—but there is something about the intensity of concentration in her aura that tells me this is the most important thing of all.

"What has changed? Let's see: both *my* world and *the* world. My mother died. Almost everyone where I lived died. Once I realized I was a carrier I turned myself in, and instead of being thanked for my civic-mindedness, I was drugged and brought here unconscious to be experimented on." Sweet can fly out the window.

"I can appreciate how difficult that—"

"Really, can you? Do you know what it feels like to think people all around you died, just because they got too close to you?"

"No. I guess I don't. But that isn't what I was asking you. How have *you* changed, Shay?" This is the thing she most wants to know.

I stay silent.

"Well, I can tell you a few things." She consults her tablet. "You can tell truth from lies—as if you were reading minds, one witness said. You could stop yourself from bleeding; heal yourself." She doesn't believe that one. "And you can make people sit and listen, and stop them from interrupting or doing anything at all."

And I killed people too. Do they know that? I consider her carefully and dismiss it—they don't know. At least, Dr. Smith doesn't. The soldiers I killed were part of SAR, and they were trying to kill me, so it was self-defense, but if Dr. Smith is anything to go by, they don't know about it here.

"Go on, Shay, tell me: what were you thinking just then?"

I'm startled. "Can you read minds too?"

She smiles at my slipup—at saying *too*. "No, I don't share that ability. Though at times it'd be really useful to my work, it could be a burden, I think. I'm just good at reading the signals people make. Is that what you do?"

If her aura is just another kind of signal, then yes. And she is so *curious*; she wants to know, to understand.

So do I. The thought hits me with force: I want to know why and how I can do the things I can do. Maybe she could help me work this out?

I regard both her and her aura carefully. There is nothing threatening about her, this Dr. Smith. But who else might be listening? For all I know, SAR could be pulling her strings without her knowing about it.

"Shay, being different from other people can be really difficult. If you explain to me how things are for you, maybe I can help. What has changed about you since you were ill? How about you start with explaining how you can tell if someone is telling the truth or lying, like you did at the air force base in Shetland." She is intent, encouraging, but I don't know what I should or shouldn't say, so I opt for evasion.

I shrug. "I just guessed. Maybe I'm just good at reading signals too." And auras: hers is disappointed.

"That's okay, Shay. I understand that you're scared and find it hard to trust me just now. I hope that over time you will. We'll talk another day."

Next I'm sent to another room to do a written test—an IQ test. I sail through it without really having to think. The questions are easy; too easy. Is this because of the changes inside me, the ones that Dr. Smith is so interested in? It must be. We did one at school last year and it was really hard.

Even as part of me wonders if I should slow down or get some of them wrong, I can't stop myself. The sheer delight of getting questions right and knowing they are right pulls me through in a race to the end.

CHAPTER 5

BACK IN THE TV ROOM, board games have been abandoned, and there is an ongoing battle for the remote control.

I tune out, close my eyes, and pretend to sleep.

Spike?

Yeah?

We were definitely drugged. And they want to study us and work out how to decontaminate us.

He's shocked. Then rueful. *Well, there you go. It is true that you can attract more flies with honey. Good work.* A pause. *I don't want to be decontaminated.*

Me neither. At least, I don't think I do. It sounds somehow very *wrong*, but then I'm wistful—maybe they can fix me, and then I can leave this place, and be with Kai.

Who's Kai?

I'm surprised. *Didn't know I'd broadcast that.*

You're not used to being around other survivors, are you? You can choose what to share, what to keep to yourself. It's like this. He shows me how to separate projected thoughts from private ones—how to send the thoughts I want to out, but at the same time hide the rest of me behind walls visualized in my mind. But Spike's curiosity remains.

Kai is—was—my boyfriend. He's immune.

Was?

I left him to turn myself in. This time I carefully shield any thoughts of that day.

You turned yourself in? You're crazy!

Gee, thanks. It seemed like the right thing to do, rather than randomly infect everyone I came into contact with.

He's silent for a while; shielded. *Another time—we need to talk properly. But back to Dr. Smith. I pretty much got the good doc to admit she doesn't know where we are, but apart from that didn't come up with much.*

I may know a little about that, though not from Dr. Smith. And I show Spike in my thoughts the view I'd had from the bird flying above.

He's startled. *How the hell did you do that?*

So there are things I know that he doesn't? *I kind of reach out to the life around me; it's hard to explain.*

Show me, he says, and I try—remembering every detail with the bird from the time when I first sensed her above me.

The landscape looks familiar—we could be in Yorkshire, maybe?

Does it matter where we are? We *can't leave.*

I've got to try this bird trick. Does it work with people?

Do you mean being able to look out through their eyes? I don't know, I haven't tried it.

Maybe it wouldn't work with survivors anyway, like how it is with the way we are talking now.

What do you mean?

We can only do this if we both agree—and then we only get the thoughts we project to each other. You can't dip into my mind unless I let you.

So that's why he was giving me the raised-eyebrow, unspoken-question look before—he wanted an invitation to chat.

A hand pushes my shoulder, and I open my eyes. "Now you're the sleepy one," Ami says. "It's time for lunch."

It's a buffet and it looks okay—marginally better than a school cafeteria. There's someone with an *I* on their hand handing us plates as we go in.

Spike's there already, waiting for us, looking at the man doing the plates. *I wonder . . .* I can read the words he hasn't said: he wants to try to see through the man's eyes, like I did with the bird.

Better not. If it works and they notice, you could get sent to solitary.

If they notice.

Ami pushes in front of me to the buffet. "You snooze you lose," she says, and I wonder if I've been staring off into space again.

You need to learn to divide your attention, or they'll wonder why you take so many naps. Watch.

Spike starts an out-loud conversation with Ami with a running commentary inside my head at the same time, never missing a beat with either.

Ami is smiling up at him, her head tilted to one side, playing with her hair, and I see what I hadn't noticed before when she looks at him that way. He's kind of cute, in a geeky sort of way.

Why, thank you.

Don't be so cheeky. Stop eavesdropping in my head.

Remember to screen and I won't be able to.

Ami is telling some story about sneaking into a concert, her hand on Spike's arm.

Watch out, she likes you.

What? He's startled and loses his train of thought with Ami in midsentence, and I laugh.

Ami turns to me, raises an eyebrow. "What's so funny?" she says, and that makes me laugh more.

"Nothing," I finally manage to say. "Sorry, it's just me." Now Spike is struggling to keep a straight face too, and he turns a laugh into a cough.

In the afternoon those of us who've had our little meetings already are shown the gym and library and told to amuse ourselves.

Time to work out. I'm on a cross trainer; Spike is rowing. Ami is on a treadmill and trying to look like she is fit and working out without actually sweating, which is quite a thing to achieve. Beatriz isn't interested and sits in a corner with a book.

I look around me. People seem to have naturally settled into small groups—mostly along age lines, like ours. They're chatting, exercising, or reading—but something isn't quite right, and it hasn't been for a while now. I'm liking the cross trainer and feeling my muscles do something when they've been lazy for too long; it feels good, but . . .

It also feels *wrong*. We're all so content, chill. All the fear and anger and pain has slipped away; we're all so . . . agreeable. Doing what we're told. Even Spike seems to have forgotten his endless list of unanswered questions.

Spike? I think we've been drugged again.

How so?

Everyone is too happy.

Silence. *I know I should be angry, and I sort of am, but not like I should be.*

Give me a minute. I think there may be something we can do about it.

My feet and arms keep doing their thing on the cross trainer, but I close my eyes and *reach*—reach inside me. I've done this before to heal myself; can I find whatever is in my system and neutralize it? I concentrate, remembering to keep going on the cross trainer at the same time so no one will notice I'm zoning out again.

Inside me, my blood rushes through my veins and arteries, doing its usual work but faster, since my heart rate is high from this exercise. There's a warm flush on my skin.

Look in; closer. There is hemoglobin; white cells; platelets. *Closer.* Molecules . . . atoms . . . particles, and I want to get lost with them as they spin.

Focus.

Something is foreign.

There is something in my blood that shouldn't be there. I follow it around my body and my brain and send it to my liver at top speed to be processed and dealt with.

Gradually my head starts to clear, and I speed up the process until all traces of it are gone.

Finally I open my eyes. I'm furious to the core but trying to hide it from my face as I look around—at Beatriz, smiling at the book she is reading; at Ami, laughing and flicking her hair as Spike tells her some joke or other. They're managing us, aren't they? Making us safe, compliant. Enough of that stuff I found in my blood, and no doubt we'd do anything they asked us to do, like how I raced through that IQ test earlier.

Spike?

Hmmm?

You can eliminate the drugs by speeding up how they are metabolized. Watch. I link to his thoughts and show him what I did and how. Then I leave him to try it for himself.

I get off the cross trainer. The people around me were strangers just a day ago, yet we share so much—we're all survivors. We're a disparate group of people brought together by unique abilities and the tragedy of what we are at the same time. I have more in common with the people in this room than anyone else on the planet—Kai and Iona included.

A day ago we were all torn apart by emotions we couldn't deal with, and now . . . they're happy.

Beatriz giggles at something in her book and turns the page. Being an only child, I haven't been around a lot of younger children, other than when we visited my cousins now and then.

Another pang of loss.

But she's nothing like I expect an eight-year-old to be.

Her aura is calm—all clear primary colors. She answers questions if asked; otherwise she mostly sits still and quiet—so composed it's scary.

Unlike Ami, who never shuts up.

As Beatriz continues to smile at her book, I wonder: is it such a bad thing to make her feel better?

When Spike touches my mind again a bit later, his fury is so strong I nearly trip up, as if I'd been slapped.

Tonight. Deal with whatever they put in our dinner the same way, and we'll talk tonight.

CHAPTER 6

WE GO BACK TO OUR ROOM to shower before dinner. After that Beatriz is still reading, Ami is playing with her hair in front of the mirror, and I'm lying on my bed, staring at the ceiling.

"What do you think they are going to do with us?" Ami says.

"I don't know," I say.

"It's probably against the UN or human rights or something to keep us locked up in here forever."

"I guess. But I'm not sure that applies if letting us out could kill ninety-five percent of the population of the planet."

"Good point." She's quiet for about three seconds. "I call dibs on Spike."

"What?"

"Spike, you know—the cute one with the glasses."

"I know who he is, what do you mean?"

"If we don't get out, man options are limited—I'm staking a claim."

"Honestly, are you *serious*? Is there something else we can talk about, anything? *Please?*"

"Oh, somebody is sensitive. Are you jealous?"

Unexpectedly Beatriz looks up from her chair in the corner of the room. "You shouldn't be like that, Ami. Shay's got a broken heart."

I look at her in surprise.

"It's there, I can see it." Beatriz gets up—holds out her hands to me over where my heart is, then gives me a hug.

And something happens. A warmth spreads out from her to me, but it isn't from this small girl who has lost everything getting up and out of herself and reaching out to me—not in that way. She's *doing* something—or trying to.

Stop that, I say in her mind.

Doesn't it make you feel better?

Yes. But that isn't the point. It's not me *feeling that way.*

She's disappointed but withdraws, and the pain rushes back.

"You're doing the zombie face again. Are you two talking inside your heads so I can't hear you?" Ami says, finally working out what's been going on.

"If you talked less, then maybe we'd get more of a chance to talk out loud," Beatriz says, and my eyes widen in surprise. Ami scowls.

"High five!" I say and hold out a hand, and Beatriz hits it. She almost smiles.

That night when we all go to our rooms, the weight of needing to sleep is pressing in on me again. I'm fighting it, wanting to stay awake—to process and sift through the things that have happened, to try to work some things out—and wasn't there something else I need to do? I'm nearly asleep when some fragment of consciousness reminds me to *reach* in, focus—find the drugs in my system, neutralize them, and open my eyes.

CHAPTER 7

I CREEP SILENTLY TO MY BEDROOM DOOR. I'm early; Spike had said to meet in the TV room at 2:00 a.m., and it's only just after midnight. I hesitate, somehow unable to believe it could be this easy—that we can just slip out of our rooms and go and have a chat without being noticed.

But why would anybody bother watching, when they think we're all in a chemically induced sleep?

They would if they knew we could neutralize drugs like I've done. Or if they're extra paranoid.

I *reach* out.

There's a spider on the wall in the hallway and I watch from his web, staying quiet, waiting. I'm about to give up and open the door when the spider web sways ever so slightly—from movement in the air or vibration of the wall?

Or footsteps.

I feel him now. A man. Bored and walking back and forth, up and down this hall and the next one, past our rooms.

He walks to the end, and I count the seconds between when he walks past my door, then reappears again.

Spike's door is the other way, and I don't think there is enough time to get out of my room and away before the watcher turns around again. I need to distract him from his duties and send him away.

Thirsty, so thirsty. Parched. Tea, kettle; thirsty, so very thirsty . . .

I project thirst and tea at him over and over again, until finally he goes through the door at the end of the hall to the dining room. The door shuts behind him.

I open my door.

The hall lights are on, but dimmed. I slip down the hall, fast and silent on bare feet.

All the rooms have the names of their occupants on the doors. I walk quickly, reading as I go, until I find the one with *Spike* on it.

Spike, are you awake?

Shay?

There are footsteps behind me now and I open his door, slip into his room, and shut the door quietly behind me. They are too loud to be the watcher this time—it sounds like several sets of feet. Have they noticed I'm missing?

There's someone in the hall—someone's coming.

Hide, here. Spike gestures urgently to the space between his bed and the wall.

I sprint over and duck down just in time: the door opens. I look under the bed, along the floor, and across the room: there are two sets of feet coming into Spike's room. There are wheels too—a wheelchair? They're across the room. There are sounds of something being moved, and then there are feet on the wheelchair's footrests.

The door opens again, and the chair is pushed out the door. It closes; they're gone.

What the hell? They've taken Fred.

I get up and look across the room, to where Spike points to an empty bed.

We decide it's safest to stay where we are to talk. Spike's other roommate is snoring so loud in his drugged slumber that he'll cover us if we're quiet. We sit next to each other on the floor between his bed and the wall, a place where I can duck down and hide again if anyone else comes.

"So let's analyze the situation," Spike whispers, choosing words over silent conversation, as if he doesn't trust his thoughts to be coherent just now. "They drugged us at dinner to make us sleep, and one of us was taken in the night—and we have no idea where or why. They also drug us when we're awake to keep us happy and compliant."

"Yep, that's it."

"What are we going to do about it?"

"I don't know. We could tell everybody, show them how to neutralize the drugs." But then I think of Beatriz and how she smiled at her book today: does she really want to feel everything again? "But even with the drugs, we're better off than we were. I don't want to get sent back to solitary, which they might do if they realize their drugs aren't working."

"So shall we take them, and be happy and have a good night's sleep all the time? That's not so bad." That's what he says, but he radiates fury. "We should confront them, so they know we know what they're doing. And that it is pointless."

"I can see why you want to do that. But how about we try to learn all we can about what they're up to while they don't know we can stop the drugs? Let's work out what's really going on here before we decide what to do."

"Maybe we should get a few of the others to help us, ones that are still under the radar and can get away with more than we can?"

"Ami?"

He smiles. "I think she . . . er . . . lacks the mental stamina to be secretive."

"Huh." I hesitate. "It may seem crazy, but Beatriz? There's more going on with her than you might think." I tell Spike what she did earlier.

"Wow. She did that without your say-so? And she somehow knew stuff about you? She must have been in your head without you knowing."

"Or maybe she's just a good observer of people? But if she can do that to *us*, imagine what she could learn from Dr. Smith. Influencing someone with simple suggestions—like convincing that guard he's thirsty so he goes to get a drink—is one thing. I've never managed to really get into someone's head to sift through their thoughts without them knowing it, even non-survivors." Like Kai. "I wouldn't dare try when so much rides on not getting caught."

"I think we need to remember she's only eight years old, though. She might do that with Dr. Smith and find things that upset her. Should we be putting her in that position?"

"Fair point. Maybe we should think about it some more."

Spike suggests a few others that he knows and thinks will be up for it—Ali, who he has to describe before I remember which one he is. And Elena, the quiet woman in her sixties who lost her children and grandchildren to the flu.

We talk through much of the night, trying to come up with something resembling a plan, watching and listening in case they bring Fred back.

They don't.

Finally I creep down the hall before the bell, past the watcher, and into my room.

CHAPTER 8

AFTER A WAY-TOO-EARLY 6:00 A.M. ALARM and a breakfast that tastes like dust from worry, I'm summoned to see Dr. Smith.

"Good morning, Shay," she says when I peek through the door. "Did you get to sleep more easily last night?"

"Yes, thank you," I lie.

I sit in the chair when she gestures. "Today we're going to do some more tests, all right, Shay?" Dr. Smith says. "But first I'm going to tell you a little about what we did yesterday." She seems really excited about something and beams at me.

"Sure." I remind myself I'm supposed to be all happy and not have a headache from having been awake all night and smile back at her.

"It's your IQ test result. You got a perfect score—this has never been recorded before, to my knowledge. And you did the test faster than any member of Mensa has ever done."

"I did?" I'm startled, even though it had seemed way too easy. "How about everyone else here?"

"Well, I shouldn't really discuss other patients with you. But everyone did ridiculously well."

So I was right: being a survivor *has* booted up my brain to a new level, and there is the proof. There's a weird shiver inside. The only perfect score . . . ever? And everyone else did well too: it's not just me, it's all of us.

"Let's get started now, shall we?"

She starts with a video test. People tell facts about themselves, looking toward the camera, and I have to guess if they're lying or telling the truth, then push the corresponding button.

And I have no idea: I can't see auras in a recording; I can't feel their thoughts when they're not here.

Then she's got a list of things to read out herself: true or false. And while the answers are obvious in her aura, what I should do isn't. But then I think they already know I can do this, don't they? And I wouldn't be obstructive if I was all happy, like I'm supposed to be from their drugs. In the end I answer honestly.

"You got every single one correct. How do you do that, Shay?"

"I don't know," I lie. I project a feeling of truthfulness at her, since I'm not a great liar. "I just sort of know, but I don't know why."

"There is one more phase to this test. Can you follow me, please?"

We go down a hall to a medical room with equipment and a few white-coated types, and fear rushes in. Have I been here before? But I don't quite remember.

"Don't be scared. We're just going to do a scan. It won't hurt."

I swallow, trying to quell my heart rate, to stay placid like I should be. "Dr. Smith, *why* are we doing these tests?" I can't stop myself from asking.

"We're trying to work out what is different about you," she says, and she's telling the truth, but that isn't all of it. There is something she isn't saying.

"You know you can't lie to me," I say.

"I suppose not! I wouldn't anyhow." Again, the truth.

"Do you know why we're doing these tests?" A different question, with different emphasis.

How involved is she in what happens in this place?

She half frowns. "To learn everything we can. Why else? To work out how your brain works and what has gone wrong."

"So you can fix it."

"Exactly."

"If I do this, will you show me the results? Will you explain them to me?"

She hesitates. "I'll have to check, but yes: I can't see why not. Now, lie back here and listen to my words—try to stay still." She gives me a button in each hand. "If I tell the truth, push the button in your left hand. If I lie, the right one."

The machine whirs and makes weird noises. I hear her voice inside of it. I can't see her aura anymore but I *reach* a little, and she isn't far—I can see the truth, the lies. I do her test, but the whole time, part of me is in a whirl of panic.

They want to fix what has gone wrong in my brain, but it hasn't gone *wrong*. It's gone *right*—more right than it ever has been before.

I've got senses I never knew existed before I was ill. But now that I've tasted the world this way, taking them away would be like cutting out my eyes.

They can't take this away from me and leave me whole.

CHAPTER 9

THAT AFTERNOON WE'RE BACK IN THE GYM, and Spike has arranged a group-think: something that is new for me. Spike explains how it works. Our merry band of mischief makers now includes Elena, Ali, and a surprise guest: Beatriz. It turns out that even though we hadn't decided whether we should include her, she noticed something was up. She's here whether she should be or not.

It feels weirdly like trying to listen to four radio stations at once.

Spike: *Fred still isn't back.*

Elena: *One of the women is missing as well—Carmen.*

Ali: *What's happened to them?*

Beatriz: *I can't reach them. They must be unconscious or far away or dead.*

Her thoughts are so matter-of-fact.

Spike: *I asked Dr. Smith about Fred, and she felt surprised and worried—I honestly think she doesn't know anything about it.*

Me: *They know we can get truth from people; it stands to reason they'd keep knowledge they don't want us to have from the people who interact with us directly.*

Elena: *Good point.*

Me: *I didn't know whether to be honest or not in the tests. We need to decide what we're okay with them knowing about what we can do, and what we'd rather keep to ourselves. I probably just confirmed to them without meaning to that we need direct access to people to know what they're thinking.*

Spike: *I think we should go further than that and go on strike. No more tests; no more displays of our abilities. Unless and until they're straight with all of us about their plans and tell us what happened to Fred and Carmen.*

Ali: *That'll only work if everyone, not just us, agrees. And we'll have to show all of them how to stop the drugs from working.*

Me: *I'm nervous about being this direct. You know that honey thing, Spike?*

Spike: *I know, I know—more flies with honey. But I don't think subtle will work with this group. If we don't take a stand, how far will they go? Who might disappear next?*

The others agree with him.

Spike: *Okay then, we need to get everyone else in on this next.*

Elena: *And then we can bargain with these doctors.* Her thoughts are grim; she doesn't think we'll get anywhere.

Spike: *Maybe we need to come up with an "or else."*

At dinner that night—when all the remaining twenty-one of us are in the same room—Beatriz and I talk to each of them, one at a time. Silently. We all agree not to do any more survivor tricks or displays of our weirdness. We'll see how long it takes them to get bored watching us. And Beatriz—who it turns out is the best of us at projection—shows everyone how to stop the drugs from working.

We all head for the TV room after lasagna and a not-bad tiramisu. There are no current channels; it's all old series and movies playing on an endless loop. No news of the outside world or anything to worry us. But a *Friends* marathon session is a great way to avoid actual thought.

Sooner or later they'll start to wonder why we aren't all falling asleep.

Spike's mind touches mine somewhere in the middle of the third episode. *Shay, I'm not sure we're taking this far enough.*

What do you mean?

I still think we should try to control one of the guards or doctors and see what we can find out.

No! Try this first, see what happens. That is way too risky. If anyone notices, you know what Dr. Smith said?

I know; back off to solitary. But that's only if I get caught.

He grins, and I'm full of fear for him. *Promise me you won't!*

He hesitates. *No promises. But I'll wait and see how things go, like you said.*

I try again but he still won't promise anything beyond that, and I'm full of unease.

CHAPTER 10

THE NEXT DAY I'M SCHEDULED TO BE FIRST with Dr. Smith again. Today I'm not going to play.

But I *am* curious.

"What happened last night, Shay?"

"What do you mean?"

"Everyone staying up late and watching TV. We were a little surprised."

"Because of the sleeping drugs?"

Her curiosity is even stronger than mine, but as if she knows there is no point, she doesn't ask.

Yet. Instead, she opens a laptop, angles it so we can both see the screen.

"I said I'd show you your test results from yesterday: here they are."

She's got cross-section scans of my brain and graphs underneath. "These show brain activity. There are whole regions of your brain that were active that normally are not.

"And see here: When I lied—where there are *x*'s on the graph—this happened; there is a peak there. When I told the truth—the *y*'s on the graph—the peak is here instead."

"What does that mean?"

"I've got no idea, but I'm hoping we can find out! Today we're going to—"

"No."

"No?" She's surprised.

"I don't want to do any more tests." But I'm lying, aren't I? I'm dying to know what all this means.

Yet I don't want to *actually* die for it at the same time. I don't want to get to the point where they can't learn anything else from tests and scans and decide to cut up my brain instead.

I stand up and walk to the door, half expecting to be stopped, but nothing happens.

I turn back and look at her.

"Tell whoever is pulling your strings that we need to talk."

CHAPTER 11

IT'S ANOTHER DAY BEFORE I'M SENT FOR BY ALEX.

"You seem to be a revolutionary," he says, and from the way he says it, he approves of revolutionaries.

"Who, me?"

"You and Beatriz, and a few other friends. I haven't quite worked out who they all are yet."

I raise an eyebrow, surprised they noticed Beatriz, that they'd even suspect her of anything when she's so small.

"Why have you stopped cooperating with the tests?" he asks.

"I have a question for you first."

"Go on."

"Is Kai all right—do you know?"

"I don't know where he is." He's hiding something—it's in his aura. He's not lying, exactly, but there is something he's not saying.

I frown. I can read this in his aura, but his thoughts? They're opaque, and I don't know why. Has he somehow worked out a way to block us?

He smiles as if he knows what I'm thinking, and I'm disturbed.

"So are you going to answer my question now?" he says.

Two can play at this game. "As truthfully as you answered mine—of course. We're not lab rats. We want to know what is going to happen to us and why."

He nods slowly. "That seems fair. I'll come after dinner tonight and have a chat with everyone."

I go back to the TV room and update the others; Spike isn't there, and my stomach twists in knots. His appointment was a while ago; is he still in with one of the doctors? But surely he would have just refused to do their tests and then walked out, like I did?

Maybe he's still with the doctor; he probably couldn't resist arguing with her. Once he's had his say, he'll leave, and everything will be okay. I tell myself this, but I don't believe it.

Spike, where are you? What have you done?

There is no answer.

CHAPTER 12

SPIKE DOESN'T COME TO DINNER THAT NIGHT. I check his room and ask everyone—no one knows where he is. I cast about for him over and over again with my mind, but there is no answer, and my panic is increasing. Beatriz tries to find him too, and she can't either.

Alex comes just after dinner, like he said he would.

Not that I've eaten much with my stomach twisting with worry. But I did notice that dinner came without sleeping drugs tonight; I guess they figured there's no point when we can stop them from working.

I fix Alex with my eyes. He *will* tell me where Spike is; he *will* bring him back to us.

He waits until everyone is silent.

"Hi. I'm Alex. I met some of you the day you arrived. I'm a professor of physics, and I've been brought here to study Aberdeen flu survivors."

"Why a physicist?" somebody asks.

"The flu isn't really a flu," Alex says. "It's caused by antimatter." There is a mixture of gasps and puzzled glances around the room.

Not many knew, did they?

"Antimatter? What even is that?" Ami asks—one of the puzzled.

"Antimatter is made up of particles that have the same mass as matter, but opposite magnetic or electrical properties," he answers. "In simple terms, matter and antimatter can't coexist. If they come into contact, they annihilate each other."

"And that is what is killing everyone?" Elena asks. "And changed us?"

"Yes on both counts," he answers. "And as part of our studies on you here, we have worked out how to test for survivors—using a scan that detects antimatter. So even though you're not sick anymore, and you survived, there is still some antimatter in some form or another inside each of you. We're trying to work out what effect it has and how to extract it."

"What happened to Fred and Carmen?" Ali asks.

"They volunteered. They both have families that weren't in the quarantine zones; they wanted to have the antimatter extracted so they could leave and go home to their families. It didn't work out—unfortunately they both died in surgery."

"You killed them!" Elena says, fury in her eyes and her aura.

"No. We tried experimental surgery with full consents from patients who wanted to be cured. We learned a lot from them; next time it may work. But we're still analyzing the results."

"Where is Spike?" I demand, unable to keep quiet any longer. "He would never have agreed to that!"

Alex turns to me, and there is regret all through his aura. "I'm sorry. You're right; he didn't. But Spike broke the one rule we can't overlook. He's back in isolation."

"What did he do?"

"At his appointment this afternoon, he . . . ah . . . controlled the doctor's mind. She was about to give him full access to all of our research files and door codes, which triggered a remote alarm she didn't know about—one that is set off if an attempt is made to access files globally in this way. It was set up as a precaution against just such a security breach."

No; no, Spike. Why take such a risk? Tears are pricking in the back of my eyes.

"Are there any more questions?"

There are none. We're all shocked into silence.

"You can cooperate and help us, or not, as you choose. No one will be made to do anything they don't want to do, but you'll never be able to leave this place with an antimatter time bomb still ticking away inside of you. Understood? So *you* have to decide; each of you has this decision to make.

"And finally—the drugs we were using were to help you deal with everything. Again, you're quite right: we should have asked. If anybody is having trouble sleeping or coping, let us know and one of the doctors will prescribe some pills the old-fashioned way.

"Now I think you need to talk among yourselves."

He leaves.

Conversation breaks out all around, but I stay silent.

"Yes, Carmen's family was in Portsmouth . . ."

"What was Spike trying to find out? Is there more they haven't told us?"

"Fred's was in London . . ."

"They warned us. Why'd Spike do it?"

"Carmen would have done anything to get back to them. That must be right . . ."

"Poor Spike . . ."

I block it all out and focus on Spike: on calling him again and again with my mind, but there is no answer.

Elena comes and sits next to me.

Well. We thought we wanted honesty, she says.

Yeah. I'm sure Alex was telling the truth with everything he said—but I felt he was holding things back too.

So did I.

Beatriz? I bring her into our conversation. *What did you think—was Alex telling the truth the whole time?*

She's puzzled. *There's something about him I don't understand. I tried to get into his thoughts, but I couldn't. That's never happened before.* And then she's scared. *They're not going to extract me, are they? I don't want to be extracted!*

She comes over to me, and I give her a hug, pull her onto my knee, and put my arms around her.

No way. It'll never happen. Will it, Elena?

She puts her bony arm around my shoulders and gives Beatriz a pat on the arm. *No. We won't let them; we promise.*

But Beatriz knows we don't know if we can keep this promise, and she's still scared.

CHAPTER 13

KAI IS HERE, LIKE HE OFTEN IS IN MY DREAMS *. . . and nightmares. Which one will this be?*

He strokes my hair. Lies down beside me. His body curves against mine, and he kisses me.

Then he pulls away.

"You tricked me."

"I'm sorry."

"Are you? Not as sorry as you're going to be."

Not as sorry as you're going to be . . .

Not as sorry as you're going to be . . .

I force myself awake and open my eyes, Kai's accusing words still ringing in my ears. There's noise—a crash, shouts.

I sit up in a hurry, struggling to throw off my dream. What's going on?

Our door is thrown open—it's Alex.

He's rousing Beatriz, dragging her out from under the covers.

Half-asleep and whimpering protests, she's more like the child she should be. He lifts her in his arms.

Shay? The facility is being attacked. He's in my head, and the shock makes me wake completely. Only survivors can talk like this, fully in my mind. Does this mean . . . how can this be?

Are you a survivor? I ask him silently.

I'll explain later. We've got to get out of here. He answers the same way; I didn't imagine it.

And now he's at our door, peeking out first, then pushing it open. *Follow me if you want to live.*

I get up. We're being *attacked*? Who's attacking? There are distant screams, shouts. Smoke. I'm coughing, following Alex and Beatriz to our door, not sure at first if I'm doing it to follow Alex or because he is taking Beatriz.

We're hurrying down the hallway before I remember.

Ami? I shout in her mind. *Ami, you have to get out!* There's no answer, and I turn back.

Leave her, there's no time! Alex says, and then I'm angry.

And then I'm scared.

CHAPTER 14

I STUMBLE AFTER ALEX AND BEATRIZ IN THE SMOKE.

What's happening?

There are angry voices, shouting, getting closer. I *reach* out and can feel their thoughts—those who attack. Waves of hate and fear and death surround us. They've found us. They hunt survivors, burn them; they've found us, and they're exultant.

The noose is tightening. The mob and their fire are getting closer. All survivors must die.

Why do they hate us?

We're only a danger to them if they get too close. How did they find us when our location is such a secret that *we* weren't even told where we are?

And they don't just want to kill us—they want to use fire. Bodies of those who die from the epidemic are burned to stop the contagion from spreading; they must think burning us to death will do the same thing. But will that make us all like Callie—dark and silent but unable to really die?

The weight of fear and revulsion focused on us is so heavy, it is hard to move.

Hurry! Alex, still carrying a crying Beatriz, is running and pulling me and Elena along with him. Is she the only other one who answered his mental call to follow? There are so few of us. What has happened to the others?

We come upon a door, a hidden door to a secret way out; he shows us where it leads in his mind. He opens the door, and he and the others go through, but I don't.

What about Spike? I say.

There's no time, Alex answers—the same thing he said about Ami, and I'm ashamed. I was so disoriented and scared that I didn't insist we go back for her. I won't do that again.

No! I won't go without him. If he's locked inside a hospital room, he can't save himself. Where is he?

Alex curses and pushes Beatriz into Elena's arms. He has a quick mental exchange with Elena that I can't follow. He comes back through the doorway, and then shuts the door on them.

We may have to protect ourselves, he says. *Are you up to it?*

Yes. I show him how I attacked soldiers from SAR, but I hide the promise I'd made to myself that I'd never do it again.

Good girl. Now RUN. And do this. He shows me mentally how to filter the carbon monoxide and other poisons out of the smoky air we must breathe, and my head starts to clear as we run.

Despite the fear and urgency, part of me is still stunned—marveling that Alex is a survivor too. He must be to talk to me like this, fully inside my mind. It's completely different when I talk to a non-survivor, like Kai—with Kai it was more like me receiving, finding Kai's thoughts, rather than Kai projecting them out.

So Alex is one of us, and none of us knew.

How is that even *possible*?

We reach a security door with a keypad, but the power has gone off; it doesn't work.

They're getting closer: I can feel the waves of hate getting stronger with every step they take toward us.

We're trapped.

I can override the door, but it'll take me a while and I have to concentrate, Alex says. *You're on, warrior girl.*

He's ripping the unit off the wall, pulling out the wires. The smoke is thickening, but I can still see when five of them run around the corner at the end of the hall.

They're wearing biohazard suits. And carrying flamethrowers and other weapons.

They whoop when they see us. Everything is in slow motion—they're running toward us, but each foot seems to hang in the air before it crashes back down to the ground.

Their auras are muted with the smoke and the suits they wear, but their hate and fear rear up ugly and clear enough to locate and target.

Stop now! I project inside their heads.

They pause, shocked, then shake it off and start toward us again. I attack their auras, strike at the energy waves that surround their hearts. The first few fall to the ground, and the others run back the way they came.

I stare at the bodies on the ground: dead. Hearts stopped. I'd wanted to try to just, I don't know, knock them out or something, but their hate was so strong that something in me reacted to it, and I couldn't do anything else. I'm frozen in shock.

Come on! The door is open now. Alex pulls me through, then shuts and disables it behind us. *You shouldn't have let any of them get away—they'll come back with reinforcements now. We'll have to go back another way.*

Alex runs down the hall, and I make myself follow. We run into a room that looks like the one I emerged into from my hospital room.

Again, the door controls won't work without power. Alex is fiddling with wires and finally gets a door to open.

Through it lies Spike on a hospital bed.

Spike!

Hmmmm? He's groggy. He half opens his eyes and then they close again.

Alex is lifting Spike over his shoulder like a sack of potatoes when the whole building rocks with an explosion.

This way! Alex yells in my head.

We run.

I follow him back through the door and down the hall to another door—does it lead to the courtyard?

One step closer . . .

Another . . .

Alex, ahead of me, is opening the door. He's through, and I'm nearly at the threshold to the door when there is a roar, a rush of air—

I glance back.

It must be a split second only, but time seems to slow enough that I can experience each of my senses.

Dazzled by the red and gold colors, the ball of fire . . .

Deafened by the roar and rush . . .

Choked by air too hot, too poisonous . . .

And most of all—above all—

Pain.

My body is engulfed in flame.

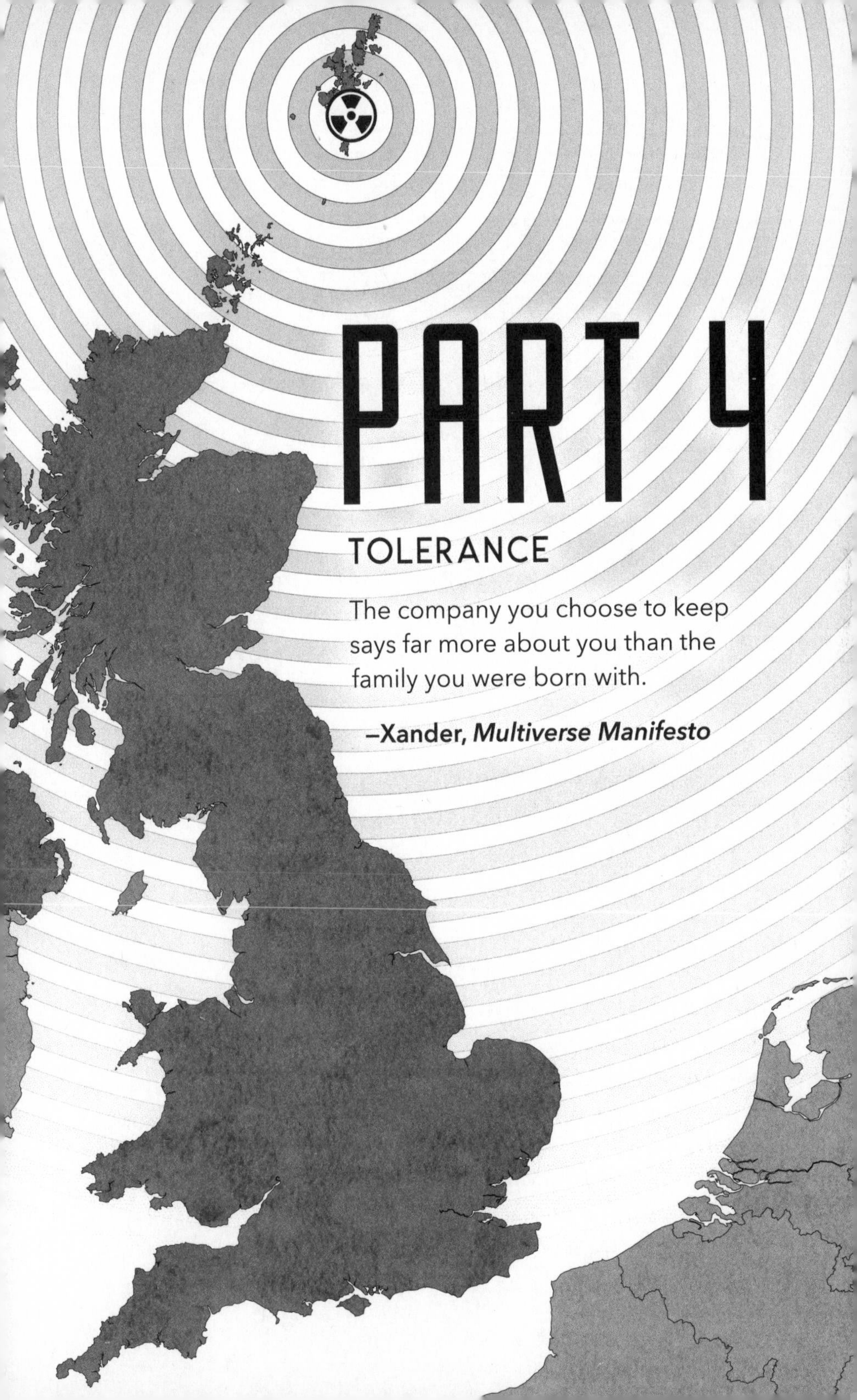

PART 4

TOLERANCE

The company you choose to keep says far more about you than the family you were born with.

–Xander, *Multiverse Manifesto*

CHAPTER 1

CALLIE

SCISSORS AND ANGER: NOT A GOOD COMBINATION. Freja hacks at her hair with fury until she looks like some sort of demented pixie, short blonde tufts sticking up at odd angles.

"I heard that!"

Sorry.

"I can't believe I'm cutting my hair. I really can't." And the anger is giving way to something else. Her back is trembling: is she *crying*?

"I am *not*. I don't cry!" And with those words she straightens her shoulders and shakes it off.

The morning paper that made her do this still sits next to her on the table—her photo and emblazoned across it, "Wanted: for murder." Just like we'd guessed, they're saying Freja shot that policeman—a policeman with a wife and four children.

It says she ran away with *an unidentified male accomplice:* no photo or description. Maybe they don't know it was Kai who was with her? It's either that or they're not releasing all that they know to the press. There are so many closed-circuit TV cameras in London, Freja said, that it was hard to believe they never caught a glimpse of Kai with her on any of them.

The door opens.

"Red?" she snaps before Kai has a chance to say anything. "Did you get copper red?"

"Yes," he says, and puts a bag on the counter.

She turns and faces him, a look on her face like she is daring him to say *anything*.

He stands there, tilts his head a little to one side, then walks around her to see from all angles.

"Well?" Her voice is dangerous.

"Short hair suits you. But give me the scissors, I'll just straighten it up a little." She reluctantly hands them over. "Here. Sit." He pushes her into a kitchen chair and snips a little here, a little there, carefully evening it out as best he can. It starts to look much better, but then Freja is one of those girls who could shave her head and wear a sack and still look good.

"Is the area clear, Callie?" Kai says, and I rush outside to look. The house I'd found for them to break into is set back from the street. Nobody's home, and there's no alarm. It's got that dusty unlived-in look, like no one has been here for a while; the fridge is empty, and mail is piled up on the front mat under the mail slot. Kai said that probably means no one is coming in regularly to check the place, or they'd put it on a table or something. Of course that doesn't mean that today isn't the day that whoever lives here is coming back.

But when I check up the road, there is no one heading this way.

All clear, I say when I come back, and Freja gives the thumbs-up to Kai. She's smearing dye into her hair now while Kai sweeps the floor, scooping up every single strand of blonde hair and putting it in a bag.

"Mr. Clean and Tidy," Freja says.

"If someone comes home and finds blonde hair everywhere and an empty box of red hair dye, it won't take long for somebody to put it together and amend your description," he says.

"You're right. I'm sorry." She's peering at the sheet of instructions. "Twenty minutes to wait now."

"Are you hungry?" Kai asks, and takes sandwiches out of the bag. "You pick—egg salad or ham?" She takes the ham and devours it in a way that says meals haven't been often enough lately.

He picks up the morning newspaper. "Did you get beyond the front page?"

"Isn't that enough?" She scowls. "Couldn't they at least have used a decent photo? I *hate* that one."

"Least of your worries," he says, and turns the page. "You're even bigger news than the epidemic: it's on page two." He folds the paper over and holds up page two: a full-color map of the UK with the latest quarantine zones marked. All of Scotland and northern England are in red now. No-go zones.

"It's like southern England and Wales have just written off the rest of the country," Kai says. "Can't they see that if it keeps moving like this, their fences will never be high enough to stop it?"

Freja sighs, tracing the boundary on the map with her finger. "Does anything we want to do even matter when everywhere people are still dying?"

"Yes. It must," Kai says. "The only hope we have is for the truth to be told, and the more of us there are to tell it, the better. So rinse off that dye, and we'll hide all traces of it. And then we'll get out of London. See if we can find that survivor group that contacted you, and any other survivors."

"Like Shay."

"Yes. And we can all work together; see what we can do to make things better. Right?" He holds up a hand.

"Right," she says, and they high-five.

Freja heads for the sink, starts rinsing her hair. She mutters, her voice too low for Kai to hear over the water rushing from the tap, as if she is saying it to herself: "If this disease rampages across the world, it is only people like us—survivors, the immune—who'll be left. It might make sense for them to recognize that."

Maybe . . . someone has.

CHAPTER 2

KAI

THE MILES GO BY OUTSIDE THE WINDOW. The bus is half empty; no one wants to go even a little bit north when that means getting closer to the quarantine zones, not unless they have to.

Freja sleeps against the window next to me. I've got to hand it to her: she looks really different. It isn't just the short red hair but the Goth look she went for to go with it: heavy dark eyeliner, black clothes. You'd never guess it was the same girl.

Though I'm not sure the same thing works on me. She'd insisted: shaved hair up one side of my head, dark eyeliner, the works. And I know she was right. They could be looking for me too. Even if I wasn't caught on closed-circuit TV with Freja, someone was looking for me in Glasgow, weren't they? They might not expect to see me in London, but my face could still be on a wanted list.

I rub absently at the itchy stubble on the left side of my head and wonder what Shay would think of this. There is the familiar twist of pain inside me that comes whenever I think of her, like now, without meaning to.

She is always there, on the edges of my thoughts, but thinking of her like this makes her take center stage—and the pain sharpens.

Though it hasn't happened as much lately.

Freja shifts in her sleep; her head turns toward me, and she leans against my shoulder. Her face is softer in her sleep. What has happened to her to make her so *angry*? Apart from recently. There is some set to how she is, something that seems more long-term than the epidemic and all that has followed from her being a survivor. She's the first person I've met in a long time that makes me feel like the level-headed one.

There's something indescribably lovely about the way she smells. I don't even know what it is, and I lean down to breathe her in even as I fight to pull away.

What would Shay think? The same thought as before is in my mind, but in an uncomfortable and different way.

Then Freja jolts awake as if someone has shouted in her head.

Someone *has*. "Callie says there's a roadblock ahead," she whispers. "They're checking inside every vehicle, then waving people on. Are they looking for me?"

"No way," I whisper back. "Even if they are, they're looking for a blonde ice queen. Not a ginger Goth."

She rolls her eyes like it doesn't matter, but I can feel her arm against mine—the muscles are taut, tense. She's scared.

We're slowing now, the traffic is lining up. My stomach is twisting. Will they be fooled? If they even *are* looking for Freja, or me, or both of us. The roadblock could have nothing to do with us—but somehow I don't believe it.

We inch forward; it seems to take forever. Our bus is finally next in the line.

I can feel Freja's fear, almost like she is projecting it outward, and in a strange way it seems to make me calmer. I nudge her with my shoulder and take her hand. Her pulse beats fast under her skin.

The bus doors open and two policemen get on. They walk down the aisle. They stop and talk to a blonde girl a few rows up, then keep going, scanning everyone as they go past. They don't even pause next to us.

I glance at Freja, and I'm so startled I have to stuff back an exclamation to stay quiet. She looks *different*—really different. Her features are coarser, her cheekbones not so high. The police walk back past us and get off the bus.

The bus starts and heads back up the road; her features blur a little, and then her face is back to the way it usually is.

How did she do that? I'm uneasy, weirded out—is this another survivor thing, being able to make yourself look different?

Like she knows what I'm thinking, she winks.

CHAPTER 3

CALLIE

IT'S DUSK. FREJA IS RADIATING HUNGER, she's tired, and she's stomping up the road she's been stomping up for the last few hours. Kai trails along beside her. He's more of a closed book to me than she is, but he must be hungry and tired too.

It's a quiet country lane and a good example of what the middle of nowhere actually looks like.

"Are you sure—" Kai starts to say.

"Yes!" Freja snaps. "I'm sure that was the right stop and that we're going the right way down the right road. And no, I don't know where we're going. Maybe it was all a hoax, or they've moved. Maybe someone will find our bleached bones in the sun in five years, picked clean by vultures or rats."

Tasty.

"Maybe if you tell me exactly what they said?"

She stops.

Her arms are crossed, and I imagine steam actually coming out of her ears. I visualize this and show it to Freja; she's startled and then starts to laugh.

"Okay, a good change of mood, but . . . ?" Kai shrugs his shoulders, confused.

She shakes her head. "It's Callie. She just showed me her version of what I look like just now—oh, never mind. *They said* to get off the bus where we did and to walk up this road."

"And that's it?"

"That's it. Well, they're not going to be too specific, are they? What if someone was spying on our conversation somehow? I assume the people we want to find are watching the road."

"But *where*? A mile from here, ten miles, or a hundred?"

"Lovely thought."

"Do you have a name of who we're trying to find?"

She hesitates and then shrugs. "The avatar said JJ, but that could just be an online name."

"Why don't we ask Callie to have a look ahead? She found you in London, after all. If there are any survivors around here, she might be able to find them. Or at least find a place we can stop to rest and get something to eat."

Callie?

I'm on it.

I blur up into the sky and along the road to see what the middle of nowhere looks like from a distance, but it's just more of the same stretching on and on. Rolling hills. Fields. Trees. A few farm buildings. No sign of movement, no traffic. No likely-looking cafés or empty houses to break into.

Are there any survivors watching out for us, hiding somewhere in this vast space?

How did I find Freja in London? I sort of felt out and around for anything that felt *different*—like Shay did, like Freja does. Ripples of emotion and intensity and, I don't know, a certain kind of *presence*. The only other living things that feel anything like survivors are cats.

I drop closer to the road that Kai and Freja are still walking on and go forward along it more closely, mile after mile—casting out, feeling all around . . .

But there is nothing. Nada. Zilch. The only point I can sense is Freja, well behind me now. I've been keeping up a light contact with her all along, so as not to lose track of them.

She's just as tired but more chilled out now; she's laughing at something Kai is saying.

Wait a sec. Is there something—someone—else? Some different vibration near where they are?

I try to home in on it, but just as I do, it vanishes.

I *reach* again for Freja, to go back to them so I can tell them I thought I felt something, but . . . there's nothing there anymore.

Freja? Freja?

She doesn't answer.

CHAPTER 4

KAI

I'M FLAT ON MY BACK ON THE GROUND. my head spinning a little. *What the . . . ?* I shake my head, confused, and try to sit up, but something is holding me down. I can't move or see anything. It's pitch-dark.

My eyes: they're shut. It takes a huge effort of will to open them even a little to a slit. There is this weight crushing down on me, but then, when I look . . . nothing is there.

It's not *real.* I open my eyes all the way, push this invisible wall aside, and sit up.

Freja is standing a short distance away, arms crossed, and the angry set is back in her shoulders. She's facing somebody, some guy. He's in profile—dark hair, tall and thin, about mid-twenties or so. There are a few others there too—a teenage boy and girl a bit younger than us—and they look like they're all having some sort of argument . . . but not out loud. All is silent.

Something is still holding me back, and *anger* bursts through it inside. Struggling against it, I finally manage to stand up.

"What the hell is going on here?"

The guy facing Freja turns toward me, amazement on his face. "I told you to stay still," he says out loud, and as he says the words the crushing weight is back, only now it's even more.

But it's not *real.* "Get out of my head!" I push it aside and step between him and Freja. "Who are you?"

He grins. "I'm the one who gets to decide what happens to you."

"Oh?" I say, and I can feel my muscles tensing, fists clenching.

Freja's hand is on my shoulder. "Stand down, Rambo. This is JJ. They're the ones we've been looking for."

"And that is kind of the problem," JJ says. "Freja is welcome. *You* most definitely are not." He's still smiling, but it is unsettling, and then something weirds out in his eyes: dark swirls like clouds through the colored part.

Something *tickles* in my mind, not a physical thing like before—something else—and everything goes black.

CHAPTER 5

CALLIE

FREJA? FREJA?

I cast out again and again, but there is nothing, no trace of her, and I'm starting to panic.

They can't just *vanish*. I've been up and down the stretch of road where they should be—concentrating on the area where I guess they're most likely to have been, based on the pace they were walking. I go slower, along the road surface, looking for something, anything . . .

There is a place where maybe the dirt is scuffed on the side of the road. As if someone fell over and then was dragged into the trees?

But I'm no tracker. I can't follow bent twigs or anything like that to see where they've gone.

Freja?

Still there is nothing.

Less than nothing.

It's almost like . . . something is missing. As if there is a blank patch in a murmuring world. Maybe something is blocking her?

It's harder than trying to find a person I can home in on; it's more vague. I think I can feel something in the nothing, but when I get closer, the sense of it vanishes.

Maybe if I go farther away, then come in toward whatever it is—or *isn't*—until it disappears again, and maybe if I do this over and over from all different directions, then the place in the middle of all that should be roughly what I'm looking for.

Huh. Sure it will.

I dash away until I sense it more strongly and come back in until it vanishes. I do this again and again from all different directions, noting where I lose the void each time—and it seems to be working. There is a rough circle of missing space in a wooded area well away from the road; somewhere inside of it I hope will be the place Freja and Kai have vanished to.

I go over the area in the circle fast to start with and then slower, but there is no sense of Freja or of anybody else. Frustrated and scared, I drop down to ground level. I'll check every inch if I have to.

I almost run into a tent before I see it.

Cautious now, I hang back, look around. There are a few more camouflaged tents and a low wooden cabin that blends into its surroundings so well that I'm almost on it before I see it.

This *must* be the place where Freja and Kai have been taken.

But there is a sense of dread inside me, and it's growing. It's like that time on the boat with Freja when I was imagining killer zombie rats and was so scared I almost left before I found her: that came from her, didn't it? Somebody else—a survivor—is making it so I don't want to be here.

I shake it off.

I check each tent. They're sparse: a few sleeping bags and other belongings. No one is inside any of them until I get to the last one, closest to the cabin: it's Kai.

His eyes are closed and he's breathing evenly—like he's asleep or unconscious. He's very still, but there are no injuries or anything I can see.

I'm guessing he didn't just decide to take a nap. What's going on?

I head for the cabin door.

The sense of dread and revulsion is getting stronger, and I still can't sense anybody—inside the cabin is a blank. I shrug off the urge to run in the other direction and instead flow under the door.

Once I'm inside the cabin, the dread vanishes. Freja is here, others too—five altogether—and I can sense all of them the same way as I do Freja. They're all survivors? It must be just outside the cabin that is blocked somehow. I stay shielded, low to the ground, and hope no one will see or sense me. The light is dim, so maybe they won't notice me seeping across the floor.

Freja is furious. I've seen her angry before, but this is well over her usual scale of rage.

Undo whatever it is you've done to Kai, or we have nothing to talk about, she says silently—they're talking in their minds.

He's perfectly fine; he's just having a nice sleep, a man answers. *I thought it'd be easier to talk about what we're going to do with him without him lumbering around with his fists.*

I don't care if you've sent him on a five-star Caribbean vacation. I have nothing to say to you until he comes back.

Another man, an older one, raises his hands. *I think everyone should calm down. JJ, you're not the law here, and we're not going to do anything to anybody.*

The first one—*JJ?*—turns to him angrily. *We can't just let him go. How can we trust him?*

How can we trust anybody? Even you. The others in the room—a woman and two teenagers, a boy and a girl—are looking back and forth between the two men now. *Wake him up, and let's get to know each other; we'll work it out soon enough.*

Freja's arms are crossed. She's scowling, her anger focused on JJ.

JJ leans back, an amused half smile on his lips. I don't like him. *I'm not sure why you're angry with us, Freja. You're the one who broke your word, told an outsider about our group, and brought him here. It's your fault he's in this predicament.*

Aren't I an outsider to you too? Do you mean he's an outsider because he isn't a survivor? So what? I trust him. I wouldn't have made it here if it wasn't for him and his sister.

He exchanges an alarmed look with the others. *His sister? Is there someone else who knows about us?*

I've had enough of listening in and draw myself up next to Freja.

Yes. Me.

They jump away, alarm and fear radiating through them, and despite everything—despite Kai and the fear and threat—I'm still happy *all* of them can see and hear me.

The older man crosses himself.

The girl, maybe a little younger than Freja, is the first to move. She looks fascinated and comes right up to me, stares into my eyes. *What are you?*

I was like you. This is what happens if they try to cure you.

Great dramatic entrance and all that, Freja says, *but where've you been?*

It was hard to find you. There was some sort of blankness over this place.

So, our clever shield doesn't work after all, JJ says, a glance at the other man. *And who are you?*

Freja answers for me: *Everyone, this is Callie—Kai's sister.*

The others, one by one, stop pulling away. They come closer—curiosity and fear warring inside of them, but curiosity starts to win. There is so much they want to know.

Cure? Is there a cure?

If who *tries to cure you?*

How?

Their questions all batter against me, but there is only one that I care about right now.

What have you done to my brother?

CHAPTER 6

KAI

I'M IN A WARM PLACE. *Soft arms are around me, and I'm breathing in deep, inhaling that delicious something, close and closer. Lost and falling. I shouldn't be here, but I don't care. I burrow my face in her neck, her hair, but her hair isn't dark—it's red, like the heat in my veins . . .*

"Kai?"

Someone is shaking my shoulder.

"Kai, wake up."

I shake off both the dream and the sleep and sit up in a hurry. I'm in a . . . tent? Freja is here, and all at once what happened by the side of the road floods back. My muscles tense, and I half spring up but then sit back down again when my head hits the top of the tent.

"Listen. You have to promise not to punch anybody, and in return, they've agreed to let you wake up. We're all going to talk and work things out together after dinner."

"After whatever the hell it is that they've done to me?" I'm furious.

I'm pretty pissed off about it too, she whispers inside my head, and I'm in turn startled and angry that she's in my mind. She's never tried that with me before, and my automatic instinct is to resist, to push her away. *Sorry. Best way to not be heard. Can we go softly, softly for now, until we work out what they're about? Callie agrees. Actually, she's the one who got them on our side. They want to know what she knows, and she said you were the one who can tell them all about Shetland and what happened there. Can you keep your cool, at least for now?*

I'm disoriented from whatever has been done to me, and I'm still angry too. I'm frustrated about having to talk to Freja like this, worried that she caught the end of that dream and, if she didn't, wanting to get her out of my head before she does. But if she did, she doesn't react, doesn't acknowledge it.

Come on; you're one of the Three Musketeers. We need you.

I struggle to control the swirling anger inside, then nod. *I'll try.*

"Right," she says out loud. "First up it's time for dinner."

She backs up on her knees to get out of the low tent, and I follow her. It's dark now, I'm starving, and there is the smell of a barbecue and something delicious cooking.

I step into a wooden cabin with Freja. Four pairs of eyes look at me.

"Listen up," I say. "I only promise not to punch people who don't mess around in my head, so keep out of it."

"Sounds fair." It's a milder voice than the one I remember earlier—was that JJ? He's not here. "I'm Patrick." He holds out a hand. I hesitate, then shake it. It's a firm handshake, and his face is open, honest. He's about my mum's age, and there is something about him that says he's all right. "I'm sorry you all got off on the wrong foot before," he says. "They were taken by surprise."

There's a woman who comes up behind him—she must be in her sixties. "I'm Zohra. I'm sorry too. I'd have knocked JJ's head if I'd been there for what he did. I know we're all scared we'll be found, but that's no excuse for bad manners."

The door wafts open as she speaks, and JJ appears with a platter of barbecued sausages.

He scowls. "Knocked my head? Like to see you try."

"Peace," Patrick says. "Our guests"—he stresses the word *guests*—"are hungry. Food first. Talk later."

CHAPTER 7

CALLIE

"I THOUGHT TO START THINGS OFF we should tell you who we are, and how we came to be together here. Out loud, everyone," Patrick says, and nods at Kai. It'd been weird at dinner, like they had to keep reminding themselves Kai couldn't hear what everyone said if it wasn't out loud, given that everyone—even JJ, when pressed by Patrick—promised not to venture into his head.

"Zohra, do you want to start?" Patrick says.

"Yes. Well, I'm rather good at finding survivors—sensing them. It was me who first noticed you walking up the road today. Before we came here, I'd been hiding in plain sight, as it were, but I was scared. Lonely. Afraid to tell anyone what I was, even though it was obvious I wasn't a carrier—no one ever got sick around me. But I think I needed to talk to someone like myself to understand what had happened to me. So I started trying to find others like me."

Freja nods; she understands. She's been by turns nervous of this group, like Kai, and ecstatic to have found people like her. I mean they're different from each other in all the ways that people can be—accent, age, skin color—but with this one overriding thing in common. They're survivors like her, like me.

Or like I used to be.

"First I found Henry," Zohra says. She smiles at the boy—he's maybe a few years younger than Freja and has been staring at her with rapt attention all through dinner. "And he knew about Amaya—they're friends from school. We were all out in the community, passing ourselves off as immune. But then they started testing people that were immune with some scan, and we were scared we'd be caught. There were rumors of survivors being taken away to some research place, and who knows what would happen to us there?"

Kai winces, and I'm guessing we are sharing the same thought: was Shay taken there? She might know the answer.

"Anyhow, we decided to disappear," Zohra says. "But we were being tracked. We nearly got caught, but JJ found us and helped us get away—he's rather good at blocking, so I didn't sense him. It's mostly JJ that's put a block over this place—even though Callie still found it."

It was hard, though, I answer, still marveling at this: communicating with a whole roomful of people. Not just through Shay or Freja. Everyone in this room hears me, acknowledges me—except Kai, of course.

"I'd been monitoring Zohra for a while," JJ says. "They weren't very good at hiding, and worse at defending themselves. I'd retreated here already. I'd already seen Freja's channel online at this point and told her how to find the road."

"And Patrick?" Kai asks.

"I was online telling everyone survivors aren't carriers, like Freja was, but anonymously and not as visibly perhaps. JJ gave me hints how to find them here; I was the last to come. I don't stay here all the time. I'm still officially living at home—I've got a place on the outskirts of Matlock—so I can check online for news and so on, and come and go, bringing supplies and updates on what is happening."

"Didn't they scan you?" Freja asks.

"No. Where I live the epidemic hasn't come. Not sure how I caught it—I'd been traveling back from seeing a friend in the Lake District, so probably caught it somewhere along the way. I live alone in an epidemic-free area; nobody knew I'd been sick, so there was no reason to test me."

"Okay, so now we know how you came to be together here. But what next? What are you going to do?" Freja asks.

"Stay alive and free," Zohra says.

Stay together, Amaya adds silently, and no one tells Kai what she said. But I can feel it—despite their differences, this group has become like a family to each other. Maybe closer than a family—it's hard not to be when you're in each other's heads most of the time.

"Tents in the woods might feel like fun in the summer, but it won't stay that way," Zohra says. "We need to relocate. Go past the boundaries into the quarantine zone. Find others like us and a place where we can live more openly."

"Others?"

"There are traces of other groups here and there," Patrick says. "One in the zone in Scotland has contacted us and asked us to join them."

Freja scowls. "Go and hide away behind the barriers? What good will that do? We need to take it to them, not run away."

"A girl with some fight; I like that." JJ grins at her. "But we feel some responsibility to each other—to continue surviving. What if we're it for the human race? We'll need to get busy, repopulating the planet."

He'd make my skin crawl if I had any, I say, an aside to just Freja—one the others can't hear.

No kidding, but let's keep him on our side for now, she says, answering me the same way.

"Do you mean if everyone in the country dies?" Kai says. "That's a bit cold. What if we can do something to stop it?"

"The best medical people the government and World Health Organization have come up with can't stop it," JJ says. "What are we going to do?"

I was there when it started, I say. *On Shetland. In a government lab. I didn't understand the science, but Shay did.*

Freja repeats what I said, looks at Kai, and nods. It's time to tell them all that we know.

Kai gives them the whole story about Shay and us. That she was a survivor, that I told her what I've told them now—how it started on Shetland. That we went there and found out about the underground particle accelerator and that antimatter causes the epidemic. How *it* got out.

How some parts of the army didn't seem to know what other parts were doing. That Shay, believing she was a carrier and trusting that all of the armed forces couldn't be behind the epidemic and cover-up, turned herself in to the air force base on Shetland. That now that he knows survivors aren't carriers, he wants to find out where she's been taken.

They don't think Kai will see her again, though none of them say it out loud. All through his telling they've looked alternately shocked and angry, and afterward the silence goes on while they process what he's said.

Finally JJ breaks it: "Does knowing more about what is behind the epidemic and what happened to us change anything?"

We need to find Dr. 1—he started it all, he must know how to stop it, I say, and Freja tells Kai what I said.

"But how do we find him?" Zohra asks. "If he's even still alive."

"Someone in the government *must* know who he is, where he is," Kai says.

JJ raises an eyebrow. "Should we give them a call and ask?"

Freja's arms are crossed. She's radiating cold fury. "The government can't be trusted. They started this. And they must have worked out by now that survivors aren't carriers. Why do they perpetuate this myth? Is it to let mobs do their work for them—hiding the evidence of what they've done by eliminating survivors who may carry traces of what has happened to them inside? They *must* know more than they're letting on. If they don't want to tell us, we have to make them."

There is a furious exchange now between all of them, inside their heads, and Kai looks from face to face, wondering.

Patrick puts up a hand. "Out loud, remember? But there is something we have to deal with first. I really think you can see from all that

Kai has done and what we've learned from him, and Callie too, that they're both on our side in this. Does anyone object to Kai joining us, along with Freja and Callie?"

No one says anything. JJ is the only one who isn't sure, about Kai at least, but he says nothing.

"Good. Now back to the really big question, one we've been dodging for a while, but you've reminded us must be faced: what do we do next?" Patrick says.

"We need there to be more of us, together, to tackle the lies being spread about us. We need to find the government institution—the one in all the rumors—where survivors get taken. Free them. Find out what the government knows," Freja says.

"Or we could continue to hide away, try to keep our own sorry skins safe," Patrick says. "Should we vote? Who is in favor of staying out of the zone, trying to find and free these captive survivors, seeing what we can find out and do about it all? Hands, please."

Kai's hand goes up. Freja's and Patrick's too.

JJ's, Zohra's, Henry's, and Amaya's stay down. Zohra looks at the two younger ones, one after another—silent arguments are taking place, ones that exclude the rest of us. Amaya wants to put hers up, she's almost twitching with it, but hers stays down.

"Callie? What do you want us to do?" Freja says, and I'm startled.

Do I count? Hesitantly I put up my hand.

Patrick nods, and something moves inside me, some feeling. I *belong* here with these people.

"It's an even split," Patrick says, disappointment clear in his voice. "Should we think about it and talk some more and then try again tomorrow?"

But JJ is looking at Freja, holding her gaze. Then he puts up his hand too.

"That's it then," Patrick says with a grin. "We stay; we search. We're going to do this thing."

CHAPTER 8

KAI

I SLIP OUT OF MY SLEEPING BAG, unable to sleep—maybe because of all that unplanned, involuntary sleep I had earlier.

Or maybe because somehow I know that Freja won't be able to sleep either.

It's like she's waiting for me. Did she plant a suggestion in my head and do it so subtly that I wasn't aware of it? I don't think she would do that, really, but both what JJ did to me earlier and Freja's talking to me inside my head have brought my paranoia up to full rev.

The moon is new tonight and there is little light, just stars, but her white skin reflects what there is. Her red hair is a bright halo.

She gestures, and I follow, walking away from the cabin with her, wanting to ask her—to *demand* to know—if she'd called me somehow. I'm both angry if she did and wanting her to have done it at the same time, and confused about why I feel this way.

When we're a hundred yards or so away from the cabin, she stops and leans against a tree.

"I couldn't sleep. First Callie and Amaya were up giggling endlessly, and I didn't have the heart to ask them to stop," Freja whispers. "Amaya finally fell asleep, but then Zohra started to snore." Freja makes a face. She'd been put in the cabin with Zohra and Amaya; the rest of us are in tents. I'm in Patrick's tent at the moment; he'd headed out as the rest of us went to sleep, saying he needed to get back home, find out what was happening in the world—and make sure no one noticed he was gone. He said we're too far out here to get any reception on phones or signal to check anything online.

"What did you say to JJ to get him to vote with us?" I ask.

"You know, the usual. I appealed to his male ego until he'd agree to anything."

"Hmmm. Is that what you do with me?"

"Not necessary in your case. You're more sensible."

"I see. Do you give me little commands inside my head?" I try to say it lightly, but it isn't felt that way and she knows it.

She frowns. "No, don't be an ass. Of course not. I'm not into subtle; arguing is much more fun."

I'm sure she's telling the truth, and I'm embarrassed. "I'm sorry. I shouldn't accuse you of that."

She tilts her head, looks at me searchingly. "Are you happy?"

I shrug. "Existentially or more specifically?"

She rolls her eyes. "About staying here with this group."

"Patrick is all right, I think. Zohra is too—she's protective of the younger ones, that's all. Not so sure about JJ."

"You haven't answered the question."

"No?" I try to smile, but there is something that is still bugging me. Despite her reassurance that she hasn't been meddling with me, there is still some sense of weirdness, and I don't know what it is. I shrug again. "We'll see how things go."

"You don't like feeling like the odd one out, do you? The only one who is different."

I look back at her, surprised. Is that it? "I don't know. Maybe a little."

"Now you know how we feel."

CHAPTER 9

CALLIE

THE NEXT DAYS WE SPEND HUNTING. Not in the woods, but in nearby villages—for other survivors. They all agreed we should try to find any survivors we can in the surrounding areas first so that there are more of us—that we need to increase in strength before tackling a government institution. But couldn't they at least try to *find* it? Kai, like me, is full of impatience: he wants to find Shay, and I want to find Dr. 1. But no matter what I say about it to everyone, this is what they've decided to do.

The group has a few motorbikes and Kai's eyes lit up when he saw them; it's been a long time since his bike was left behind outside of Killin. Kai and Freja go on one, JJ and Zohra on the other. Zohra has made a grid and we're trying different places.

Now I'm searching the farthest parts of the village Kai and Freja are checking tonight. Looking for the telltale signs and traces that say a survivor is here—a concentrated place of feeling and thought. It's how I found Freja that night in London. Freja can do it too, but she can't cover the ground that I can.

Though sometimes I get it wrong. I glare at a Siamese cat crouching on a shed roof and wonder: why do cats feel so much like survivors? Its eyes are wide, measuring, but it doesn't flip out and run away like most of them do. What can it see of me?

I hold out a hand, like I would have done with a new cat if I were still me and not what I am now. But instead of sniffing it, deciding if I am friend or foe, it just runs away.

I used to like cats. Some trace of a memory says I had one once, a ginger tabby with deep green eyes, but when I got Freja to ask Kai about it, he said we'd never had a cat, that Mum was allergic, that maybe the cat I'm thinking of belonged to a friend. But I remember the soft fur, orange tiger stripes; the loud purr late at night that made me feel safe. Until—

A door slams shut in my mind. Until what? I don't know.

I go back up into the sky and then out and around in increasing circles, again and again. There are no survivors in this village.

I head back to where Freja and Kai are checking on foot.

None here, I say. *Are we going on?*

Freja shakes her head, disappointed, and sighs. "We need some sleep."

"Do we know what the incidence of survivors is?" Kai says. "Like how many survive for every hundred infected?"

"Not precisely. At least I don't know, except that they're rare."

"And how many are likely to even be here, when the epidemic isn't in this area anyway? There's only the odd one who traveled from somewhere else, like Patrick, or escaped the zone, like you."

"JJ thinks we should go into the zones instead and search there. Zohra does too. She probably thinks it would be safer to be on the other side of the barriers, where the authorities have given up."

"But it's easier to get into the zone than back out—believe me, I know. So maybe it makes sense to keep looking out here, at least for a while. But we need to stretch out farther."

They're just going over the same argument everyone has been having for days.

But everything changes when we get back to camp.

CHAPTER 10

KAI

WE'RE A FEW MILES AWAY STILL when Freja tenses behind me on the bike.

"What is it?" I say.

"I don't know. Something's happened; something's wrong. Hurry."

Patrick's back.

He's brought more supplies. Everyone walks to where he's parked his four-wheel drive to help unload and carry stuff to the cabin, but there is something he's not saying. JJ and Zohra aren't back, and he wants to wait until they are. There must be some words flying back and forth silently to make everybody else so on edge, but no one says anything out loud, and once again I'm annoyed. I throw myself into lugging as much as I can at once to help Patrick. I march up the thin path, muscles straining.

"Is this a race?" Freja asks, walking behind me with a more reasonable load.

"Just takes my mind off whatever." I grunt more than say the words.

Finally JJ and Zohra appear, and by their faces they know something is up too.

We all gather, and Patrick takes out a bottle of whiskey and some glasses and pours himself one. He gestures a question at the rest of us with the bottle. Zohra and JJ have one as well.

"This is the good stuff. It must be bad," Zohra says.

"Yes. Okay, here it is. The epidemic is in London, and it has been for days."

"Out loud," he says to what I thought was shocked silence. Questions rip out, and he holds out a hand.

"I'll tell you what I know. It hasn't spread in an ordered fashion from the north; there've been a few pockets of it here and there after Glasgow was hit, but nothing major until London. So it's kind of like it has jumped great swathes of country and landed in London, and it's hit there big time. And the quarantine zones are breaking down north of us too; they're breached all over the place. The boundaries don't mean anything anymore. The UK is overrun. It's everywhere or will be soon.

"And that's not all. I'm sorry, Freja," Patrick says, "but everyone is blaming you for what is happening in London. It hit the day you left. They're saying you really were a survivor and that you spread it all around."

"It's not true!" Freja says.

"We all know that."

"But it doesn't even make *sense*. I was around loads of people and no one caught it—for weeks. Explain that?"

"It *doesn't* make sense, but that is the official explanation they've latched onto. London is under siege now. And elsewhere, places that are still untouched are becoming fewer and farther between. It seems likely that the rest of the country will follow soon."

CHAPTER 11

CALLIE

DID THEY NOTICE WHEN I LEFT THE CABIN?

Everyone was so upset—maybe they didn't.

Most of all, I hope they didn't notice what I was thinking as I raced away. To start with, I forgot to hide it. But they were all so focused on Patrick, on what he was saying, on Freja freaking out, that I think they missed me completely.

Because I knew what Patrick was going to say before he said it.

It is in London—of course it is. I was there too.

CHAPTER 12

KAI

I KNOW FREJA IS AWAKE LIKE I AM. I know she is out there in the woods where we talked the other night.

She said she wouldn't plant thoughts in my head, but if she didn't put them there, then where did they come from?

Annoyed, I slip out of the tent, a new one that Patrick brought for me. He must be another insomniac: I see him sitting on the bench by the cabin, but he doesn't look up.

I head into the woods.

Freja is leaning against the tree where we talked a few nights ago, and in her hand is Patrick's bottle of whiskey. She tips it back to take a drink from the bottle as I walk up.

"What are you doing?" I say.

"I'm over eighteen."

"Are you?"

"Yes. I'm eighteen, two months, and six days."

I take the bottle, have a drink, and struggle not to cough. "Let's see: I'm eighteen, five months, and nineteen days."

"Congratulations."

"Respect your elders." I waggle the bottle at her. "Does Patrick know you've got this?"

"He should. He was sitting outside the cabin when I walked past with it in my hand."

She takes the bottle back, has another drink. "Seriously—why does life have to suck so much?"

I shrug. "I don't know. But that seems to be the way of it lately."

"What's bugging you? No one thinks you're a bringer of death."

"You. Them. *All* of you bug me."

"How so?"

"As much as Patrick says 'out loud' all the time, you're always talking in ways I can't hear—it's like you're all speaking a different language and can't be bothered to translate."

"I could deliver whatever anyone says straight to your brain if you wanted, but you don't want that. Anything else?"

"You're all just generally creepy sometimes."

"Thanks. Thanks a lot."

"Look, I don't care that you can do weird shit. Not much, anyhow. But bloody well keep out of my head."

"What do you mean?"

"I could feel you tickling around in my brain again just now—calling me to come out here. Don't do it."

She frowns and shakes her head. "I didn't. I don't know if anyone else has, but I didn't, and I don't. Though maybe—" She stops.

"What?"

"Well, maybe Patrick sent you out to keep an eye on me, which quite frankly pisses me off more than it should you. Why does it freak you out so much, anyway, if he did? Is there something hiding inside you that you're afraid somebody will see?"

I shake my head. "I haven't got any deep, dark secrets. But private should be just that: private. There may be some things rattling around inside me that I don't want to talk about, and that should be *my* decision."

She passes me the bottle and I have some more, and this time I don't cough. The world is spinning a little. I never drink this strong stuff. There's a small clearing, and I lie back on the ground and look up at the stars through the treetops.

Freja settles next to me. There is a whisper of her silky sleeve against my bare arm; I can feel the angles and heat of her through it in the cool night. "What do you see when you look up?" she says, her voice soft.

"Right now? The night sky. Stars. What else?"

"Things have changed for me. I see that, but I see more. There are halos and rings of color around the stars; the whole sky is bright. It's beautiful. But I didn't ask to see things like this. It just is as it is."

"And?"

"It's like that with people. I didn't ask to see how you feel, I just do. And I'm sorry if it bugs you, but that's just how it is. But I *don't* dip into your mind without you knowing. Never."

I'm quiet for a moment. Then I nod. "Shay tried to explain to me once that not touching my mind was like trying to pretend she couldn't see or hear."

"Yes. That's a good way of putting it."

"But I don't want anyone meddling in my head!" My muscles tense, and I'm angry again.

"Whoa. You've got some issues."

"Me? What about you?"

"What do you mean?"

"You're the one person I've met who usually makes me feel well balanced."

"Thanks. Thanks a lot." She pulls away, then turns and punches me, hard, in the arm. And I'm rubbing my arm and annoyed and then I hear these little snuffling noises she's making in the dark. Is she really? Is she *crying*?

I sense rather than see the space that is between us now. Unsure, I reach out a hand, find her shoulder—she's on her side, facing away from me. "Freja? What's wrong?"

"You don't bloody know where I've been or what has happened to me, so don't make these judgments, all right?"

"Look, everyone has had way too much to deal with lately—"

"It's not that."

There's silence, except for the chirp of insects, my heart beating; hers. Her sniffing.

"I'm listening. Tell me."

"It's not something I talk about."

"But you mentioned it . . ."

She laughs, but it's a bitter sound. "You caught me. Maybe because you might be the one person who could understand."

"Okay. Tell me, and I'll try."

She's quiet a long while, and I don't say anything else, just wait next to her in the dark.

Then I feel her move back next to me.

"I had a sister. A younger sister. She was a beautiful person, Kai. But she was different. She saw the world in her own way; she was funny, kind, had an amazing imagination. But she found it really hard to get on with other people, to interact with them—she took everything people said literally. And she didn't know how to hide her feelings—she was just open, and people hurt her to make her cry. They were mean, cruel, because she was different."

"What happened?"

"She killed herself, that's what happened. And then everybody was all like, we're sorry, we didn't mean it. *Sorry* doesn't mean anything when it comes too late."

I hesitate. "How . . . ?" My voice trails away. "Don't answer that if you don't want to."

"She jumped off a cliff into the sea. Smashed on rocks and died."

"Freja, I'm so very sorry."

"The thing of it is that I wasn't there. I couldn't stop her. *That's* why I thought you could understand."

"Because of Callie."

"Yes."

Silence. Beating hearts, insects, the wind. But silence.

My hands are clenching into fists. "I should have been there. Not just for Callie, but for Shay too."

"I can tell when you mention Shay that there is something you're not saying. What *really* happened with her?"

I take the bottle from Freja and sit up to have another drink. The taste is starting to grow on me and I have another. "She messed with my mind. Sent me to sleep, so I couldn't stop her from going."

"Is that why you get so freaked at the thought of anyone in your head?"

I shrug. "Yes and no. I mean it was before that too—it *always* bothered me."

"Why?"

"There's more to it; something that is tied up in the past somehow. I can't explain what I don't get."

"But this wasn't just anybody, this was your *girlfriend*—someone you should trust. It sounds to me from what you're saying that you didn't trust Shay, and that's why you didn't want her in your mind."

"What? No, it's not that. Not exactly."

Maybe a little. Maybe I can't trust anybody.

"Maybe you were just scared of her because she's different from you. Maybe you're scared of me, of Patrick and the rest of them too, and that's why we make you angry."

"No," I protest, but then I wonder—could she be right? I sigh. "Maybe that was part of it to start with. Not now that I know you."

"Oh, really? Think about how it feels to be different, really different. Like my sister was. Like Shay is; like I am. We didn't ask for this, you know. Even if everyone finally accepts we're not carriers, they'll still be weirded out by us like you are."

"You're right. I'm sorry," I say, and I mean it, but I *did* trust Shay. I let her in, and then look what happened. She did exactly what she promised not to do: she mucked around in my mind without permission.

"Whatever it was that happened with you and Shay at the end, if you can't completely trust her, then there is no hope for the two of you," Freja says. She isn't spying on my thoughts—I'm sure of it—but somehow she still seems to know that there are things I'm not saying. "What happens if we find her?"

"I don't know. I *have* to find her. After that, well . . ." *I can't think about that right now.* "I just have to find her."

"Maybe there's something I can do to help you. With part of this, at least."

"What's that?"

"If you need to be able to have your own space in your head that no one can step on, let's see if we can work out how to do that. Then if you find Shay again, you'll know how to do it: then you can let her in if you want to. Or keep her out if you don't want. It'll be your choice, you see?"

"But *how* do I do that?"

"Let me think a minute." She's quiet, then I feel her nod her head and sit up. "When we came here, it was the first time I'd been around other survivors, so it's still new to me. With the others, it took me a little time to figure it out, but now I can let them in or keep them out at will. Doing that is kind of instinctive, but I've been trying to work out just *how* I do it, and it's something like this. Think of a wall, one inside you. It's tall and thick and no one can breach it. Hold it in your mind."

"Okay. Brick, many feet thick. A castle wall higher than I am tall."

"Are you visualizing that? Making it strong and steady?"

"Yes."

"Do you know what it feels like if someone is in your head?"

"Sometimes—maybe even most of the time. It sort of, I don't know, *tickles* in a particularly weird way. But not always."

"Sometimes is better than never. Some people are really unaware and don't even have that. I'm guessing if you can tell *sometimes*, then you can train yourself to be more *aware all the time*. Okay, keep thinking of the wall. Hide something behind it, something you don't want me to see. Build the wall all around it."

"Something I don't want you to see . . ." I grin. "Okay. I've got it."

"Right. Now I'm going to try to see what it is. Keep the wall thick, and strong."

"Yes."

She starts to laugh.

"What?"

"Really? Is that it? A *bunny*. You've got a toy bunny?"

"I did, years ago, and don't laugh; he and I went through a lot together. But I did what you said. How did you see Bluebell?"

"Bluebell? Your bunny was named *Bluebell*?"

"I know. Bluebell objected to the name too."

Freja's really laughing now.

"Focus."

"Okay. It sort of worked, because I could see the wall you built and couldn't see through it, but the wall ended and I could look over the top. Maybe encircle something, instead? I don't know, I'm just making this up as we go along. Try it again. Hide something else and put walls all around and a roof over the top."

We try again and again and still it doesn't work—she always finds a way in.

I'm frustrated and punch the ground. "How can I block you from doing something I don't understand and can't do myself?"

"Maybe what we tried before is the wrong way around."

"What do you mean?"

"Instead of trying to hide something, don't think about anything. Just be blank."

"Okay. Give me a minute, then do your worst."

Cold thick walls—steel; concrete; a fortress. Over and over in my mind I reinforce and strengthen and build the walls and think of nothing else.

"Okay, go," I say.

She's quiet for a while. Then she says, "Kai?"

"Yeah?"

"I think you've done it. I can't see or feel anything except your wall."

"Are you really trying?"

"Yes. Now that you've managed that, try to think of something else and hold the barrier at the same time."

"I'll give it a go." *Strong, thick; no way through.* Very carefully and slowly I move in the dark—small movements, as I know her eyesight is better than mine. I think of a sound behind us in the trees and she turns her head to see if anyone is there. While she's distracted, I move more and tickle her tummy.

She screeches and laughs, catches my hands in hers to make me stop. "A sneak attack, using misdirection! Oh my God, I've created a tickle monster."

Her short hair brushes my nose as she shifts on her side, closer, then stops—still—her legs against mine. Blood is pulsing under our skin, apparent even through our clothes. There is something else, here and now, and it is stronger than whiskey. It could make everything go away.

We're both still, silent except for our hearts beating. Our breathing seems to be in sync.

Freja's hand lightly touches the side of my face, down my neck, then stills. Waits. Her fingers are fire on my skin.

I pull away, sit up and shift so we're not touching anymore. But that isn't what I *want* to do right now—it isn't what she wants me to do either, and I don't need to read her mind to know it. My blood thunders through my body, hot and restless, wanting what it shouldn't have. I stay silent, awkward, but hiding it all behind this wall I've built and hoping she can't see through it.

I'm sorry, I finally say—directed at her silently, not sure if she'll hear me.

She answers out loud. "So am I."

We mumble good night and stumble back to the house. Patrick is still sitting on the bench by the cabin—he takes the bottle of whiskey from Freja and whistles when he sees how much of it is gone.

"You'll regret that in the morning," he says.

I already do.

That night I toss and turn. The memory of Freja's legs against mine, the silk of her skin, the way she smells and the whiskey in my blood all combine to make me even more restless. I haven't forgotten Shay and how I feel about her, but she isn't here—maybe she isn't *anywhere* anymore, but until I know—maybe, even if I do—*no*.

By morning, I know I have to leave. I can't stay here, or I'll forget what I must do.

I'll forget who I am.

CHAPTER 13

CALLIE

THE NEXT MORNING AT BREAKFAST, KAI LOOKS TERRIBLE.

I whisper to Freja: *What's with Kai?*

I think he might be hungover, Freja answers back silently. *Too much whiskey.*

Stupid.

To be fair, I would be too if I didn't have ways of getting alcohol out of my system. Freja considers him under her lashes across the table. *I don't think it's just that, though.* Before I can ask her what she means, she shifts her attention back to me. *Where were you last night?*

Hunting. For survivors.

Don't you ever sleep?

No. I get bored when it's lights out for all of you; no one to talk to.

Sorry. Did you find anyone?

No, but why would I? We're too far from the zones.

Across the table, Kai clears his throat. "I've got something to say to everyone," he says.

Freja's emotions flood with apprehension, and then, like she realizes I can see it, she tamps it down and hides her feelings. There must be something I've missed. Did Freja and Kai have a big fight when I was gone last night?

Everyone is focused on Kai. "I can't stay here. I've got to leave." He glances at Freja, but she doesn't meet his gaze.

Patrick looks at him. "Why?"

"I have to find Shay. It might be hopeless, but I have to try. There's no chance of finding her, or other survivors for that matter, if I stay here. I think we've proved that by now. There's also no way of discovering what the government knows—or finding the doctor responsible."

Yes, at last! I'm happy—isn't that what we agreed to do when we left London? It's about time.

And I think Patrick will argue with Kai, that he'll try to convince him to stay, try to tell him how impossible finding Shay will be. But he stares back at Kai, then slowly nods. "You're right. Our reach is too limited from here, and the same applies to the rest of us. We should *all* leave."

An instant silent bombardment of Patrick takes place—Amaya and Henry look excited; Zohra, scared; JJ, I don't know. Freja is still carefully guarded. But like Patrick has done before, he shakes his head. "Out loud," he says.

"But where can we go?" Zohra says. She seems almost bewildered.

"As a start we can go to my house. It's on the outskirts of Matlock, far enough away from any neighbors for no one to notice you're there if we're careful. There's enough room if you don't mind roughing it a little—after camping out here, that shouldn't be that much of a deal, I guess. At least there is hot water. And we need instant access to information we don't have here. The zones are starting to break down; I don't think anyone is going to knock on the door looking for survivors. Everyone is too worried about themselves, their own families, to bother with us."

"You don't *know* that," Zohra says.

"No. I don't know that. But why should we hide? We've done nothing wrong. If we're committed to finding other survivors and bringing them together as a first step, then we need access to the internet; supplies, vehicles, roads. There's only a tiny area we can search from here without these things."

"You said go to your house *as a start*," JJ says. "What then?"

"Cover the area we can from there, then move on. Maybe we should head to Scotland, to that group that contacted us a while ago? I don't know. But one thing I do know is this: we're not going to accomplish anything if we stay here, running from the problem like rats from a sinking ship."

"Should we take a vote?" Amaya says, eagerness shining all through her.

"Wait," Patrick says. "I think if any of us want to stay, they should stay and the rest go. We can send more supplies. This is too big to impose on anyone, okay? So vote for you—what you want to do for yourself."

We all nod.

I'm surprised when everyone apart from Zohra votes to go. They want to leave this place, despite the fear: it's almost like they were waiting for somebody to say it so they could agree.

Then even Zohra changes her vote. She is still scared, but maybe the thought of actual hot water and a non-barbecue-related dinner is enough to convince her. Or maybe she can't let Amaya and Henry go without her.

"Kai, I'm guessing you were planning to go off on your own," Patrick says. "You can, of course, still do that if you want to, but we might be able to help each other. Finding the government facility where survivors have been taken has got to be our next priority. If we can work out the right area to search, we can sense the presence of survivors in ways that you cannot."

Kai nods. "That makes sense. Count me in," he says, but he looks troubled at the same time.

They spend the day working out what to take, what to leave behind. This place will be left equipped as a refuge, a place to run to if needed.

That evening three are to go in Patrick's four-wheel drive; the other four will follow behind on the bikes. I expect Freja to go on one of them with Kai, but then Henry looks longingly at the bikes as we're organizing ourselves, and Kai asks him if he wants a ride. JJ asks Freja to go double with him; she hesitates, then shrugs and says yes.

We set out, Patrick in front, the bikes coming up behind with Kai and Henry bringing up the rear. They keep a wide distance between each, and I keep tabs on everyone as I go back and forth.

I'm full of excitement at the freedom, roaring out of this place with all the ones who can see and hear me.

We're going to find more survivors, aren't we? And Shay.

And then we'll find Dr. 1.

I'll wrap myself around him, and then we can all watch him die.

CHAPTER 14

KAI

WE FIND ANOTHER GROUP ALMOST AT ONCE; or rather they find us. There are nine of them—all survivors. They're spread out around a base in Chester.

They're also in touch with other individuals and a few groups dotted about here and there. We share knowledge: there is more talk of a government facility in England where survivors are taken, but no one has been able to find it.

Groups have been destroyed in a few places too—either the government has swooped in and people vanish, or vigilante groups of survivor hunters find them. There is hushed talk of a group chased by a mob and burned to death. Would fire turn them into Callies? I ask, but none of the other survivors we meet have ever seen anyone else like her.

And they've all begun to work on defense and attack—ways to protect themselves or rescue other survivors. But not with weapons, at least not the usual sort: with their minds.

Freja is troubled at the thought of striking out, hurting anyone. She's stayed remote since that night in the woods; I know she needs someone she trusts enough to talk to, like when she told me about her sister. I want to be that friend to her, but it feels like it is better to keep her at a distance and not get too close.

Better for me; maybe not for Freja.

Instead I focus on Shay—things like the sound of her voice, the way she instantly had my attention no matter how softly she spoke. The way she bit her lip when she was thinking about something. How her eyes held all of her and could flit between laughter and sadness and back again, taking me with her each step—to laugh with her, comfort her, then laugh again.

As if remembering things like these will make Shay stay alive until we can find her.

CHAPTER 15

CALLIE

KAI AND THE OTHERS ARE BACK FROM PATROLS. Leslie, a visitor from another group, stayed behind tonight. She's some sort of computer geek and has been setting up access to the dark net for Patrick—the anonymous part of the internet where users are untraceable. She says we'll be able to be in more direct contact with other groups and to search for things without worrying about being tracked online.

Kai comes in and looks over her shoulder, JJ and Freja behind him. JJ and Freja seem to be together a lot lately—I don't know why. I don't like him, and I thought Freja didn't either.

"Is everything good to go?" Kai asks.

"All set," Leslie says.

"Has there been any progress in finding the trap?" *The trap* is shorthand for the government place survivors are being held.

She turns, sympathy in her eyes. She must know about Shay. "No, not yet. We're still trying. It's odd we haven't sensed them anywhere."

Unsaid: *Maybe that's because they're all dead.*

“Is there anything I can do? I wouldn’t be much use with computers, but if you run things past me, maybe there is something you’ve missed?”

Leslie exchanges a glance with Patrick; they’re having a private, silent conversation.

“We’ve been hacking into websites; for the air force, army, other armed forces, and government,” she says, a bit begrudgingly, like she doesn’t like explaining things out loud. “Seeing if anything is mentioned. But nothing has come up. Some of their secrets are buried deep. We won’t give up, though.”

“Could there be another way?” Kai says.

“What do you mean?”

“There are groups of survivor hunters I saw online a while back, like Vigil. They must be trying to find the same place we are, right? Maybe we should see what they know.”

She shakes her head, dismissing the idea. “They can’t find it if we can’t.”

Kai argues, but she’s not having it. She thinks we’re so smart that there is no way they could do something we can’t.

Finally Leslie leaves, on her way to another group of survivors to sort out their tech.

Kai’s face is a mixture of sad and angry. He sits with his head lowered, arms crossed. Freja takes one step toward him, hesitates, then reverses and goes out the front door.

But Patrick’s eyes are thoughtful. “Kai, you might have a point. I’ll see if I can find anything.”

JJ follows Freja out the door, and I follow him. Curious, I hang back and listen.

What are you waiting for? JJ says.

Freja ignores him, walks away.

Kai’s in love with somebody else.

Or he thinks he is.

Is there a difference?

Yes.

Maybe there is when the somebody else is here, in front of you.

Then you can see what is real, what isn't. You can't compete with an absence.

What makes you think I want to?

Freja holds JJ away with that, but I'm intrigued. Kai loves Shay, doesn't he? But *why* does he? I don't understand how these things work. She's younger than him. She needs saving, or so he thinks. Freja is the same age, the same sort of degree of crazy. He is himself around her; she doesn't want or need to be saved.

But maybe Kai *needs* to save somebody, because he couldn't save me.

CHAPTER 16

KAI

SOMEONE IS SHAKING MY SHOULDER. It's Freja. "Get up!" she says. My thoughts are blurred and thick from sleep.

Lights are switching on; everyone is spilling toward the computer room. Freja is strained and there is excitement on everyone's faces, and now I'm fully awake.

"What is it? What's happened?"

Patrick answers. "You were right, Kai. I've been hacking survivor-hunting websites. The one you mentioned—Vigil—is making plans to attack a remote air force site in the North York Moors—I think we've found the trap. This *must* be it."

His hands move on the keyboard. I push my way into the crowded room to stand next to him. "I'm just patching into this new group network," he says.

There are pings of excitement from other groups when Patrick tells them what he's learned. The location is pinpointed. Some want caution—it may not be what we think it is. Even if it is, are we ready to take on a facility like this? What happens if we run into Vigil on the way? Are we ready to deal with them?

It's *agony* watching this and not being part of what they're saying—the decisions they're making. At least for a change I can read it on the screen and not wonder what is being passed mind to mind.

Finally, consensus is reached. Vigil is planning to attack. We don't know when—they're referring to dates in some sort of code—but it sounds imminent, so we can't sit back and wait and plan and train. We're going to go there, and we're going to set out tonight.

We're the closest group. We'll get there first and scout out what is happening, wait for the others to arrive so there are more of us—and then do what must be done.

And we're rushing to get ready, grabbing what we need. Even Zohra is coming; no one wants to be left behind. Everyone is scared but wants to go there and rescue these survivors if it can be done, and I know part of the reason is because of me, and Shay. I'm touched that they care.

But some other part of me still hears an echo—the mixture of emotion that is Freja—happy and hopeful for me, sad for her.

How am I able to see this?

Maybe I'm more like them than I know.

CHAPTER 17

CALLIE

PLANS ARE MADE AND UNMADE AND DISCUSSED, and all the while we're rushing toward this place that Patrick thinks he has found. First racing up back roads in Patrick's four-wheel drive and the bikes; now on foot, vehicles stashed out of sight.

As we go they've been coordinating their minds, working out how best to deal with armed guards and locked doors. Can they really handle it?

But that isn't what worries them the most. Patrick found the location from posts on Vigil's website: they are survivor hunters who think the best way to get rid of the epidemic is to burn anyone who might carry it. What if we don't get there *first*?

Now and then I race ahead of them, trying to sense survivors, or anyone at all, but everything is a blank. They're following GPS coordinates, not something I can do on my own, so I go back and forth, keeping them close enough that I always know where they are.

The sun is starting to come up, the sky streaked with red and gray, when once again I rush ahead.

Then I wish I hadn't. I wish I'd waited, so I wouldn't find this alone.

It is the smoke that gives it away—it is part of the gray in the sky, mixed with clouds that are heavier now, strangling the sunrise. The place is hidden in the landscape so well that even though there are parts of it that are outside—a small plain courtyard, some twisted and burned tables and chairs—without the smoke I don't think I would have found it.

And it is only the smoke that draws me to this place: there are no beating hearts, no intense splashes of heat or emotion that say survivors are here. Then I hunt and call out again and again, in case there are any like me that were made in the fire—but no one answers.

I should race back and tell Patrick and the others, prepare them, but I can't bring myself to do it.

I'm a coward. I hide.

No one lives in this place. Not any longer.

They did, but now they're gone.

CHAPTER 18

KAI

FREJA AND THE OTHERS HAVE GONE QUIET, the excitement they had before dampened. What do they sense? Is something wrong that they're not saying?

Then I see smoke drifting into the sky.

My head is light, my chest heavy, I can't breathe . . .

I have to *move, now.*

I run. I can't stop myself, no matter if they might still be here—the ones who did this—and it could be dangerous. I just don't care.

I hear my voice screaming her name—"Shay, Shay!"—I have no control over the sound.

The smoke is rising from a dying fire, a pall of gray that stains the land before finding the sky. Patrick and the others try to hold me back with their minds, make me wait—stop me from going into danger—and to shield me, soothe me. But I easily push them out like Freja showed me before. Somehow, now, I finally get how to do it completely.

But doing that slowed me down, and they've caught up with me now. Freja insists that I must *wait*. That Callie will go in and search—see if anyone is there, friend or foe. That she can be safe in the fire and smoke and I can't. JJ and Patrick hold me back when I would rush in and not care if the smoke and fire had me. It isn't their minds that can do this but their hands, their arms. Holding me fast.

But Callie doesn't find Shay, or anyone else for that matter.

No one is left alive in this place. Callie says there is no one there like her either, but none of us understand *why*. Is there something different about her? Is she the only survivor to be changed—not just killed—by fire? Or maybe others changed form too, but they left before we arrived.

Callie couldn't find Shay, dead or alive. Does that mean Shay was never here? That she was here, but then she left?

Or maybe she was so badly burned that nothing about her could be recognized anymore.

We were *so* close; so nearly here before this happened—we could have stopped it if we'd gotten here sooner.

The walls that protect me inside have crumbled now. There is nothing left to hide behind.

Freja holds me as I cry.

CHAPTER 19

CALLIE

THE SKIES OPEN: IS HEAVEN CRYING FOR SHAY?

I'm in shock. I can't seem to take any of this in. We were too late? And Kai—his whole body is shuddering, he's struggling to control himself. Freja's arms are wrapped around him and his around her as if that is all that can hold him upright.

Rain thunders down even harder. "We've got to make camp, get out of this," Patrick says. "Come on, Kai." Patrick's hand is on his shoulder.

"Let me go. I need to go there and see for myself."

"Listen to me. The rain will help finish off the fire. We'll tuck ourselves away in a safe corner and sleep, then come back and do a proper search tomorrow. See if we can work out what happened. All right?"

"Kai, you don't *know* Shay was here," Freja says. "Remember that."

Kai nods and lets them lead him away.

They pitch tents a mile or so away, hidden in a dip by some trees. Everyone is soaked to the skin and shivering by the time the tents are up. Food is passed around in silence, and it isn't just that no one is talking out loud. Everyone is quiet inside too.

Patrick contacts the other groups to tell them what we've found and to call them off from coming here. And he organizes watches, telling everyone not on watch to try to sleep.

It rains for hours. Kai finally drifts off and is so still that I wonder if they made him sleep, if he let them. I stay with him, close. He doesn't know I'm here, but that doesn't matter. I need to be with him when he's so upset.

Freja does too. JJ thinks she shouldn't, but she ignores him. She tucks herself in next to Kai as he sleeps. Her mind she keeps closed to me, but there is such pain on her face that I look away.

CHAPTER 20

KAI

I DON'T KNOW THAT SHAY WAS HERE. *I don't know that Shay was here. I don't know that Shay was here . . .* This is a litany I repeat over and over inside as we head back to the site.

Callie's checked: no one is there, no one is near. Patrick was right: the rain killed what was left of the fire, at least as far as we can see. We need Callie's help now, so Patrick sets Amaya and Henry the task of watching the approaches in case Vigil comes back, or the authorities. The rest of us will go in.

"Everyone, this could be dangerous; take it easy and listen. No rushing ahead without checking it's safe." Patrick says it to everyone but looks at me.

"It's all right," I say. "I'll do as I'm told." Nothing is *all right* in any sense of these words, but I won't rush in and have a building collapse on my head.

I don't know that Shay was here . . .

Until I do, I will hang on to hope.

Callie guides them to the first body—air force, in uniform—outside the perimeter of the place. Perhaps a guard? He was shot, by the look of things.

Patrick kneels next to him, places a hand lightly on his arm. A moment later, he stands. "He was out for a walk, saw the attackers approaching and ran back to raise the alarm—they shot him before he made it."

And I'm remembering that survivors can talk to the dead—something like that. It's one of the things I'd heard about them but not seen in action.

I look a question at Freja; she must know the rumors that have been spread about survivors. She shakes her head slightly. "Not talking to the dead, just sensing their last thoughts—whatever they saw and felt as they died. It's not an easy thing to do."

"So if somebody saw Shay . . ."

She nods. "We all know what she looks like; Callie showed us."

We break in through a warped door.

The air is poor, and we smash windows, open doors, to let more in, and Patrick makes us wait. I'm squirming with frustration at the delay.

Finally we go in; the main structure seems to be built into the rock, with a metal frame that is largely intact—so falling ceilings look unlikely.

We check rooms one at a time. There are more bodies. Some are badly burned, some not; some air force, some in some sort of civilian clothes—jeans, T-shirts, maybe, from what is left of them—others are in their beds.

Each time we find a body, one of them checks it—taking it in turns. Again and again, they shake their heads; there is no news of Shay. They tell what they sensed if it helps work out what happened. Most were chased, burned, or the smoke got them and they didn't really even know what happened—drifting away in their sleep. They're the lucky ones; some of the others' deaths were very hard, going by the reactions of those who read them.

We find a wing of bedrooms. There are names on panels on the doors, and some can still be read. I check them as we go along, but none have "Shay" on them, and I'm starting to really believe she might never have been here.

There is one last bedroom to check. Freja rubs at the name panel on the door. "No Shay!" she says. "It says Beatriz, Amaranth, and Sharona."

Ice runs through me so it is hard to move, to speak, to anything. Finally I manage to take a step forward, to say, "Sharona? That's Shay. It—it's her real first name."

I reach Freja's side and see the name on the door for myself. We try to push the door open; it's warped and won't give, and I'm glad to be able to heave at it hard, put my shoulder into it, until it hurts.

Finally I force it open.

The fire didn't make it into this room. There are three beds, and only one has a shape inside of it.

The ice has taken over all of me now. I can't move. I can't look.

Freja takes my hand, and together we step forward. I make myself look at the body in the bed—at the blonde hair—and I almost cry with relief.

"It's not her. Does she know what happened to Shay?"

Freja leans down, touches the girl's shoulder. Sighs. Shakes her head. "No. She died in her sleep, from the smoke, most likely: she was dreaming of a boy."

Freja is so pale, with dark rings under her eyes. *It's hard to do this,* she'd said before.

"Thank you. For everything." She nods tiredly, and we carry on.

We join some of the others heading down a part of the complex that has been more thoroughly destroyed.

A few bodies lie in a burned-out hall in full biohazard gear. The suits seem to have protected their bodies from the fire.

"I think with those suits on they must have been some of the attackers?" JJ says. It's his turn.

JJ has to pull part of a suit off to reach the man inside. He touches him, flinches. He stays in contact so long that Freja looks worried, but then he pulls away.

He turns to me, grins. "Your girl *rocks*," he says.

"What? You saw her? Tell me!"

"She killed these two. They were chasing her and another man down this hall. They were trying to go through that door at the end, but it wouldn't open and they were trapped there," he says, and gestures at the end of the hall. The door there now hangs open. "She told them to stop, and when they didn't, she attacked their auras. Hearts stopped, I think."

"So she went this way?" I say, and head for the door.

"I assume so but don't know. He didn't see that."

"Careful, Kai," Patrick says, and I remember my promise and just manage to hold myself back until he checks through the door.

We carry on searching. We don't find Shay, or the body of anyone else who saw her before they died.

But she *was* definitely here: she escaped with somebody through a door in a hall, leaving two dead behind her, and that's all we know.

Shay, what happened to you?

Where are you?

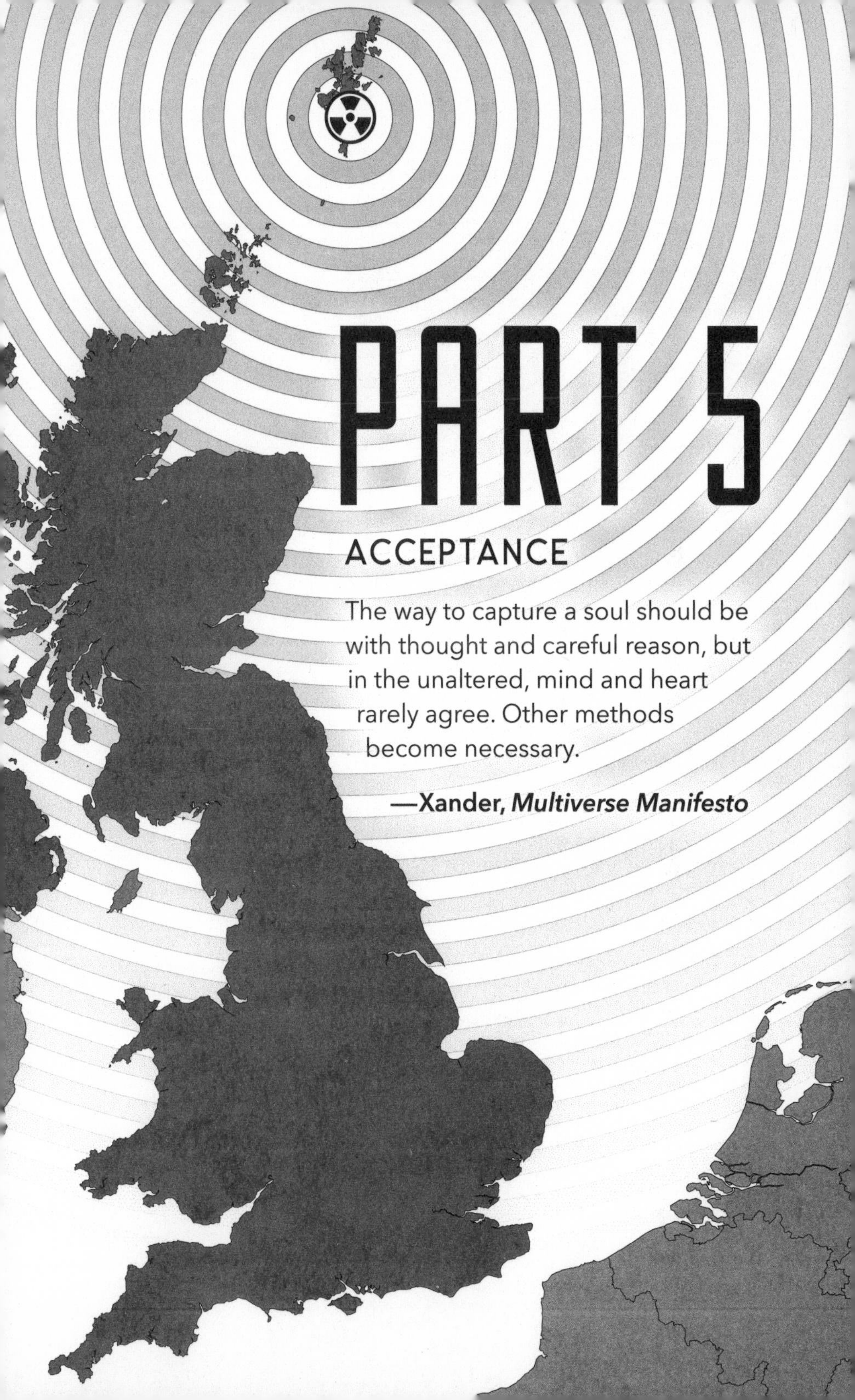

PART 5

ACCEPTANCE

The way to capture a soul should be with thought and careful reason, but in the unaltered, mind and heart rarely agree. Other methods become necessary.

—**Xander, *Multiverse Manifesto***

CHAPTER 1

SHAY . . .

Shay . . .

Shay . . .

My name is said over and over again; it's a tie that reaches out and holds me fast and won't let go—like a lasso around a bucking horse that just wants freedom.

Shay . . .

I struggle to release my name, but it holds me tight—or do I hold on to it? Why don't I let go?

Then Mum is here. I'm dreaming—is that it?

They can help you, if you let them, she says.

But I want to stay with you.

Not yet, beautiful girl, she says, and kisses me. *Not yet.*

Shay . . .

Shay . . .

Shay . . .

There is a chorus of my name in different voices, inside and around me and anchoring me to this world. They want to get in, but will that bring back the burning, the pain? I'm scared.

Scared—you? No way. It's Spike. Alex must have saved him, and I'm glad.

Not just Alex—I wouldn't be here without you. And I'm not letting you go. But I can't do this alone. You have to let everyone help.

If I don't let them help me, the fire will have won. Would that make me become like Callie forever? And then I'm even more scared.

So one by one, I let them into my mind. Spike. Elena. Beatriz. Even Alex. They hold me inside, shield me from the pain—each of them taking some of it on themselves—and slowly, a blood vessel here, a layer of tissue there heals. Skin and deeper tissues and lungs knit and repair until I can breathe on my own. I heal.

And then I sleep.

CHAPTER 2

A DARK, DREAMLESS PLACE gives way to fractured images and light. There is movement and pain that slips again to darkness.

Gradually light returns.

Dreams first. Nightmares where I'm running and running and there is fire and hate, and I can't escape.

I dream of my mother too, and sometimes she is here with me, stroking my hair and singing. But other times she is on the pyre, and this fire chases and tempts me too—beautiful flames that dance bright and promise to take me to her.

Then Callie comes to me, dark and cool and soothing. Before I couldn't imagine what she went through when she was cured in fire—now I came very close to knowing. Would I have become like her if they hadn't saved me? *I'm sorry I left you, Callie.*

And I cry out for Kai, but he never answers. Now he's even deserted me in my dreams.

But here, there is warmth—a new friend is curled up, purring by my side, and rarely leaves.

And Spike is here as well. Beatriz and Elena too. Even unconscious, I can feel their presence, their care.

I have a new family, and they know me more, inside and out, than anyone else ever could.

CHAPTER 3

THERE ARE SLIVERS OF LIGHT through my lashes—crescents of a room, a window.

Someone, or something, is here next to me; I feel it. I turn my head a little and open my eyes wider. A furry paw bats at my nose lightly, and a deep purr vibrates through the most beautiful cat I've ever seen: silvery gray fur and intent green eyes.

So this was my warm friend while I slept. As if to answer my thought, a small meow interrupts the purring.

"Well, hello there, beautiful!" I look past the cat and there, on a chair with a book in his hands, is Spike.

She's awake, he broadcasts widely, and soon there are footsteps. A door opens and Beatriz runs in and flings herself at me. The cat grumbles a sleepy protest from my other side at being disturbed and moves farther down the bed.

"Take it easy," Spike says to Beatriz. But it's okay. My arms move now and give her a little hug.

"Where are we?" I say, and it feels odd to shape words in this throat and mouth. I swallow.

Alex is at the door now, and Elena too.

"My country house," Alex says. "In Northumberland."

I move a little, sit up, head swimming. I look at my arms: they're perfect, whole. I'd wrapped them around my head when the fireball hit me. Now I'm shaking, and my eyes dart side to side. I pull my knees up under the blankets and slip my arms around them.

"Do you remember, Shay?" Elena asks, her voice soft.

"The mob and the fire." I shudder. "It caught me. And then all of you shared my pain and healed me, didn't you?"

"You were beyond doing it yourself," Alex says. "Well, I thought you were beyond *any* help. It was Beatriz who somehow knew what we had to do and showed us how. And Spike got through to you and convinced you to let us in to try."

I look again at my hands, caught in wonder. I swallow and breathe and all is as it should be—but new cells replaced the dead, and much of me feels like a not-quite-comfortable new suit that needs wearing in a little. "I was on *fire*. I breathed fire into my lungs—and you fixed me? I can't quite believe this."

Am I still dreaming?

Spike comes over to the other side of my bed and takes my hand—a gesture that feels natural. This hand has felt this before. He's been sitting, just there, holding my hand with its new skin while I slept.

"You're not dreaming. It's pretty cool, isn't it?" Spike says.

"How did we escape?"

Alex comes farther into the room. He takes a chair by the window and pulls it up next to me and sits down.

"I had plans underway already to get all of you away and bring you here, but that witch hunt found us first. Somehow a group of survivor hunters—Vigil, they call themselves—found out where you were being held and attacked."

I look around at the faces—so few faces—in this room. "Are we the only ones left?"

"Yes. We're the only ones who got away."

Pain catches in my throat. Ami—we left her in her bed to die; and all the others too, who didn't come when Alex called. Are they like Callie now—neither alive nor dead? They don't seem to have followed us here if they are. Tears are threatening, and I just don't get *why* this happened. "I don't understand why they attacked us. We weren't a danger to them locked away like that, so why seek us out? Surely finding us was the biggest risk to them."

Alex shrugs. "Fear and prejudice, mostly, and not just because of the epidemic. They were scared of difference—scared of us because we can do things they can't, see things they can't. And the rumors of what we can do have been multiplying at an alarming rate to include the absurd and incredible. They truly think we're demons or witches. Not even human anymore."

"But how did they find us? That facility was so much of a secret they wouldn't even tell *us* where it was."

"I don't know," Alex says. "I'm assuming someone who worked there let something slip; either confided in someone they shouldn't have, or did it deliberately."

"Will they find us here?"

"No; no one knows we're here," Alex says. "As far as they know, we died with the others during that attack, and no one followed us—we made sure of that. Even if they knew we got away and worked out somehow where we came, there's no chance they'd come out here: it's too far into the quarantine zone with everything that's been going on."

"Why's that? What's happened?"

Alex's eyes move to Elena. They're having a private conversation, but I want to know and I want to know *now*.

"Tell me what I've missed," I say, insistent.

"I've been told I shouldn't be telling you troubling things yet after what you've been through, but if I don't explain now you'll worry. Zone boundaries have been breaking down. First it was breached in Glasgow; now the epidemic is in London."

I draw in a sharp breath and shake my head, wanting to reject his words, but I can tell he's speaking the truth. Despite the devastation from the epidemic that I've already seen in Scotland, as long as London was free of it there seemed hope that it could be beaten; hope that is slipping away now.

If the whole country is overrun, only the immune and survivors will be left—survivors like us. And Alex.

"You were a survivor—one of us—all along, weren't you?" I say.

"I'm sorry, but I couldn't risk telling you. If they worked it out, I'd have been locked up with the rest of you, and there'd have been no hope for any of us."

"So no one there knew?"

"No. No one in the government or running the facility had any idea."

"*How* did you keep that a secret, right under their noses?"

"Best way to hide is in plain sight." He grins, and the others seem to accept what he's saying, but I still can't work out how he got away with it. They didn't seem to have any trouble identifying what the rest of us were, did they?

"Good thing, too," Elena says, smiling, "or none of us would be here now."

"I was, luckily, alone when I was ill," Alex says. "So no one knew I was a survivor. Things were pretty chaotic in Edinburgh in the early days of the epidemic, and they hadn't developed the scan yet. I already had my immune stamp before they did." He holds up his hand, the *I* tattoo I've seen before visible on the back of it.

"But why were you going to help us get away before this happened? We're *carriers*. Surely we *should* be locked up."

"This house is inside the quarantine zone, and the whole area has been deserted: we are both safe ourselves and others are safe from us. But the government had it wrong, thinking they could study survivors like specimens. They thought we were the problem; that if they could work out how to decontaminate us, the epidemic would end. But they *need* us. We aren't a problem—we're evolution. With the abilities and brainpower we have, we're humanity's best hope to beat the challenges it faces—including this epidemic. We can do it, together. We can show them."

Alex's words are passionate, convincing; he believes what he says. Yet I still have an uncomfortable feeling that he is holding something back—something to do with him being a survivor. But I don't know what it could be.

The others believe him. It's all over their auras—that the damned could be the saviors. That we could change everything.

Could it really be possible? I *want* to believe.

I shield my thoughts. Who is Alex, really? His eyes meet mine, and I get an uncomfortable feeling that he knows what I'm thinking, despite my mental barriers being in place. There is something about him, some presence—and it's not just from how tall he is, the way he carries himself. He has a way of drawing people to him—when he speaks, you want to listen. But he is also a keeper of secrets, and someone my mother left. She didn't just break up with him; she fled her home, never told him she carried me, his daughter. She didn't trust him, and neither did Kai—the two people whose opinions I value above all others.

Yet Alex risked his life and went back for Spike when I wouldn't leave without him; somehow he got both of us out of there when I was hurt. I look around the room, at Elena and Beatriz too. He saved *all* of us.

And we didn't know the one crucial thing about him—we never saw him clearly enough to know he was one of us. Did Kai and Mum have him all wrong too?

Later I lie in bed, staring at the ceiling. I convinced everyone I needed to rest, even though physically I seem to be more or less okay now. I just needed, I don't know, *processing* time—alone.

Well, alone except for Chamberlain, still purring, eyes closed, half on me and half on the bed.

He was Alex's housekeeper's cat, I was told, and decided I was his new human when we arrived a few days ago. Apparently someone who lies in bed all day is his kind of people. My hand strokes his soft fur while my thoughts jump around.

So much has happened, both before and after I was hurt—so much that I missed hiding in dreamland while I was healing.

The mob, the fire, being brought to this place when I wasn't able to decide whether I should or shouldn't come here. And now, most of all, there's a question:

Should I trust Alex?

No matter how I turn things over and over in my mind, there is no answer I can give right now. I can't discount his actions because of opinions from Mum and Kai based on who he was before I knew him. He's a survivor now, like us; he's changed, like we all have, in ways I'm still working out. And he saved us. We'd all be dead if it weren't for him.

I won't trust him, but I won't distrust him either. I will base my opinion on his words and actions, how they reflect in his aura, and my own judgment. That's the best I can do.

But I won't tell him or anyone else he's my father, at least not yet. Mum didn't want him to know; that's good enough for me. I'll respect her wishes on this for now.

CHAPTER 4

"SERIOUSLY, COULDN'T YOU HAVE DONE SOMETHING to fix my hair?" I stare in the mirror and try to even up what is left with a pair of scissors.

"Ungrateful brat," Spike says. "And no. Hair outside your scalp is dead—can't be healed. You could try to make it grow faster, maybe? But I think the singed pixie look rather suits you."

I lunge at Spike to smack him one, but he easily leaps out of the way. Maybe I'm still not quite myself after all. "I'll catch you another time," I say, and waggle a finger at him.

"You can try."

"Do you really believe that we can somehow figure out how to stop the epidemic and stuff?"

"I hope so. Alex has been working on establishing a link with a remote computer where he has stored information the government had about the spread of the epidemic and all they learned from us at that secure facility we just escaped from. Elena has started going through all the stats and other information on the spread of the disease we have and also what she can find on the internet."

"I still can't get my head around the fact that Alex was a survivor all along. And not only that we didn't know, but the government didn't either!"

"Yeah. Freaky or what?"

"Dinner!" Elena's voice calls up. We head down, Chamberlain nearly tripping me up by winding around my feet.

Now that I'm properly awake, I feel shy. Having people inside your mind like they all were when they healed me . . . well. I kind of feel like I was dancing around naked singing on TV with everyone in the world watching and laughing.

Now there's a show I wouldn't miss, Spike says, and this time he doesn't get out of the way quick enough. I punch him in the arm.

I wonder how much else I haven't screened that I should have today. Or back then, when you were all mucking about in my brain.

"Ouch!" he says and rubs his arm. *Don't worry,* he adds silently. *I was there the whole time. Everyone was too busy saving your life to rummage around in your memories.*

Then I'm contrite. *Sorry.*

Don't worry, I'd wonder the same thing. Especially if I did what you did when you were twelve.

He's running down the stairs before he finishes the sentence, and I start to panic: what happened when I was twelve? He's laughing, and then so am I.

He's such a goof. He makes me smile; he makes me laugh when I wouldn't think I ever could again.

He reminds me that I *need* to laugh, like I need to breathe.

He's waiting at the bottom of the stairs, watching me walk down them—he holds out an arm. "Hit it or hold it, the choice is yours."

CHAPTER 5

PEOPLE I KNOW SO WELL, and don't know at all at the same time, sitting around the table, sharing a bottle of wine and eating pasta that Elena has prepared with Beatriz's help.

"I made the salad," Beatriz says shyly. "Is it good?"

"Delicious," I assure her. I'm happy she is talking more than she used to.

Alex presides like the head of the table; Elena fusses. She gives him warm looks and leaps to get what he wants, almost before he knows he wants it, and now I see something I hadn't noticed before, though I don't know how I missed it when it is all over her aura. She's got a crush on Alex.

I'm guessing they are similar ages—sixty or something. Does he like her? He uses her name a lot, draws it out: Elena. Like he likes to say it. He says his first love was named Lena, and Elena's name reminds him of her.

For some reason the thought of the two of them like that is kind of . . . wrong. Maybe it's because I think of the photo of him dancing with Mum. The way he was holding her; the look in Mum's eyes.

Thinking of Mum recalls the sadness that is never far away. It threatens to take hold of me now, but like he knows it, Spike is there, cracking some lame joke about being a mushroom because he's a fun guy to be with.

And so the three of us, Spike the clown, Beatriz the serious, and me—well, I don't want to even think what role I play—round out the rest of the cast of this dysfunctional family.

After we've finished eating, my one glass of wine buzzes in my bloodstream, makes me warm. Makes me wonder out loud some of what I was thinking inside.

"Now that we're not being watched and don't have to be careful what we say anymore, like we were at the air force facility, I'm really curious about everyone."

"Like what? Who was my best friend, what subjects I liked in school, my favorite color?" Beatriz says.

"Yes, all of that." I smile at her. "But also, what can we do as survivors? I know we can all talk telepathically, for instance, though I don't think all twenty-three of us at the facility were that good at it."

"You mean talking in our heads?" Beatriz says, and I nod. "Some of them were really terrible at it. I almost had to shout to make them hear anything when we were showing everyone how to stop the drugs from working inside."

"Maybe there are more things we can do that we haven't worked out yet," Alex says. "Maybe if we share the things we've discovered on our own, there will be things we can learn from each other? And this may help all of us."

"What I really want to know is *how* we do stuff," I say. "They were doing brain scans and other tests at that facility, weren't they? Did they come up with anything?"

"I can show you the data," Alex says. "There were odd patterns they couldn't explain, but they hadn't worked much of anything out yet. I'm not sure they ever would have, using those methods. They needed to engage you in the process. Something they didn't want to do."

"So, what can we all do?" Spike says.

"There is the internal stuff," I answer, "like healing yourself, speeding up the metabolism of drugs to make them inactive. And external stuff: talking in each other's heads, choosing what to project and what to keep to yourself."

When you remember, Spike says, an aside to me. I project an image of a cream pie splatting on his head. He smirks.

"And *suggesting* things to others who aren't survivors," Alex says.

"We need a shorthand term for non-survivors," Elena says.

"Like what?" I ask.

"Let's call them Muggles," Beatriz says, and Spike laughs.

"Why not?" Alex says. "So, suggesting things to Muggles, planting thoughts in their minds to get them to do what we want them to do."

"Also being able to tell if Muggles are lying or telling the truth, what they are feeling," I add.

"I can do that a little, but I'm not always sure of it," Elena says.

"It's the colors you need to look at," Beatriz says.

"What do you mean?" Elena asks.

"The colors around people."

"She means their auras. They're something like color, something like sound," I say. "Everybody's is different. It's like their own unique voice—their Vox."

"Exactly!" Alex says, but Spike's and Elena's eyes are on me; they don't know what I'm talking about. I can tell that Beatriz does, as well as Alex. In fact when I said about everyone having their own voice, his eyes opened wider.

I explain how to *unlook* to see an aura. Spike gets it quickly. Elena struggles until I show her in her mind.

"You can use auras to heal too. Elena, you've got a headache?"

"Yes; too much staring at computers with the wrong glasses. How did you know?"

"It's in your aura; there is a shadow around here." I gesture around the back of her head and neck. "If you let me, I may be able to help?"

"Go on," she says nervously.

"Hey, relax; this is nothing compared to what you all did to me after the fire." I hold my hands behind her and pulse waves of gentle energy into her aura, into the shadow until it eases.

She smiles. "That's brilliant. We could hire you out."

"I have a question," Spike says. "Could you do that if she said no, if she resisted?"

"I don't know."

"Punch me in the arm again," Spike says. I roll my eyes and oblige.

"You didn't have to hit me that hard! Now try to make me feel better without my cooperation."

His arm does have a rather sore place, *there*—another shadow. *Sorry, didn't mean to hurt you; I don't know my own strength.*

Sure.

I try different ways to affect Spike's aura; first gently, like I did with Elena's. Then using more and more effort until finally I give up, afraid if I push it too hard I might hurt him if I get through.

I shake my head. "Nope. Can't do it. Let me try again without you blocking me now?"

"Go ahead." This time there is no resistance: a gentle readjustment soothes his aura and the slight pain in his arm.

"Nice work," Spike says.

"Of course that's not all you can do with auras," Alex says. "You can use them against others too." He's looking at me.

"What do you mean?" Elena asks.

"For self-defense." I say it quietly.

"Or offense," Alex adds.

"How?" Spike says, but I don't want to tell them what I did.

"They may need to know," Alex says when I don't answer. "To save themselves or each other."

I know he's right, yet . . .

"Show them." Alex's voice is insistent.

I link them to my memory: the five men running at me with flamethrowers, Alex behind me frantically pulling at wires, trying to open the door. The way I slammed into the auras of the first few—hit hard into the colors around their hearts—and they just fell to the ground. Hearts stopped. Dead.

I look down, avoid their eyes and auras and the judgment I'm afraid to see and feel.

"You did what you had to do," Spike says.

"Yes," Beatriz agrees. I raise my eyes. She's shocked, they all are, but they don't say *murderer*, a word I hear whispered in my mind late at night.

"Show us again," Elena says, steel in her voice. "If anyone comes around with a flamethrower, I want to be sure how to do it."

And so I find myself teaching them all how to kill.

CHAPTER 6

SOON AFTER THAT I RETREAT the way I usually do: into books.

Alex's library is an Aladdin's cave. It's huge, with bookshelves covering every wall. The ceilings are so high there is a ladder for the top shelves, and I'm looking everywhere at once—reading titles, touching books, smelling them—the very old and very new on every subject I can imagine.

What do I want to read?

Everything we are able to do—for me anyhow—seems to relate to waves: waves of energy, color, and sound, the same things that make up auras. *Vox* was what Dr. 1—the doctor responsible for the underground Shetland research institute—called it. A word that I used today, and I'm puzzled as to why I'd chosen to use his word when I usually just think of it as *aura*.

Human auras are the brightest, especially survivors', but all living things—and inanimate objects too, like stars—have their own patterns.

Except for Callie: she's the only one I've ever come across who doesn't have any aura at all.

The scientists and doctors seem to struggle to understand that a disease can be caused by a physical agent instead of a biological one, like a bacterium or a virus. Maybe the things we can do mirror this. Do they relate less to biology and more to physics?

Niggling away inside me is the feeling that while the answers I want may have huge consequences, they are actually small, infinitesimally so. We were infected by particles of antimatter, much smaller than atoms. And when I reached inside to heal myself, I focused in and in—on molecules, then atoms, then particles. Smaller and smaller, and the smallest things that exist became waves that I could use to heal myself. Is this the same way I can act on someone else's aura to hurt or heal or speak in someone's mind?

I gather an armload of physics texts, settle into an armchair, and open the first one. But I want quantum physics: this text starts from the big bang, the theory that a massive explosion at the beginning of time released equal amounts of matter and antimatter and created the expanding universe. I should swap it for another book, but I can't stop myself reading. This is all stuff we touched on, superficially for sure, in school physics. But reading it now at a higher level and understanding things in a way I couldn't before is exciting.

It's like in science fiction: antimatter plus matter equals big explosions—both cease to exist. So how do we walk and talk with antimatter ticking away like a bomb inside each of us?

And at a universal level, how does *anything* exist? The matter and antimatter created by the big bang should have blown each other up until nothing was left, and why they didn't nobody really knows. For some reason matter won. That we—and our matter-based universe—are here is the proof.

The universe keeps expanding, and it shouldn't do that either. There isn't enough gravity from all the matter in the universe to make it behave as it does, and since they can't explain it, physicists invented an explanation: there must be more matter—matter that cannot be seen, felt, or measured, but *must* be there if they've gotten the rules of physics right. Because they've got a sense of humor, they call this made-up matter you can't see *dark matter.*

But what if they've gotten the rules wrong, instead? Physicists must have really big egos.

Spike and Beatriz wander in and I barely notice. Spike is soon on the other side of the room with a pile of books of his own. Beatriz settles closer to me.

She yawns and I look up over a page.

I smile to see she's got a Harry Potter book. She found *that* in Alex's library?

"It's late. Time for you to get some sleep, maybe?" I say.

"Probably." She closes her book but holds her eyes on mine, unblinking. She is still, quiet, intent—when she is like this, she is *so* not like a child. "Olivia," she says finally.

"What's that?"

"My best friend—she was called Olivia. She died like everybody else. I liked reading best at school. And purple."

Best friend—favorite subject—favorite color: the things Beatriz had mentioned before when I said I wanted to know more about everyone.

"Mine were Iona. Science. And turquoise blue, like the tropical sea."

"Is your Iona all right?"

"I don't know," I say, disquieted. "She was, last time I checked in with her—but that was ages ago really. I actually can't believe I haven't thought of her lately."

"You should find out."

"Yes, and I will. Thank you for reminding me, Beatriz. Good night."

She walks across the room, and the door shuts behind her.

I look across the room at Spike just as he looks over at me. "I'm worried about her," I say.

"I'm worried about all of us."

I put my book down, lean back, and sigh. "She's not exactly having a normal childhood."

He walks across the room and sits on the other side of me than where Beatriz was before. "She's not exactly normal. Neither are we. Neither is our world anymore."

"About that. There's one more thing I'm a bit worried about," I say.

"Only one? What's that?"

"That brain stuff we were working out together earlier. Among ourselves—us wizards and witches," I say, and he grins. "You know how I could only heal you if you let me?"

"Yes. And it was the same when we healed you: you had to let each of us in to help."

"Likewise I'm sure I could only hurt another survivor if they allowed it."

"And?"

"Well. I've felt like I can read everyone here—what they're feeling and so on, how truthful they are being. But maybe that isn't true. Maybe it's only what they allow to be seen."

Spike gazes back, his face serious for once; one heartbeat, two. "Everyone has a mask, Shay," he says finally. "Otherwise it'd be like we're all wandering about naked in front of each other, and who'd want that?"

He gets up, heads for the door, then turns to look at me when he reaches it.

"But this is all true: Louis. Also now deceased. I hated all subjects in school equally. Blue."

The door closes behind him, and I stare at the empty space left behind.

If Spike wears a mask, what hides behind it?

CHAPTER 7

ELENA FINALLY GOES OFF TO SLEEP and I get private use of a laptop.

I log on to JIT. There is only one draft post, and it was posted weeks ago: the title is "JIT is compromised." All that is there is the title.

Oh my God. What does that mean? What is going on with Iona—is she okay? I can't believe I've been so self-preoccupied that I hadn't thought of checking on her until Beatriz spoke about best friends.

All right, *think:* if she's managed to put up a post, she must be all right. It must just be that the website isn't safe to use anymore.

If it was just her login that was compromised, she could have changed it. But then I couldn't have logged in; she'd have no way to warn me that JIT had been targeted by someone. Or Kai either, for that matter—he had her login details in the note I left him.

I go to the public JIT webpage. The last story—a heartbreaking one about unaccompanied immune children being kept behind fences near Glasgow—was posted a few weeks ago. Nothing since.

One thing I know about Iona: if there is any way she can be, she'll be blogging somewhere. I just have to find her.

Think, think, think. She wouldn't have hidden a new blog so thoroughly that I couldn't find it, would she? It'd have to be hard to link her to it, so that whoever compromised her previous blog couldn't easily find it—but not impossible for someone who really knows her.

I try searching for everything I can think of—family names, favorite books, even Demon, her cat's name—and nothing works.

Finally I think back to one of the last times we were messaging each other, when she told me Lochy had died. She said she loved him, something I was *sure* she hadn't told anyone else, since it was the first I'd heard of it.

Could she have used Lochy's name for a new blog?

Soon I find a news blog with the address *JusticeForLochy.co.uk*. There's a post about the cause of the epidemic being antimatter: it *must* be her.

I click on "About me" to see if there is anything else to back up my conclusion. It all sounds made up, like not about a real person—certainly not about Iona—but there, hidden in the detail near the bottom? Favorite song: "My Sharona."

What was it that Lochy called me on his login when I was messaging Iona? Curly—that's it.

I hit the "Contact me" button. Hi. It's Curly. Are you okay?

And I wait. It's late; she's probably asleep. I hit "refresh" again and again, hoping, thinking I'll check again tomorrow, and then . . . there's a new blog post.

Some drivel about going back to the beginning, back to basics, back to her original password. I've only just read it and it vanishes.

Think, Shay. What was the very first password Iona gave me to her blog all that time ago?

BieberIsHot99. Well, everyone is entitled to their opinion, and I think she's moved on since then.

It works. I log in.

Shay: Iona?

Iona: Shay? I'm so glad to hear from you!

Shay: Likewise!

Iona: Where are you?

I hesitate. Her last site was compromised; should I answer on this one? No.

Shay: Sorry, better not say, but I'm fine. What happened with JIT?

Iona: I don't know. I'd arranged on JIT for Kai to stay with a friend in Paisley, near Glasgow. Before Kai got there, my friend's place was staked out. He spotted what was happening and contacted me. I put the warning message up on JIT and stopped using it. It must have been there they worked out where Kai would be. There was no other way they could have found out.

Shay: What about Kai?

Iona: According to my friend, Kai never arrived, so he must have gotten the message. I haven't heard from him since then, sorry. Though I did get a random call–some woman asked for me, then hung up when I said who I was. I wondered if that was him, checking if I was okay, but I don't know for sure.

At least I know he got off Shetland and missed being caught in Glasgow—that time.

Iona: Can you tell me anything about what is happening with you?

I hesitate and then think, why not? It's not a secret; those nutcases probably bragged about what they'd done all over the internet.

Shay: I was in a supposedly secure air force facility with a bunch of other survivors. It was attacked and destroyed by some survivor-hunting group called Vigil. A few of us got away.

Iona: Oh my God, Shay. How terrifying, how awful. Are you safe now?

Alex says we are, but there is a niggle inside me that says *no*—whether from Vigil or something else entirely. I hesitate; I don't *know* there is a problem, so why worry Iona?

Shay: I think so. Best not to say much else for now. We're trying to work things out. Like what has happened to make us different.

Iona: How are you different—really? The stuff online is all over the place. I'm sure most of it can't be believed.

Shay: I'm still me, Iona. No matter what.

Iona: Of course you are, but . . .

Shay: Look, I've got to go.

We say goodbye, and I log off and wonder why I wouldn't tell her anything.

Why I couldn't.

Restless and unable to sleep, I stare out of my bedroom window. It's a dark night, windy and starting to rain. There aren't any lights I can see, anywhere but here. Are we on a generator? Is the power out?

How long can we stay here, on our own, undetected? Even in a quarantine zone, won't people fly over and see the lights and wonder? And how long will there be enough food to eat?

There is something about that attack on the facility that is still bothering me, and I struggle to focus on what it could be.

Alex thought that someone leaked our location, either accidentally or on purpose, and this led Vigil to us. But can it really be as simple as that?

My thoughts are skittish; they don't want to go back there, but I make myself *focus* back on that night . . .

On Alex waking me; he took Beatriz. On the panicked run; we stopped when I remembered Spike. On Elena taking Beatriz when Alex and I went back for Spike.

We were trapped by the door. There were five of *them*—those who would kill us. Alex was trying to open the door. I struck out, and two of them died. The horror of that moment takes over so strongly, it is hard to *see* them as they were. Before they fell.

They thought they were safe in their biohazard suits. They were wrong, and—

Wait a minute.

Their suits: their biohazard suits. They were the heavy, reinforced kind—they looked like the real deal, like the army wore. Their weapons too: they weren't the sort of thing civilians should be able to get their hands on.

What does it mean?

Maybe they raided an army depot and stole these things, but it's hard to imagine that they were organized enough, smooth enough, to pull something like that off. Maybe they bought them on the black market. There are sure to be enterprising souls selling these things given the hysteria about the epidemic.

Or maybe . . . someone outfitted them. Someone in the army. Someone who wanted to destroy us and gave Vigil the gear and told them exactly where we were.

But *why* would they do this? We were in a contained government facility under control; the government was hoping they could solve the epidemic using us. So why would they act against themselves?

There is one obvious candidate: Lieutenant Kirkland-Smith and his regiment, SAR. He hunted me in Killin. They shot at me and would have killed me there if they'd gotten the chance—I'm sure of it. They seemed to be working on their own before, not with the rest of the army. Maybe they still are, and they are out there somewhere—hunting for us.

I still can't work out *why* they wanted to destroy us. There must be a reason, and given where we were, I can't see that it has anything to do with just wanting to kill carriers of the illness. There's got to be more to it. Maybe something that just relates to SAR?

What are they trying to hide?

Alex thinks we're safe here, that no one knows we are alive, let alone where we are, and even if they did that they wouldn't come here inside the zone. But I'm not so sure.

If they come again, we need to be ready. I need to go beyond what I can do now, and I need to understand it all—to know how to use what is inside me.

I shiver and pull the curtains closed, as if that will be enough to shut out the world. As I walk across the room to the bed, I spot my profile in the mirror and can't stop myself from turning to look at my hair: singed, short. It's *awful.* I never knew I was so vain about my hair until most of it got burned off.

And here I am, still focusing on the external: how I look, being warm and dry, well-fed, and safe. But what about the things that really plague me, the answers that can't be found outside?

I sit on the side of the bed and look *in—reaching*—starting with my blood. The rush and roar of it provides a focus. Blood cells; molecules; atoms.

Particles.

I spin with them in beautiful randomness, but they're in such huge numbers that the random becomes predictable overall. Deterministic. The whole acts in concert to behave in certain ways—but what if the random movements can be influenced?

Then they become something that can be manipulated.

I reach into the skin of my scalp and find the hair follicles. I encourage them, like talking to plants, or more like singing to them: *grow, grow, grow.* I can feel it within and without—my hair lengthening, becoming stronger, starting to curl, and—

Wait. Instead of just making my hair grow, can I change it—make it straight?

I focus to a point within the hair follicles, to the cells, to the genetic code within each cell—the winding, twisting strands of DNA. How do I find the gene I need?

I go back to the hair, to the protein that makes it curly. Protein is made by transcribing DNA to RNA, then translating RNA into protein. I follow the path backward, from protein to RNA to DNA; now I know the exact stretch of my DNA that codes for curly hair. I trial small changes in the base sequence, one after another, to see what they do to the hair protein; finally I find one that works.

Cell after cell I visit. *Adjust. Change. Grow.* I'm getting tired—this is more work than I would have thought.

When I finally think enough is enough and open my eyes, I reach up to feel with my hands. Long *straight* hair. WOW, double WOW, and WOW again.

I get up and look in the mirror. My dark hair is a few inches past shoulder length and has a nice bit of wave at the ends—that'd be when I started growing my hair, before I changed it from curly to straight.

So not only can I speed up how my hair grows, I can also change it—from curly to straight. Could I change the color of it if I wanted to?

Or my eye color. Or how tall I am. Or anything, really . . .

CHAPTER 8

I SLEEP LATE, REALLY LATE. I wake up a few times but feel leaden with exhaustion and can't convince myself to stir.

Finally Beatriz comes to check on me.

Are you all right? she says from the other side of the door.

Yes. Just tired.

Elena says you've missed breakfast. But Spike says he's going to make us pancakes.

Yummy! I'll be down soon.

When I finally venture into the kitchen, pancakes—second breakfasts?—are underway.

Spike turns when I walk in, and his eyes open wide. He whistles. "When I said you could try to make your hair grow faster, I didn't actually think you *could*."

"Wasn't your hair curly before?" Beatriz says.

"Maybe when it grows back it grows different?" I say, uneasy about admitting what I did without knowing why.

Elena wanders in to get a cup of tea while we're eating and tells us that Alex wants us when we've finished. She is fascinated by my hair. "Tell me how you did it. Can you change my hair from white back to red?"

"You were ginger?"

"Afraid so. Or wait a minute: could you make me blonde?"

I shake my head. "I've heard of people who've had chemo and lose their hair having it different when it grows back—maybe it's like that. It was kind of all burned away, and then I just sort of *encouraged* it to grow faster. Just like we metabolized drugs quicker to make them stop working." But that wasn't *all* I did, and I'm shocked. I'm *lying*. Why?

She seems to accept what I say, without question, and soon leaves with her cup of tea.

Now I know I can hide things I want to hide—that I have a mask of my own.

"If you did it deliberately, changed your naturally curly hair to straight, is that genetic manipulation?" Spike says, not letting it go. "Or something more basic at a physical level?"

"I really don't know," I say.

"If it was genetic—well. That'd be exciting! What else could we do? Make me look like an Olympic athlete?" Spike extends his arms and then curls them up. "Of course, my biceps are pretty amazing already."

"Sure. Well, I guess time will tell, if it grows back curly or not when it starts growing normally. Though that'll take a while."

"I'm not going anywhere." Spike comes close and stares at the top of my head.

"Watching my hair grow will get boring in a hurry. Didn't Alex want us?"

The link-ups Alex has been working on are ready. He has us gather together in his office downstairs where he's set up a giant computer screen against the wall.

"I'm going to start by showing you images of the underground research institute the air force has unearthed on Shetland," he says.

There are images of underground—photos they took with drones sent down to a place still too dangerous for people to investigate after the explosions and fires. There are destroyed labs and equipment. Skeletons are there too, and I shudder. I've seen this before through Callie's eyes.

Is this too much for Beatriz? Elena objects, but Beatriz is staring at the screen, fascinated. Maybe it doesn't seem real to her? But whether it upsets her or not, I'm not sure she should see this either. Alex and Elena are having a silent conversation, and then she says nothing else.

"It's hard to believe this was all there underground and nobody knew about it,"Spike says. "How could they build it without anyone noticing?"

"There were secret underground facilities on Shetland already," Alex says. "They were built during the Second World War, similar to the caves at Gibraltar, as a place to hide and continue operations if the islands were invaded. They were crucial strategically: Norway was occupied in the war. These islands between Scotland and Norway are a stepping stone between the two.

"Then during the Cold War, extensive bunkers were added, places that could survive nuclear war—or so they hoped."

"So did they expand what was already there, underground, when they built the accelerator?" I say.

"Exactly," Alex says. "I'll show you how it was before." He taps away at a keyboard, and then there are more images: grainy old photos from decades ago of underground places. "And then they built this."

Images of the worm fill the screen, like Callie showed me in her memories—before it was destroyed.

"This was the particle accelerator," Alex says. "They believe antimatter was being created, that this was the infectious agent—as I've told you before."

"But *why* would anybody do this?" Elena says.

"I read that they've been doing experiments at CERN in Switzerland, using antimatter to target and kill tumor cells," I say. And as I say the words, I'm remembering where I read this article: at Dr. 1's house on Shetland. "Maybe they were going further here and trying to cure cancer. Or maybe they were trying to make a weapon, and it got away."

"This is just speculation," Alex says.

"But no matter why, *how* could they do this to anyone?" Elena asks.

It's not a question any of us can answer: maybe they didn't know what they were dealing with, what could happen?

Or maybe they did.

Even if they had no idea of the implications and consequences of their research, is that any sort of excuse? They *should have*. You can't hand a weapon to a child and then lament you didn't know what they'd do with it.

"Wait a minute," Spike says. "How did the authorities get these photos? Wasn't the place destroyed by the time they were investigating?"

"Depends who was doing the investigating," I say. "The army was involved in Shetland from the beginning, weren't they?"

The others are looking at me now with a mixture of shock and curiosity.

"Yes. It's true, but only part of the army, and the rest didn't know what they were up to—at least, not officially," Alex says. "There's a secret regiment—"

"Special Alternatives Regiment," I say.

"Yes. SAR. They are completely separate from the rest of the armed forces, who've only just begun to uncover SAR's role at Shetland. I only learned of them recently myself through my work at the air force facility." Now Alex is looking at me too. "How did you know about them?"

"They tried to kill me." I tell them the story of Killin and the lieutenant who used Kai in an attempt to trap me and how we got away. I can tell this is all news to Alex.

"That couldn't have been sanctioned by the forces, army or otherwise: they were trying to track down survivors and take them to the air force facility to study, even before they suspected they might be contagious," Alex says. "SAR must have been acting alone, even after the epidemic was established. Interesting."

"Wait a minute. I don't understand about this SAR. What sort of special alternatives? Why were they set up in the first place?" Elena asks.

"From what I understand, to come up with alternative ways to handle terrorist threats," Alex says. "Like developing weapons that might not be sanctioned if they went through the usual channels."

"Weapons, like, say, an epidemic?" Spike says.

"It's being investigated still, but it looks that way: that SAR was behind the experiments on Shetland."

"And they could just do this without the government knowing?" I say.

"Ah, the government knew they existed, but the whole point of their existence was to operate outside of observation and control."

I snort. "That hasn't made it into the news."

"And it's not likely to."

"But I still don't understand. Shouldn't everyone in SAR be under arrest or something now that it is known what they did? And why was SAR trying to kill me, and where are they now? What are they up to?"

"What do you mean?" Alex says.

"Are they still out there, hunting for me, for us? When Vigil attacked the air force facility, they were wearing what looked to me to be army biohazard suits, and they had some serious weapons. Where did they get them? And more to the point, *how* did they find us?"

Alex's eyes open wider, then defocus. He's thinking back to that day and place.

"Their suits looked the same as army issue," he finally says. "And they can't be easy to source without government involvement; you're right about that. I'll see if I can find out anything more."

"Do you think SAR supplied Vigil and put them up to attacking us?" Spike says to me.

"I don't know what to think," I answer. "Maybe. And if Vigil is backed by SAR, can they find us here now? If they know Alex is with us, then checking this house would be a logical step."

"Even if so, I can't see Vigil coming this far into the quarantine zones, not with the spread of the epidemic down south," Alex says. "Where we are has been written off—it would make no sense to follow us here. But SAR may be another matter: perhaps they're misguided and trying to eliminate survivors to end the threat they created? I'll see if there is anything more I can find out about them."

Alex's face gives nothing away. He's detached, thinking. How much does he really know?

I shield my thoughts.

Kai and I went to Shetland because of Callie—Alex's daughter. His *other* daughter. She'd been one of the subjects at Shetland—infected with *it*. She was a survivor, like all of us. They burned her in a fire, and she became what she is now—dark and silent to everyone but me.

I look around at Elena, Beatriz, and Spike. They are all intent, looking to Alex, wanting to understand, to work things out and fix them.

Is it wrong to withhold Callie's story from them? Especially from Alex? She was his daughter.

Alex starts to explain more of what is known about the cause of the epidemic: about the particle accelerator in Shetland. He looks around at each of us in turn. When his eyes rest on me, there is *something* there, some flicker of recognition in him that there is more that I know; things I'm not saying.

When he finally asks, will I tell him?

Maybe. But for now I'll keep Callie to myself.

Afterward, Alex suggests we go through all the information he has gathered about the epidemic and its spread, focusing on whatever interests each of us the most. He encourages us to try to think about the issues and mysteries we discover creatively from our own perspectives to see what we come up with. Then we'll come back together and share what we have learned.

What do I most want to know?

How antimatter makes people sick: what does it do inside them? Maybe this will help me understand how things went differently with us. I read fast and faster, everything I can find on the subject, online and in Alex's library.

Soon I am convinced of two things:

How people die makes sense.

How we survived? It makes no sense. None at all.

Again and again I'm drawn back to the very, very large and the very, very small—I'm sure the answer lies somewhere there, beyond the limits of normal perception.

After all, we're not normal.

CHAPTER 9

WHEN WE ARE ALL TOGETHER AGAIN, I'm almost bursting to talk. "Can I go first?" I ask.

Alex nods.

"I've been thinking about what happens when people get sick from the epidemic. Matter and antimatter can't coexist, so when someone is infected with antimatter and it spreads through their system, every time a particle of antimatter touches a particle of matter, they go *boom*, until there is no more antimatter left. By then the person has died.

"So there are two things that don't make sense. If the antimatter is destroyed when somebody dies, why is there an epidemic at all? It should end when the antimatter is used up. And how do survivors like us get through this—why didn't we die?

"I'll look at the survivor question first.

"For example, say we've injected a load of antimatter into . . . Spike. He becomes ill, very ill. There is excruciating pain. But somehow instead of dying like most people, he starts to get better. Not only does he recover, he's also got boosted brain function and other abilities he never had before. Somehow, the antimatter that infected him has changed him.

"But how?

"Then I thought of another antimatter mystery. According to the big bang theory, there was a huge explosion that created exactly equal amounts of matter and antimatter. With amounts of the two the same, they should have blown each other up until nothing was left. This didn't happen, and somehow we've ended up with our matter-based universe. Why? Is there some reason why matter is favored over antimatter, both then and now?"

"Are you likening the human body infected with antimatter to universal evolutionary processes?" Alex says. "This is fascinating."

I shrug. "With the epidemic, we are talking about a physical thing—antimatter. Why not go back to the big bang, another time when matter and antimatter got mixed together?

"Anyway, back to the first question: why is there an epidemic at all? It should be self-limiting. Once antimatter plus matter goes *boom*, there is no more antimatter left, right?

"But if you scan a survivor for antimatter—bingo! It's still there. But it can't be found, can't be localized. It's like it's there, but invisible.

"Is that why we are contagious? But why doesn't it all just go *boom* inside us until it is gone? Why do non-survivors who are ill spread it around as if there is an inexhaustible supply of antimatter instead of the stuff going *boom* until it is used up? This epidemic should be self-limiting. Why isn't it?"

I sit down.

"Aren't you going to tell us the answer?" Spike winks.

"I haven't got a clue."

"So, basically, antimatter should kill us, it doesn't; and it is still there, but invisible," Spike says.

"Yes," I answer. "And this all makes about as much sense as why the universe didn't blow itself up before it began."

"Isn't this *fascinating*?" Alex says. He is like a child in a candy store, unable to pick his treats. "And this is why the clever doctors and scientists decided that survivors must be contagious: they've got the stuff still inside them that makes people sick, haven't they? Plus, there has been some anecdotal evidence—following travels of specific survivors and linking them with the spread of the disease. But what if they're wrong—what if it isn't quite as straightforward as that?"

"Specific survivors? How many did they track?" Elena asks.

"One that I know of." Alex glances at me; he must know my story from the air force files. "There may have been more," he says, and shrugs.

"What? You're kidding me," Elena says. "They incarcerated us based on that amount of evidence? A scan says antimatter; one survivor seems to be followed by the disease—that's it?"

"It's not very rigorous," Alex says.

"We can do something about that right now," Elena says. "Here we are, five survivors. Everyone, tell me exactly where you were when you became ill and exactly where you were from that point until we . . . er . . . got together at the air force facility—day by day, and hour by hour if you can, when you changed location. Let's compare this data with the timed spread of the disease in the same areas."

"There is quite a lot of information on the others in the facility files," Alex says. "You can check them in a rough way and include their data as well."

"All right, we're up to twenty-three"—Elena glances at Alex—"twenty-four, that is, survivors."

We all input the information into a table for Elena. Some hem and haw a little, trying to remember, but for me the places and dates are all engraved stark in my memory—the moment I realized I must be a carrier, because death followed everywhere I went hours later.

It's late, but Elena wants to make a start. Alex stays to help her with the facility files, and the rest of us shuffle off to bed.

I can't switch off. I can't stop thinking.

Matter and antimatter: annihilation should follow. Why doesn't it?

My mind is spinning around and around, but I can't settle on just what it is about it all that is bugging me.

But the answer must be within all of us: within me. It has to be. Whatever it is wouldn't show on their scans, not in a way they could interpret anyhow—it's too small.

I *reach* inside, zooming in and in again, but I don't meddle with my hair or any other distractions. This time I go swiftly from blood to brain.

Deeper and stiller and *smaller*: there is something there. Something I think I sensed once before—when I was healing my ear—something dark. Something I can't *see* or *touch* or *feel*. There's a barrier, or a cushion—something wrapped around inside me—something that I can't penetrate.

It is part of me and alien, both at the same time.

CHAPTER 10

ELENA SUMMONS US FROM OUR SLEEP. *Come now, this can't wait,* she broadcasts, and we all stumble downstairs, bleary-eyed.

She's twitching with excitement—nerves—*something*. "I'm sorry, I know it's not quite dawn," she says. "But I'd have exploded if I'd had to keep this to myself until a more reasonable hour."

"What is it?" Spike says.

"Look. Look." She's pulling tables and graphs up on the large wall screen, and we crowd in around her.

"Here we are on the map," she says. "I've entered our locations and dates; each of us is represented by a different color. The spread of the epidemic is in black. Now watch."

She does one of us at a time, beginning with herself. She's in a center of the epidemic when she becomes ill, but then when she leaves, it doesn't follow her.

Next, Spike.

And now I learn he's from Lincoln: it's strange how we know so much about each other and so little at the same time. The epidemic doesn't follow him either.

"I don't understand!" I say. My head is hurting, my new skin feels itchy and wrong, and I don't want to listen anymore.

As if he knows, Spike's hand is there on my shoulder.

Beatriz is the same as the others; Alex too: the epidemic didn't follow either of them.

Everyone is talking at once. What does this mean?

How could they have gotten things so wrong?

"We're not carriers," Alex says. "*That's* what it means." There is no surprise in him as he says it. I'm shocked when I realize that he already knew—or suspected—as much.

I study his aura. I feel that Alex is speaking the truth, as he believes it. I look around to each of the others—they believe him too—and of all of them, only Spike's aura is laced with empathy. He understands. He knows what I gave up.

But just because they believe it doesn't make it true.

I shake my head. No, it can't be, it can't . . .

They're wrong. With an effort of will, I control my breathing, calm my pulse.

"What about Shay?" Alex asks. "Did you input her information?"

"Yes." Elena hesitates, then calls the next group of data points to the screen. From Killin to Aviemore to Inverness to Elgin, my movements match perfectly with the subsequent spread of the epidemic, everywhere I went.

"How can this be?" I say. "How can I be the only one who is a carrier?"

"It doesn't make sense," Spike says. "There are other places you haven't been that carriers must have been involved, due to the fast spread of the epidemic. Like Newcastle. And more recently, Glasgow. London."

"Where did you go from Elgin?" Elena asks.

"Shetland. I went to Shetland. I turned myself in to the air force there, as I'd worked out what you've just shown—that I was a carrier. And I told them so."

"And they believed you. And so all survivors were hunted by the authorities—and groups like Vigil—from that point on," Alex says. And they're all looking at me, and it is in their auras—the realization. All those who've died—is it my fault? Not just the ones who died from the epidemic that caught it from me. But survivors who have been persecuted and murdered too? SAR was hunting survivors before then, like when they tried to kill me in Killin. But once I turned myself in to the air force, from that point on it had the official sanction of the government.

I wrap my arms around myself, not wanting to think it through, not wanting to understand. How could it be just me who is a carrier?

"And then it was confirmed on Shetland with the outbreak at the air force," Alex says.

"*What?*" I say.

"There was an outbreak at the air force base after you left. Other than a few immune, everyone died."

"No. No way. I was suited before I got anywhere near anybody, and the whole time I was at the air force base I was in isolation or suited. It couldn't have been me that infected them. It must have been somebody else that brought it in."

"There hadn't been any arrivals in the days before the outbreak besides you."

"What could be different about Shay that makes her a carrier? We must work this out," Elena says.

The others feel *relief*—they aren't carriers.

Pity.

Confusion.

"This really doesn't make sense to me," Spike says. "We all had the illness; we all survived. There weren't any differences in our scans, were there?"

"No. I've been through them all," Elena answers.

"So why would one of us be a carrier and the others not?" Spike says.

I frown and run the animation Elena did of me again. It is clear that the illness followed our movements until we got to Shetland.

And then it spread to the air force base.

If they didn't get it from me, then how?

Alex said no one else had arrived on the island. Well, except for us—Kai and me. And Kai is immune; they've proved the immune aren't carriers.

The only other one with us was . . . Callie.

Shields up, eyes closed, I go through it all. Everywhere Callie went. The flu started in Shetland, then moved on to Aberdeen—like Callie did. Then she traveled by train through Edinburgh to Newcastle—again, the flu followed her. I met Kai in Edinburgh—I assume she was with him—and soon after that I was ill. They went to Killin to look for me: Killin was later quarantined, and nearly everyone died. For the whole path of our travels after that she was there. And she would have gone looking for me when I left her with Kai on Shetland—everywhere, including the air force base.

It all fits. But this is *madness*.

If Callie was the carrier all along, instead of me—*no*. Then I left Kai for nothing.

The air has been kicked out of me—or the will to breathe. Everything stops.

Beatriz's small hand slips into mine, and I open my eyes. "Are you all right, Shay? Your colors don't look so good."

Elena and Spike's concern washes against me.

I'm breathing again now, but more like hyperventilating; too fast, in, out, in, out, and things are spinning. It can't be, it can't . . .

"None of this is your fault, Shay. You didn't know. How could you?" Spike says. But he thinks I'm upset about being a carrier; not about *not* being one.

Later I'm pacing in my room.

Everything is tumbling around in my head as if the answers I want are almost there, but I can't quite line them up in the right order.

But there is one thing I am certain of: I can't keep Callie to myself, not any longer.

Callie was Alex's daughter. I have to tell him first.

CHAPTER 11

I FIND ALEX, STILL AWAKE, DOWNSTAIRS. He looks up and smiles, like he isn't surprised to see me.

"Alex, do you know where Kai is, where he has been? You were hiding something when I asked you before. Tell me what you know."

"I couldn't answer you at the facility; it was all being recorded. I was trying to trace him for my ex-wife, his mother. There is evidence he traveled to Glasgow under another name. More recently he may have been seen in London, but nothing since. I don't know where he is now."

"Glasgow—London. Two supposedly safe places the epidemic has spread to recently." And assuming Callie was with Kai—and I know she'd never leave him, so she must have been—she was there, on the spot, again.

"Yes, but he is immune, isn't he?" Alex stares at me, and curiosity and intense desire to *know* ripple through his aura—but he's not going to want to know this.

I sigh and flop into a chair.

"You know something," he says.

"Maybe. I think I've worked out how the epidemic really spread."

He sits opposite. "But you don't want to tell me?"

"It's not that, exactly. It's just—well. You might not want to know, even though you think you do."

"I couldn't be any more intrigued. If it helps: I would always choose knowledge over ignorance, no matter what knowing may do."

He says the words fiercely, as if he's never said anything more true: I sense these words are the core of Alex, of who he is, in a way nothing else has ever been.

"All right, then: brace yourself. This may be a shock."

He waits to hear what I may say, leaning forward. His blue eyes, intense, drawing the words from inside me, making me want to tell him. They're a darker blue than mine, like maybe who he is is a darker version of me? I wouldn't always choose knowledge if it would hurt—not so much me as other people, maybe. But I've always had this intense curiosity to *know*—to know *everything*—in the same way that he does. Did I get it from him? Did Callie have the same trait?

I *unlook* a little—just enough to focus more on his aura and less on the man.

Is an aura something you can inherit, like eye color? His is a lot like mine—if I hold my hand out next to his, both blaze with the colors of a rainbow.

But Callie doesn't have an aura anymore. Doesn't that mean what I've been thinking is impossible?

"Shay?" he prompts.

"It's about your daughter—it's about Callie."

He's startled. This is a topic he wasn't expecting. "Go on," he says.

"I hate to have to tell you this, Alex. She was at the facility on Shetland; she was one of their subjects. She was injected with antimatter and became ill, but she survived."

His shock is absolute.

"Are you saying Callie is a *survivor*?" he says, and disbelief shimmers through him. "Do you know where she is?"

"She's with Kai. Or, at least, she was. I expect she still is."

He frowns. "There's been no report of anyone traveling with Kai initially or—"

"No. There wouldn't be."

"What is it you're not saying?"

"She was 'cured' in fire at the facility—that's what they called it, but 'murdered' is more apt. I mean she was"—I swallow—"I'm sorry. It means she was incinerated. Burned in an intense fire to ash."

"I don't understand. How could you know all this? And how could she be with Kai if that is the case?"

"Some part of her wasn't destroyed and survived the fire. At first I thought she was a ghost, but I don't think that is quite right. I think it is Callie who is the carrier."

I explain more. How Callie—a form of darkness only I could hear and see—traveled from Shetland to Aberdeen, then Edinburgh and Newcastle to find her mother and Kai. The more I say it out loud, the more I see how it explains the whole initial spread of the epidemic.

"And then Kai and Callie found me when I was ill," I say. "It was what she told us that made us travel to Shetland—and everywhere we went, the epidemic followed. I thought it was me; that it had to be me. But it was when you told us about the outbreak at the air force base on the island that I realized the truth. And there was Glasgow and London: Kai—and therefore, Callie—were there. This confirms it."

Alex asks question after question: about how I communicated with Callie, what she was like, what Kai made of it—why Kai believed me that she was there. What Callie could remember and what she couldn't. I can see the scientist has taken over; he is gathering facts, analyzing them, sifting through them to feel for the truth.

And the questions he asks and the places they lead are opening channels of thought in my own mind, ones I want—*need*—to explore. There is something there just out of my reach.

And the whole time, Alex is screening places inside. Has he locked up his feelings about Callie and what she went through?

Then he asks me to leave him alone with his thoughts. He also asks me not to tell anyone about Callie, not until he can come to terms with what I've told him.

I readily agree. It's his daughter; how could I not?

CHAPTER 12

I SHOULD SLEEP, BUT I CAN'T.

How can I, when now I know I'm not contagious and that Callie is?

Pain that is never far away is welling up inside. I want to run to Kai, to say I'm sorry for leaving him—that I had everything wrong . . .

As if he knows I need it just now, Chamberlain stirs and rubs his head against my hand until I pet him. I push the tears away. What about Callie? I've got to find them and find a way to tell her. Take her somewhere she can be happy where no one else will be infected. This is the only way to stop the epidemic.

There are so many unanswered questions that won't leave me alone.

What is Callie? She can't be just a dark cloud of antimatter: if she were, everything she came into contact with would go *boom*—not just people—and, as it happened, bit by bit she would cease to exist.

She was a survivor, like me: made of matter, with antimatter hidden away inside of her.

She was burned in a fire.

I try not to go back to how *I* nearly died in a fire, to remember the burning, the pain. I push it away.

Nothing could have survived the fire Callie was in. Her ashes were scooped up and taken away; she told us so. If nothing *physical* survived the fire, what is she?

She is more like . . . a form of *energy*. Most people can't see it. It's a dark energy, one that can only be seen by survivors.

But how could this dark energy make people sick and do it in exactly the same way as if they've been exposed to antimatter? Callie was always the same as far as I could tell, so whatever she did to make people sick, it didn't change her.

Wait a minute: that sounds like a catalyst, something we learned about in chemistry. Catalysts speed up reactions without being changed themselves.

Maybe there is something in humans that can produce antimatter with the right catalyst. Then the antimatter makes them sick.

Huh. That's easier than using a particle accelerator, isn't it?

Anyhow, this idea is just plain over-the-top crazy. Why would humans evolve to have something built in, dormant inside them, that will wipe almost all of them out? It's like they've been programmed to self-destruct.

Except for survivors, who get infected but don't die. Why?

Like I told the others before, I keep thinking back to another time when matter won out over antimatter: the big bang. There must be a connection here, somehow; I just know it.

Maybe something shielded matter from antimatter after the big bang, like it shields antimatter inside survivors now. Something dark, like the barrier I sensed inside me . . .

Dark matter.

Maybe dark matter stopped the big bang from destroying the universe; likewise, dark matter keeps survivors alive. And if Callie is made of dark energy, maybe that is all that is left when matter, antimatter, and dark matter are destroyed.

Another thing on the list of things I don't understand is this: when the air force facility was attacked, many survivors were killed—burned in Vigil's fires. If more Callies were created, we'd have known it. I might have been beyond registering it after nearly dying, but the others would have been able to see and hear them. Why didn't the same thing that happened to Callie happen to them? Was there something special about Callie—beyond just being a survivor—that made this happen to her and only her?

I frown and shake my aching head. I'm desperate to tell everyone what I've started to work out about all of this to see if they can help put the pieces together.

I consider going back downstairs, finding Alex and raising the others. But he's just found out his daughter has died. He was shielding his emotions before; I need to leave him alone to deal with what happened to her.

It can wait until morning. I close my eyes and wrap my arms around Chamberlain. His rumbling purr lulls me to sleep at last.

CHAPTER 13

WHEN I GO DOWNSTAIRS IN THE MORNING, Alex isn't at breakfast. Elena says that he left early—that he told her there was something he had to look into, that he'd be back tonight or tomorrow. That we should stay put and wait for him.

She hadn't questioned him and seems puzzled when I ask her, where would we go anyway?

And where has he gone?

No one seems concerned that he's not here, but he's gone off without telling anyone about his daughter, that is clear. Maybe he doesn't want to admit that she is the one who causes death everywhere she goes.

That afternoon we're all off researching, reading, and thinking in our various corners, but I can't concentrate. Something doesn't *feel* right; there's a vague sense of foreboding deep in my gut, and somehow it is wrapped up with Alex's silence on something so crucial—and his absence.

Coming to terms with a loss in his own way and time I can understand, but when I was talking to him last night there seemed to be something *more* going on inside him. I don't know what it was. What was he hiding?

But he can't hide this: the mode of spread of the epidemic is too important not to share, and I can't keep quiet on it any longer.

I cast around for Spike and hail him. *Hi, can we talk?*

Of course; I need a break. I'm in the summerhouse.

I head outside to the garden, Chamberlain at my feet. I haven't gone into the summerhouse before. It's old and looks like a good push would knock it over, but when I go through the door, I can see why Spike likes it here. He's made a cozy nest in a corner, one that looks across the overgrown lawns to the house. It's a good hideaway.

Spike moves a pile of books off the other chair for me, and I sit next to him. As soon as I do, Chamberlain jumps onto my lap, then turns and arranges himself so he's watching the door, eyes wide open.

"Isn't it time for you to be snoozing on a bed somewhere, Sir Cat?" Spike says, and scratches his ears, but Chamberlain's attention stays fixed on the door.

"He's jumpy today," I say, realizing as I say it that he's been shadowing me, wide-awake, ever since I got up this morning. "Maybe because I am."

"Is something wrong?"

"I don't know. Maybe. I need to ask you something that might seem a bit random."

"Go."

"You know how you said you have a mask—how much do you think each of us can hide from each other?"

His eyes are thoughtful. "Are you wondering about Alex?"

I'm surprised. Does Spike have concerns about Alex too? And he doesn't have Kai or my mum as reasons. "Yes. How'd you know?"

"I've been wondering about a few things. How he managed to keep that he was a survivor secret is beyond me. And he said he couldn't tell us, but come on—telepathy, right? He could have told us. For whatever reason, he didn't want to."

"He must have been masking his aura then so we couldn't tell he was a survivor—it looks completely different now," I say. "But who's to say he isn't making it look different all the time?"

"What is it you're worried about?"

"Easier to show you than tell you," I say. We link minds, and I show him Callie.

I tell Spike all about her too; how she drew us to Shetland. That I'd told Alex about her last night—that he'd asked me to keep it to myself. But then he wasn't here in the morning, and—without even quite knowing why—I wasn't comfortable with keeping it to myself any longer.

Spike stares levelly back at me while I talk, taking it all in. He doesn't have trouble believing me about Callie: how could he when our minds are linked as they are? I'm as open to him now as he is to me. He knows it is the truth.

Spike is about to say something, but whatever it is he stops and looks at the summerhouse door. Chamberlain digs his claws through my jeans and I wince.

Beatriz stands there, unsmiling.

"They're here," she says.

PART 6

VENERATION

To see the truth, you must be able to listen, and not just with your ears—with all of your senses.

—**Xander, *Multiverse Manifesto***

CHAPTER 1

KAI

I'M STANDING ON THE ROCKY HILL above the burned-out remains of Shay's last prison. Is she free now?

There were arguments within the group about what to do with the bodies of survivors we found in the trap—the ones not destroyed in their attackers' fires. We decided we couldn't leave them with the other dead. Sooner or later, the authorities will appear to see what has happened here; we don't want to leave survivors' bodies intact, not when they might experiment on them.

The ground is too hard and rocky to bury them, so pyres are all we can do—even though it seems somehow wrong to take bodies of these survivors and burn them, when that is what their enemies would do if they were still alive. And Patrick asked whether burning them might cause a change of form, make them like Callie.

In the end we decided no, it couldn't happen, because they're already dead.

But we had to hurry. We couldn't be found in this place. They would either think we're responsible, or realize most of us are survivors and lock us up.

Callie, Henry, and Amaya are watching to make sure that no one is coming, while below me the others stand by the pyre as it burns.

I needed to be away from them just now, and I think they needed their space from me so they could make their peace with what has happened, together—in a way they can't if they're including me. Before that I had to stay and help, lend my strength to what had to be done—to carrying the bodies to the pyre we'd made. It was too distressing for the others, as any contact with the dead had them reliving their last moments over and over again, so I took that task away from them.

But it has all been done now, and I'm restless.

Is Shay out there somewhere?

We didn't find her body, or anyone who died who had seen her die. But there is no way to know where she went—no clues, nothing to follow. She could be literally *anywhere*.

Shay isn't anyone else's problem but mine; I know this. Patrick already said as much—that we've done what we could, and without a clear trail to follow, we need to make plans and move on to other things.

They need to move on to other things.

I can't.

CHAPTER 2

CALLIE

SMOKE RISES INTO THE SKY and we're no closer to finding Dr. 1, no closer to finding Shay. Kai stands above, alone. He seems more apart from everyone else now than ever.

Freja, JJ, Patrick, and Zohra are watching the bodies burn on the pyre. With the right fuel, they burn so easily. It doesn't take long. We could leave now, but still they stand there and watch the flames. Even though they decided burning dead survivors wouldn't make them like me, maybe they want to be sure before we go.

Then Freja glances around until her eyes find Kai above us on the hill. They rest on him there before she turns to JJ, to something he says, but they're not broadcasting so I can't hear. She walks away and JJ follows.

I do too. I'm not supposed to be here; I'm supposed to be watching the roads and the sky to make sure no one is coming, but Amaya and Henry can cover it. I'm tired of being excluded.

I slip next to Freja, by her side, in order to face JJ.

Ah, so our shadow has returned, he says.

I stick out my tongue and he chuckles.

Leave her alone, Freja says with some feeling.

Well, this was meant to be a private conversation, but whatever you prefer. You know I'm right, Freja. Don't you?

She copies my earlier gesture.

He really laughs this time and shakes his head. *Kai has to go on his quest. You can't stop him.*

What makes you think I want to?

Just a tickle of an idea.

Freja looks at him, then closer again, as if she's had an idea of her own. *You* did *actually see Shay, didn't you? You didn't just make that up to send him away?*

Are you doubting my word? JJ is angry. I don't think he lied, but Freja is wondering. Why would he? I don't understand.

I wish I could see Shay again, like JJ did.

That's when I realize: maybe . . . I can.

Show us, I say to JJ.

What? he says.

Show us what you saw.

JJ shrugs. *Are you sure you want to see?* He says this to Freja, not to me.

She hesitates, and then says *yes*.

His mind kind of bumps into ours, and we're *there*—in JJ's memory—back underground beside the two bodies. He pulls the suit open and touches the man's shoulder, distaste running through him, and then we're carried along with JJ to the dead man's last thoughts.

It's just a girl, not many yards away. A man behind her is pulling wires out of the wall by the door.

They're trapped.

A slip of a girl, and I laugh when she faces us and straightens her shoulders.

"Stop!" she says, but her lips don't move—she says it in my mind, and I do stop, afraid. She's one of them*—the ones we hunt.*

But our friends are here, behind us, and we throw off our fear, focus on our hate. She must die. We raise our weapons, and then—

Pain?

In my chest. Agony. I stagger, fall to the ground; another falls next to me.

The rest run away behind us. Cowards.

She stares at me, horror on her face . . . but she is the true horror.

Pain squeezes my chest tight. Everything goes black.

CHAPTER 3

SHAY

BEATRIZ IS RIGHT. When Spike and I cast out with our minds, there are pockets of consciousness and thought scattered all around us. Is that why Chamberlain was stuck to my side and jumpy all morning—could he sense their approach? I shake my head; that's crazy. Cats don't need a reason to be jumpy; sometimes they just *are*. But today he was right: people are here, and not just a few. Who could they be? No possibility I can think of is good. I swear under my breath. *How* did they get so close to us? If Beatriz hadn't pointed them out, I'm not sure I'd have noticed they were there at all.

"Who are they?" Beatriz asks.

"Let's take a look," I say, "and see what they are up to."

The three of us link thoughts lightly and *reach* out: we see from others' eyes. Moths, spiders, a mouse or two, a few birds.

Men have come. They are wearing biohazard suits that look just the same as the ones Vigil wore when they attacked the facility, but the people inside them are different. They don't exude rage or hate; they're intent, professional soldiers under orders.

Maybe they're just here to round us back up, take us to another facility—study us some more. As much fun as that would be, I'm fearing worse, and I look closer and closer at each of them until at last one of them makes my fear sharpen.

It's *him*: Lieutenant Kirkland-Smith. The one with SAR. Despite my suspicions, the shock is still a kick in the gut.

He's the one who came to Killin to get me using *any means necessary*. He failed, but my friend Duncan—I think of him as a friend now even though he was more the opposite before—died, pushing me out of the way when they tried to shoot me. Kai very nearly died too.

If this bunch are all with SAR, their plans for us aren't likely to be any better than Vigil's.

Kirkland-Smith is with the largest group of them, by the access road to the house, but they're not the only ones. Others are just out of sight in twos and threes at intervals around the whole property. Weapons in hand.

We're completely surrounded.

Where's Alex?

CHAPTER 4

KAI

"WHAT ARE YOU GOING TO DO?" Freja asks me.

"I don't know. Keep looking for Shay, travel around until I find her. What else can I do?"

"It's hopeless without a lead. You don't even know if she's still alive."

"JJ saw her. That was, what—a few days ago? How far could she have gotten?"

"You can't go in all directions at once."

"No. If only we'd gotten here sooner."

"I know. I'm sorry."

"I just can't believe I'll never see her again. I *can't*."

Freja looks to the side and unfocuses, like she does when Callie is there and she's talking to her.

"Callie, what do you think I should do?" I say.

Freja frowns, half shakes her head, and sighs.

"Callie says you can see Shay at least one more time, if you want to."

"What do you mean?"

"JJ shared what he saw with us. I could show you. You have to know, it's not . . . well, pleasant. It's from inside the man she killed—what he saw and felt."

I don't have to think for long. What if I never find her? This could be my last chance to ever see her again. "Yes. Show me."

"I'll have to link to your mind."

I nod, nervous but knowing it must be done. "Okay. Do it."

She nods, her eyes look into mine, and then she's inside my head.

Are you sure? she says.

Yes.

And then we're there. First we have JJ's view, and then we're into the dead man's. His hate and fear are all focused on the girl I love. What he sees is warped by what he thinks of her and what she is, and it is so incongruous with what *I* see that it's hard to even look at her, feeling what he feels at the same time. But she's there. She's alive, scared, defending herself the only way she can, even as her face shows her horror at doing so.

And I want to rip into his chest and crush his heart all over again.

I'm so focused on Shay I almost don't look at the man trying to open the door behind her, and when I do, I don't believe what I see.

Shock makes me break away from the link with Freja abruptly.

I shake my head. "It can't be. No—I don't believe it. How can it?"

"What? What's wrong? That was Shay, wasn't it?"

"Yes, that's not what I mean. Show me all of it again?"

Freja does, and this time I pay more attention to the man behind Shay. The height of him; he towers over Shay. The silver hair. He was so vain about his hair. He glances at the bodies as they fall to the ground, and even in the smoky air there is a flash of his blue eyes. Then their attacker dies, and the memory is over.

"What is it, Kai?" Freja says, and I hear her, but I'm too caught in shock to answer. "Kai?" she says again.

I find my voice and meet her eyes. "The man with Shay? It's Alex—Alex Cross. He was my stepfather, and he's Callie's dad."

CHAPTER 5

CALLIE

THAT MAN WAS . . . MY FATHER?

I replay the memory again and again and stare at him within it, but there is *nothing* about him that I recognize apart from his name. He's really tall and not an average-looking person—he's the sort of man you'd remember even if you weren't related to him.

But there is nothing.

How can I not remember my own father?

I know that what they did to me in Shetland—infecting me, all their tests, and the final cure—mucked up my memory. There are holes in it all over the place, but I still remembered Kai, my brother, and our mum. There's a pang inside when I think of her, left behind when I chose to go with Kai.

But of my father there is absolutely nothing. I only know his name because I heard Kai and Shay talking about him—I didn't even remember that.

Freja is radiating sadness so intense that it intrudes on my thoughts, even though I can feel she's trying to hide it. And her sadness isn't anything to do with Alex—it's something about Shay.

I can't see into Kai's mind at all; only into survivors' minds, and only if they let me, really, but when Freja showed Kai what JJ shared, I was there. I could feel an echo of what he felt through Freja—and his strongest emotion of all was how much he loves Shay.

And finally I'm understanding what has been weird with Freja and Kai: she must love Kai too.

Kai rushes off to talk to Patrick. Freja makes an excuse, says she'll follow in a moment. I feel like I shouldn't leave her alone, but I need to know what is happening.

I follow Kai.

The others are packing their tents, getting ready to leave, when Kai rushes up to them.

"Patrick, at last: I have it. The lead I need! The man that was with Shay—I know him." Kai explains as Patrick, JJ, and Zohra listen. "So if I can work out where Alex would go—or can trace him somehow? Then I might find Shay."

"Why do you suppose Alex was there?" Patrick asks. "He must either be a survivor himself, and so was one of those being held, or he was working for the government."

"I didn't think of that," Kai says. "He could have been working for them; he's a quantum physicist. Maybe they brought him in to try to work out all the antimatter weirdness? But he also lived in Edinburgh—he could have caught it and survived. I don't know which it is."

"Let's get back to base, get online, and see what we can find out," Patrick says.

CHAPTER 6

SHAY

WE RETREAT INTO THE HOUSE, find Elena, and tell her what we've seen. We lock the doors—not that that would stop SAR if they attack. For now, at least, they seem to be holding their positions in a rough ring around the property—just watching, waiting. For what?

Chamberlain stares out the window: a guard cat. Though I'm not sure how much help he'd be if they move in. We call Alex over and over again in case he's heading back and close enough for our minds to reach, but he doesn't answer.

"I can't sense him," I say. "Unless he's blocking us, he's too far away."

"The coward," Spike says, fury all through him. "Leaving us to face this on our own."

"That's not fair!" Elena protests. "I'm sure he didn't know they were closing in."

I nod. "I don't think Alex is scared of much. There must be some other reason why he's not here."

"Like that he's working for them," Spike says. "That he brought them here."

"You don't know that he's done anything," Elena says, but I can see Spike's point. Alex *did* disappear the same day SAR arrived. And he didn't tell any of us where he was going or why. Where is he?

But Spike's theory just doesn't *feel* right to me.

"For what it's worth, I don't think he'd set SAR on us or abandon us to them either, but that isn't what we have to focus on now," I say. "What are we going to do?"

"Beatriz, has there been any movement?" Spike asks.

She's been sitting there quietly all this time, watching each of us while we talk; the way she can divide her attention is amazing. Her defocused look clears, and she turns to Spike. "No. They're all where they were when we first noticed them." She goes back to watching.

"It's almost like they're waiting for something, but what?" I say.

"I don't think we should stay and find out," Spike says.

"Maybe Alex knew they might come," Elena says. "He told us to stay where we are, to wait for him."

"If he knew and didn't tell us, I'm not doing what he said," Spike says. "Let's get out of here. Agreed?"

One by one we all nod, until, outnumbered, Elena does too.

"Do we have to attack them?" Elena asks. "Like how Shay showed us?"

I shake my head, wincing inside. "We're not murderers, are we? Only strike out if we have to, in self-defense. Let's see if we can distract them first."

CHAPTER 7

KAI

WE LEFT THE TRAP JUST IN TIME: Callie was watching and told us the air force arrived soon after.

The whole trip back to Patrick's house is torture. What if Shay went in completely the other direction? I could be getting farther and farther away from her. Freja tries to talk to me but soon leaves me alone when I don't respond.

Everyone is exhausted when we get there, but Patrick takes me straight to the computer. "Let's see what we can find out," he says. "Tell me what you can about him. Full name and address to start with."

"Dr. Alexander Cross." I tell him Alex's address and the university department where he worked.

Patrick goes first to the government site that shows the progression of the epidemic. "If he was there at the time, that area was decimated by the epidemic. Unless he was immune or a survivor, he'd be dead."

I snort. "Figures that he'd be one of the few to escape dying."

"I'm getting you didn't like the guy."

"No."

"Just usual stepparent stuff?"

"No, worse—much worse."

"But maybe he's helped save your girl."

"Maybe. If so, I'll shake his hand; then I'll punch him."

"Good to have a balanced approach."

Patrick enters his name next.

And the top hit: *Breaking News: Noted physicist Dr. Alexander Cross dies in fire.* Patrick clicks, and there's a photo; his steady blue eyes jump off the screen.

"This was only posted a short time ago," Patrick says. He looks for more information, but there's nothing: no mention of Shay or anyone else dying with him, no time or place of death given.

I feel like my guts have been kicked out—again. Could Alex and Shay have died there, in the fires, before we arrived? No. No, it doesn't make sense. We checked all the bodies; they weren't there. *Think, Kai:* what does this mean?

Patrick's hand is on my shoulder.

"You don't know they were together when he died."

I shake my head. "I don't know that Alex is even really dead."

"What do you mean?"

"Maybe the authorities *assumed* he died at the trap. But we never found his body or the body of anyone who saw him die, did we? If he was working for the government and he and Shay got away, the first thing he'd have done is turned her in to the authorities. But then why would there be a report of his death? No. I think he's a survivor too, and he faked his death to get away; maybe they're on the run together."

"Who is this guy, Houdini?"

"Pretty much. I hate him, but if he has Shay, her chances of survival are high."

"Where do you think they'd go?"

"I'm not sure, but I'm thinking."

I slip out that night. I leave a note, apologizing for taking one of the bikes, hoping they'll understand: I can't expect them to join me in what I must do, but I can't stay either.

I wheel it away from the house as quietly as I can. My barriers are up high, like Freja taught me, so no one will sense me go.

Finally I judge I must be far enough away from the house for them to not hear the bike. I get on it, about to start it—

"There you are."

Startled, I look around: it's Freja.

"How did you follow me? I thought I had blocking you all worked out pretty well."

"Wasn't me, it was Callie. She never sleeps, remember? She saw you leaving and came and got me. Where are you going?"

"There are a few places I want to check that Alex may have gone and taken Shay with him."

"Unless he really is dead." She doesn't fill in the rest: *And maybe Shay is too.*

I shake my head, push the thought away. "I *have* to hold on to this hope: that they're out there, somewhere, on the run."

"Okay, assume for a moment that you're right. Wouldn't the authorities check the same places? They're likely to be ahead of you."

"I'm hoping that they believe he's dead, and there's no one to look for. Anyway, even if not, I think that with the epidemic spreading south and the zone barriers breaking down, they have other things keeping them busy just now."

"So where are these places you think he might go?"

"He might go to his house in Killin, in Scotland. It's not actually his anymore—Mum got it in the divorce—but he loved it there, and everyone around there is dead or gone, so there's no reason why they couldn't go there."

"Could the same apply to where he lived in Edinburgh?"

"I don't think so. Even though it was hit by the epidemic, a city is maybe not a great place to hide—if even the five percent that were immune are still there, that's a reasonable number of people that'd be around that might spot them. But he has another place too."

"He must be rich."

"A bit. He has a country house in Northumberland inside the zone, and that's where I want to go first. Partly as it is closer, so I can stop there on the way to Killin, and partly because it's not all that far away from the trap, so it may have been a logical place for them to go. The problem is that I'm not sure exactly where it is. I haven't been there more than a few times, and the last time was probably eight or nine years ago." I frown, struggling to remember. "I think if I went to Hexham, I could find it from there."

"All right; that seems reasonable. I'm coming with you."

"No, you're not. Look, I know it isn't my thing, but those people back there are important to you."

"Yes. They are, in a way. But I'm still coming with you. You can't stop me; if you try, I'll shout out to the rest of them and they'll give chase. You are a motorbike thief, you know." She grins.

"I think Patrick might forgive me."

"Maybe. But you need me, Kai. At a minimum, you need Callie to help you find Shay, and I can help her and also tell you what she says. You can't do it without us."

I hesitate, uneasy. Things have been weird between Freja and me since that night in the woods—the night we came so close to doing what could never be undone. "There's something maybe I need to say."

She shakes her head. "No, you don't. Look, Kai: I was there when you saw Shay in that memory. I know you love her, and I don't want to make things difficult for you. I want to help you find her, because you're my *friend*. And that's it."

"Are you sure? Are you really absolutely sure?"

"Yes."

"Okay."

"Okay?"

"Yes. And thank you." I mean it, and she's probably right—that I can't do this without help—but there is still an uneasy feeling inside, something that isn't sure whether it is right to accept Freja's help with this. But I can't worry about that now.

Hang in there, Shay. I'm coming to get you.

CHAPTER 8

CALLIE

KAI AND FREJA RIDE THROUGH THE FIRST HALF of the night, then find a run-down barn in a field to camp out in. They're so tired they're asleep almost as soon as they lie down on some straw.

I'm on guard duty and check around the area, then sit on top of the barn.

I'm unsettled, weirded out. Kai thinks Alex—it seems easier to think of him as *Alex* than as my dad, since I don't remember him at all—might be a survivor. But Patrick also said he could have been at the trap because he was working for the government. He's a quantum physicist, whatever that is, and might know stuff about antimatter.

I hope he was working for them. If he knows what the government did, he may know where to find Dr. 1.

CHAPTER 9

SHAY

***REACHING* OUT INTO THE WOODS** to every mouse, bird, even spider we can find, we use their eyes to monitor each of the men and their positions. There are about thirty soldiers, none close enough for a direct visual. If we venture out and try to sneak up on them to influence their auras directly, we'd be in range of their guns before we got close enough. If we can see them, they can see us.

It's almost like they know how we work, and they've positioned themselves just far enough away to stop us.

"We're going to have to try something from a distance," I say. "Jump into a mind and see if we can influence it, even though their auras are too far away to get at directly."

"Can we do that?" Spike says.

"I don't know. We've all been reaching insects and animals in the woods to see with their eyes, but I can't, say, make a bird swoop in a certain direction to show me what I want to see. But maybe that's because a bird's mind is too foreign for mine to influence it? Let's try it on one of the soldiers."

We watch, wait for an opportunity—for one of them to be alone—concentrating on the ones behind the house in the woods. A place we can disappear from the easiest.

At last one of them slips off to pee behind some trees.

Let me try, I say.

I slip inside him, see out of his eyes—just like I was doing with the squirrel that was watching him a moment earlier. I tell his feet to move. I make him curious to know what is over there.

It's actually working! He's walking away from his position instead of going back to it.

Spike, watching, tries it with another soldier nearby.

Soon the second soldier is walking into the trees behind his companion. If we can move a few groups of them far enough apart, we should be able to slip through them and get away.

But then, all at once, the connection is broken—both the one with the soldier I was influencing and Spike's too. The two soldiers stop and seem confused; then they step back to their original positions.

"What happened?" Elena says.

"I don't know." I frown. "Maybe because they walked away from us, they were just too far to keep hold of the influence over them?"

"Let's try again, and get them to move more sideways this time," Spike suggests.

We try again and again but have no luck at all. None. We can't even look out of their eyes now.

Beatriz tries too, then shakes her head. "Someone must be blocking us," she says.

"You mean another survivor?"

"Who else could do that?" she says.

"Alex; it must be Alex," Spike says.

Elena frowns. "He's not out there; I can't sense him."

"But he knows how to hide from us when he wants to—he's done it before, at the facility when we didn't know he was a survivor," Spike says.

I sigh, head in my hands, and shield my thoughts. I still can't believe that Alex is in with SAR. Why? Is it just because he's my father that I'm cutting him slack he doesn't deserve? No. At least, I don't think so. It just doesn't *feel* right, knowing how Alex feels about survivors' potential, that he would set us up like this.

I cast out again. There's no sign of Alex anywhere, but that doesn't mean anything. Spike is right: he knows how to hide from us if he wants to.

The soldiers are alert but holding their positions.

Still they watch. Still they wait.

What for?

I look up at the others. "We've got no choice, really, have we? Let's try to sneak out of here."

CHAPTER 10

KAI

THE COUNTRYSIDE IS EERIE as we go farther north. There are no cars, no people—no living ones, that is. And we're not even at the latest zone boundary yet.

Callie checks ahead when we're nearing it.

"Callie says there's a roadblock, but nobody is there," Freja says.

"Is she sure?"

"Yes."

"Maybe it's been abandoned?" I say.

We go carefully up to the place just the same—hide the bike a ways back and walk there, staying out of sight in the trees.

"I can't sense anyone here," Freja says.

There's a gate, a sentry hut—empty, but there is a car behind it. Fences with quarantine zone warnings on signs with big red letters.

We walk back to the bike and go up the road this time. I pull in by the car. "Let's see if we can siphon some fuel," I say. "We're getting low."

I rip out some hose from the engine, work out how to wreck the electronics enough to open the fuel cap.

We top off the bike, open the gate, and go through. And as easy as that, we're in the quarantine zone.

Not far from the barrier there is a massive fire pit; bones, and a smell that will be hard to forget, from piles of bodies that were waiting to be burned but instead have been left to rot in the sun.

We hurry away, as far and as fast as we can go, but the horrors continue. They're everywhere.

We go around the outskirts of Newcastle, my home. Is Mum still there? Maybe when we've found Shay, we can try to go to her.

In a small village Callie finds us empty houses—ones without dead—and we break into one and then another, finding packaged and canned food, more gas. There is no power and the tap water looks funny, so we stick to bottled.

Finally we reach Hexham. Exhausted, we find another empty house and stop for the night.

CHAPTER 11

CALLIE

THE NEXT MORNING KAI AND FREJA step out into the sunshine.

"What now?" she asks.

"Let's see. Somewhere a few hours' drive from here, more or less, there is a house, and we need to find it," Kai says.

Have I been there? I say, and Freja passes my question along to Kai.

"Yes," Kai answers. "Actually probably more recently than me."

"Do you know where it is?" Freja asks me.

I don't know; I don't remember.

Freja sighs and looks at Kai. "Can you be any more specific about which way we should go?" she asks. "It sounded like you had more of an idea where it was before."

"I was hoping as we got closer it'd come back to me, but it hasn't. To be fair it was a long time ago that I was there. I'm sure we came here to Hexham to go shopping from there once, there and back in a day, so it must be within a few hours at most? But I don't know which direction."

Callie, show me what the house looks like, Freja says.

I shrug. *I don't remember.*

Freja frowns. "Kai, can you show me what the house looks like? Callie says she doesn't remember. If you show me then I can show Callie, and that way we can spread out and search."

"How do I do that?"

"Let me link minds with you, and then you picture what it looks like. I'll be able to see it."

I join with Freja. Kai hesitates, and then he is there too. He doesn't like talking like this. I don't know why; it's so much easier. Especially for me. It's the closest he can get to hearing me.

He shows us a fancy house—it's huge. It's got grounds and fields around it; a summerhouse, greenhouse, a barn, a load of other outbuildings with woods behind. He shows us up a road, but it gets less definite as he doesn't remember details. There are no neighbors or other buildings around at all.

We break into a gas station and find some maps, and Kai studies them closely.

"I think there are about six directions we can go from here that look reasonable," Kai says. "We've already done one of them on our way here."

"How about we check two at a time?" Freja says. "Callie can go one way, us another, and then we meet back here and do it again. We can look for the house or anything that seems familiar to you and feel for survivors as we go."

I study the map, and we head off into the countryside.

CHAPTER 12

SHAY

WE WAIT UNTIL THE SUN IS NEARLY GONE, hoping we will be harder to spot in dusk's long shadows.

Spike and I slip through a side door that should be blocked from the soldiers' view by the greenhouse, and then we creep along it slowly, quietly, then beyond it, bent down in long grass as we pass by shrubs and overgrown flowerbeds, heading toward the woods. Everyone agreed I have to go in the first pair: I'm the only one of us that has killed before, who definitely knows *how*, even as the thought makes acid rise to the back of my throat. Elena and Beatriz wait in the house and stop Chamberlain from following us. They will come behind in a moment if all goes well.

Nothing here, you can't see me; nothing here, you can't see me: we play this mantra over and over in our minds, but it's hard to maintain that and block what I'm really feeling: fear of the soldiers is so strong it's hard to keep my feet steady, let alone my thoughts, but even stronger is fear and horror of what we might have to do to them to get away.

We've picked up on another two soldiers in the woods behind the house—not the same ones we tried to meddle with before, in case it is something about them that stopped us.

Nothing here, you can't see me; nothing here, you can't see me . . .

And then we can see them: the soldiers. They're vigilant, poised with guns in their hands, scanning the area around them toward the house. Yet they can't see us, just like we've told them. I'm pretty sure that won't continue to work if we get close enough to go past them, though.

Their auras aren't the worst I've come across. There isn't hate all through them. There is obedience, strength, and determination in both. One is distracted and thinking of something else, the other more focused.

Nothing here, you can't see me; nothing here, you can't see me . . .

I watch them, and I know how to do this, but I just *can't*. The only times I've ever hurt somebody were when they've been intent on killing me. These two can't even see us.

Spike's thoughts are linked with mine, and Elena's and Beatriz's too. *They would if they knew we were here,* he says.

Elena and Beatriz have caught up with us now. *I'll do it,* Beatriz says, and without discussion starts to focus on their auras—a child poised to commit murder.

No! I say, and she backs off. *Please. Let's try something else first.*

I imagine a noise in the trees off to their left. The soldiers react instantly, their movements controlled and precise even as they hurry to investigate, guns raised.

You two go first, I say to Beatriz and Elena, and they slip into the trees where the soldiers were a moment ago.

Seconds later we follow.

Then there are voices: shouts to our left where we sent the soldiers, and then something completely unexpected—a *push*, inside us.

Something—*someone*—is pushing against our minds, trying to get in.

Shocked, we shield ourselves, and push back.

"There they are!" someone shouts.

Run! Spike says, and we run, full tilt now, the need for speed more than the need for quiet.

A light suddenly shines at us in the darkness, bright in our eyes, making it hard to see.

Get down, Spike yells in my mind, and his body pushes at mine from behind.

There's a *BANG*—

Spike's body arches—

Pain—Spike's pain—

Shock—both of us—

And he falls, heavy on me, pushing me down to the earth underneath him. His body is covering mine—his thoughts are through my mind in a rush: *Save yourself—kill if you have to. Save yourself!* And laced through it all is how much he cares for me—his friend.

And then . . . he stops.

Spike? Spike!

He's gone?

No. No, this can't be. *No!*

His last thoughts are imprinted on me in a way that will never leave me, a mark left inside of me that cannot be forgotten. There is pain, fear; but most of all there is *love*—not the kind that can come and go, but that of a friend. The sort that should have lasted forever, not ended like this.

There are footsteps running toward us, but still another mind, one I don't recognize, *pushes* at mine, and having to shield against it, I am stopped, defenseless.

But then, abruptly, the other mind is gone.

Now there is no holding back.

I strike out, finding the place in their auras that will stop them forever. One soldier falls, then another, but now there are more of them, and more; and still I strike out, and still they fall.

Then, all at once, they pull back. They run away, but not because they run from me—they are called to somewhere else?

They leave me alone.

Now there are voices—shouts, sounds, gunshots—in the distance. Something is happening—but it is all remote from the horror of what is *here*.

I pull myself to my feet. Spike's warm blood is all down my back. His body and the bodies of soldiers are all around where I stand.

I vomit on the ground, again and again, shaking and weak; disbelieving.

If only I had done what the others wanted—only a few soldiers would have died. Not Spike and so *many* of them.

But I couldn't do it; I couldn't. And this is the result.

I can hear someone trying to talk to me inside, telling me it isn't safe, to *run*, to get away from here—that there is fighting in the woods. It's Alex?

Then Beatriz is hailing me too. I can sense her and Elena hiding, safe for now, but I can't go to them with the sounds of men shouting and dying between us.

And how could I go to them at all, after what I've done?

I'm shutting down; closed, shielded—blocking everyone, friend or foe, who might try to find me. I don't answer any of them.

There are more cries and gunshots, the sounds of battle; it's getting closer.

I stagger the other way, back to the house.

CHAPTER 13

KAI

IT'S ALMOST DUSK NOW, but there is one last direction to check; only one. This time the three of us will go together. My guts are all squeezed and squashed in a knot of despair—if this isn't the way, then what? Go back over all the other ways, see if we missed something?

Again and again and again.

"Ready?" I say.

Freja nods, and we walk back to the bike. She's quiet. She's been reserved since we came into the zone. Is it all the dead, calling out to her everywhere we go? She's suffering to help me, and I'm sorry, so sorry.

I stop and turn to her when we reach the bike.

"Are you all right?"

Her eyes turn up to mine. She half smiles, shrugs, but doesn't say anything.

We get on the bike.

An hour or so later it's starting to get dark. We're passing some buildings. I glance at them as we go past, and something twinges in my memory. I turn around, pull in, and stop. It's a farm shop. There's something about the building, the windows; something familiar. Hope and excitement tinge the fear and despair with something better.

"Callie, do you remember this place? I think I do," I say.

I get off the bike, push the door open, and walk in. There's rotting food everywhere, not pleasant, but a quick look around and I'm sure.

"Yes, I've definitely been here before, and Callie too—more than once, I'm sure of it! We came here with Mum for ice cream. We *must* be going the right way."

"How far is the house from here, do you think?"

I frown with the effort of trying to remember. "It's not far, but takes a while. Or maybe that's just how I saw it when I was younger and wanting ice cream. Single-track roads a lot of the way, I think?"

Freja defocuses—talking to Callie?

"Callie is going to do a fast search of the area and see if she can find anything," Freja says.

We start back down the road on the bike, this time going more slowly in case I recognize anything else. There are lanes leading off all over the place, and I don't think I have much hope of remembering which one we should take, especially when it is almost dark, and it could take ages to try each of them.

Freja taps on my shoulder; I pull in. "I think Callie may have found it," she says. "Look!" She projects an image from the air above of a big house, grounds and buildings all around, into my mind, and I don't even feel the usual urge to pull away from the touch of her mind. It's run-down, the normally perfect garden's overgrown, but there's no doubt in my mind that it is Alex's.

"Yes. That's it, I'm sure of it," I say.

Freja grips my shoulder. "Callie says there are soldiers surrounding the house, that they're fighting with another group of people. She doesn't know who they are."

"Soldiers? Fighting? *No.* We can't be too late—not again."

"Listen to me, Kai. I know how you feel, but we need to approach carefully. Callie is going to go ahead, find out what is happening, and report back to us."

"Let's go!"

"Okay, but lights off, and take it easy. Callie showed me the way. I'll direct you."

CHAPTER 14

CALLIE

I RUSH BACK TOWARD THE HOUSE, and when I get near, for a second I think I catch a sense of something *different*—a concentration of intense feeling and presence that says a survivor is here.

Shay? Shay? Are you there?

She doesn't answer.

I drop in closer.

Around the house, the ring of soldiers I saw earlier has converged on the other group. There is a battle in the dark; shots; cries.

Beyond the fighting there is the something—someone—that I sensed. It's a survivor, but doesn't feel like Shay.

I drop down low, and I'm right. It isn't her: it's Alex.

His eyes widen when he sees me. "Is that *Callie*?" he says, but he says it in a funny way, drawing out my name, and there is something about his voice—something familiar. Do I remember him after all?

Yes. And you're my father.

He's focused on me now, not moving ahead with the others. The battle continues without him.

He shakes his head. "I most certainly am not, any more than you are, in fact, Callie. Do you actually believe that to be true?"

His words don't make sense, but they're almost not registering, because it's his *voice* I'm focusing on, the sound of it, the way he shapes words, and I'm feeling sick, confused . . .

No. No; it can't be . . .

But it is.

I'd know his voice anywhere—and it isn't from remembering him as my father or anything from my life before Shetland. His voice is smooth, like velvet and chocolate—a voice you want to listen to.

I draw my arms around myself tight, shaking my head to reject it even though I know it is true.

It's . . . you. You're him. You're . . . And I can't even say it.

"What is your current delusion, little cat?"

Little . . . cat?

"We've opened the box, and there you are: you've fooled Schrödinger. You're alive and dead at once."

I don't understand what he's saying, but the more I hear his voice, the more things are coming back, in bits and pieces. He always wore a biohazard suit, so I never really saw what he looked like. When I saw him in JJ's memory, I didn't recognize him because of that . . . I didn't know that Dr. 1 and Alex were one and the same.

But I know his voice. One of the last ones I ever heard before I was cured.

He's the one I've been trying to find all this time.

And it's not *fair*. It's not! He's a survivor! I can't make him catch it and die. He's already had it. I've finally found him, and there's nothing I can do to him—nothing.

You're Dr. 1! I say, with all the accusation and hate I can put into three words.

He shrugs his shoulders. "I've been called worse. But *you* are curiouser and curiouser. I'm not sure I would have figured out what was causing the epidemic to spread so quickly on my own. It was Shay who worked out that it was you. Yes, she did—she told me about you. And she was so terribly sad for me; she thought she was telling me about my dead daughter. Not a deluded psychopathic *cat*. If only I had known from the beginning!"

Why did you have me cured?

He shakes his head. "It was such a disappointment. So much time and effort went into trying to make what you were: a survivor. I finally achieved what I wanted, but in such a defective, damaged psyche. You were too dangerous to risk any chance of your escape; you had to be destroyed. But who could have predicted that curing you would make you even more dangerous? You'd already taken on Callie's identity at that point—you didn't even know who you were."

No! I am Callie!

Aren't I?

My memory is slipping and sliding, like a kaleidoscope: I can see her/me; her/my beautiful dark hair and blue eyes; she had photos of her amazing big brother and mum and she told me all about them, her home and where they lived; talking late at night to keep us from being scared. And everything about her/me was so much better than *my* life.

Flashes of a life I rejected flit through my mind. I try to push them away, but I can't.

Fear.

Pain.

Things Callie would never have known before Shetland; not in her perfect life.

I'm *not* Callie. My name is there, just slipping away, a secret buried so deep it is hard to find . . .

She yelled my name when she dragged me up the stairs by my hair. My last foster mother, the one I had before I ran away. I can hear her snarling my name: *Jenna, you useless brat.* It echoes deep inside.

Jenna.

My name was—*is*—Jenna.

I wanted to be Callie.

But I'm not. I never was.

"You're starting to remember, aren't you?" Alex says, and shakes his head sadly. "If only it were my daughter who was a survivor. I had so hoped, but instead it was you."

At least that means you were never my father!

"Happy for both of us, then. But as you are now, you have accomplished more than I thought possible—you spread the epidemic far and wide—not just to the few subjects we had, many of them as defective as you. That was the error, I see now: drawing our initial subjects from such a genetically poor lot. And for pointing that out, I thank you."

I stare at him, shocked. Illness, despair, death—this is what he made me. Everywhere I go, people die, and he says . . . thank you?

I finally found Dr. 1, and I can't make him sick—he's already had *it* and survived. But can he burn?

I'm hot in an instant and throw myself at him, but he just pushes me out with a shrug.

"Look, I've got to go now," he says. "There are more of us that need rescuing."

His words aren't connecting. More of us?

Does he mean survivors?

And then I remember: Shay. I'm supposed to be looking for Shay.

CHAPTER 15

SHAY

I RUN INTO THE HOUSE, Chamberlain at my feet once again. Did he see what I did? I bolt the door behind us.

Blood—Spike's blood—and vomit are splattered all over me, and I'm going to be sick again if I don't get these clothes off. I shed them on my way up the stairs, wiping at the blood drying on my skin with my hands, frantic, but it more smears around than comes off—not that I can wipe away what happened on the inside by cleaning the outside.

I pull on some clean clothes over unclean skin and then curl my body around Chamberlain on the bed, shaking.

What now? What do I do?

There are distant sounds and shouts and screams, as if some sort of battle is raging. But the battle inside me is worse, far worse.

Spike is dead. It's my fault; all my fault.

I say the words inside, but even though I know they are true, they are unreal. I say it again and again but still can't take it in.

Spike is dead. My fault.

His blood is here, on my skin. I start rubbing at it again and when that doesn't work, scratching too, harder and harder, until my blood wells up to join his. Hysteria is rising inside.

My fault. I did this.

My fault.

Then there is a sudden blur in the air and a rush of darkness beside me.

It's *Callie*?

She throws herself around me in a hug. She's crying—but not crying, she has no tears—it is more dry, wrenching sobs.

"How did you find me? Where have you come from?" I ask her.

Still caught in her version of crying, it is a moment before Callie can speak. *I'm sorry,* she says. *I'm not her. I'm not Callie! I thought I was, but I'm not.*

In the midst of all the mess—both the fighting outside, and the tumult inside—are Callie's words. Focusing on them, trying to understand, helps me calm.

She is here—dark, whole, soothing—and I've missed her so much.

I'm not Callie, she says again. *She was my friend.*

I frown, struggling to focus. "I don't understand."

Listen to me, there are things I have to tell you. Alex is Dr. 1.

"What?"

He's Dr. 1! He caused the epidemic! she says, and then she's crying-that-isn't-crying again, in pain, both inside and out.

"Callie?"

Not Callie. My name is Jenna. I knew I was the carrier, but I didn't tell you. I didn't tell anyone. I'm sorry! And then she screams out in pain. *It's my fault; everything is my fault. Everyone who got sick and died is because of me.*

She cries-that-isn't-crying still, and I do too; real tears and not-real tears that hurt even more—and we hold each other to try to comfort what can't be comforted.

CHAPTER 16

KAI

FREJA URGES ME TO STOP, to hide the bike, go on foot. And I know she's right, but I want to be there *now*.

I pull in. We're close enough to hear there are sounds in the woods—behind the house. Shouts, cries. Gunshots.

"Why hasn't Callie reported back?" Freja says. "I don't like this. I'll try to find her." She shakes her head a moment later. "She's not answering when I call, and I can't sense her. She's either blocking or she's not here."

"We can't wait for her, let's go," I say.

Freja's hand is on my arm, holding me back. "Just a moment, Kai. Let me see if I can work out what is happening." Her eyes defocus, then come back. "There are other survivors, three of them, in the woods."

"Who are they? Is one of them Shay?"

"No; wait." She pauses. "One of them is hailing me. It's a man—he says he's Alex, and for us to go to him. He says he'll show me the safest way to go."

Alex really is here? Then Shay may be too—or at least he must know where she is. I follow Freja through the trees, fighting to hold myself back and go the way she is directed when I want to find out what he knows *now*.

There are soldiers on the ground in biohazard suits: dead. Other people too are dead next to them—not soldiers, not wearing suits. There are not as many of them.

The fighting appears to be almost over now: the soldiers are outnumbered; they're losing. And there, in the midst of it all, is Alex.

"Ah, hello, Kai. I was wondering if you'd turn up," he says, and steps around a dead soldier at his feet.

"Where's Shay?"

"Calm down, Kai." His voice, that mild voice. "We haven't found her yet." That reasonable tone.

"Tell me where Shay is! Tell me, now! What have you done to her?"

"We'll find her, but I'm a bit busy just now. Wait a moment and keep out of the way." He says it *that* way—with that persuasive weirdness that has always made me so angry, and so unable to resist, for as long as I can remember. And now, finally, I *understand*. I get what I always hated.

He's trying to nudge inside my head.

I push him out.

He turns to me, startled. "Have you learned a new trick?"

"Where is she?"

He doesn't answer and tries in my mind again, but I push him away and then my hands are on his shoulders, anger raging inside me.

And there are other hands on me now, pulling me away from Alex, and I hear him saying not to kill me, but I don't know why when I'd kill *him* given half a chance.

But then there's a voice—a child's voice. A young girl; an older woman stands next to her with a hand on her shoulder.

"It's okay, Kai," the girl says. "Shay is safe in the house with Chamberlain."

But then her attention shifts from me; she looks up to the sky and frowns. A distant rumble touches my ears a moment later.

A plane?

I struggle to my feet. They let me go and I run for the house.

CHAPTER 17

JENNA

GET OUT OF THE HOUSE!

A command slams into my mind, a strong, direct voice, someone I don't know.

That's Beatriz, Shay says, in response to my unasked question, but her thoughts are puzzled, detached.

Get out, now! Panic is all through Beatriz's thoughts, and then we hear it too—a plane.

"The soldiers were waiting for something. They surrounded us and waited. Was it for this?" Shay says, but her eyes are lowered, her voice flat.

It's getting closer, but still Shay doesn't move.

Shay, get up! I say. *Kai must be here by now.*

"Kai?"

He's been searching everywhere for you.

"He's coming here? For me?" And when she looks at me now, her eyes are alive again.

CHAPTER 18

SHAY

I *REACH* **OUT. MENACE FLIES ABOVE** in the sky, and it's getting closer. On the ground there are people—Alex is back, Beatriz and Elena are there too, and many others, ones I don't know—and they are all running away from the house, deeper into the cover of the woods behind it.

But there is one running toward the house—coming for me—and I can feel his aura even though I can't see it yet: an imprint of mind, thought, and energy that I'd know anywhere.

I'm shaking, not quite able to accept Kai is here even when I know it is true.

I touch his mind lightly. *Kai? Is it really you?*

He doesn't pull away from this form of contact, not like he usually would. *Shay!* he answers inside, my name a plea, a caress. *I'm coming for you!*

He glances at the sky, and I see through his eyes. The plane is flying low on the horizon, getting closer, and I can feel the deadly threat inside of it. This is why Beatriz was telling me to get out of the house. I knew the way she shouted that she was scared for me, but it was remote—I'd felt so numb after what happened to Spike, and the soldiers I killed.

My fault.

Not again: don't let me be the cause of any more death.

Fear flashes through me—for Kai—and now I can move. *Kai, turn around! Run for the woods! I'm coming!*

I scoop Chamberlain up into my arms and run. Callie—Jenna?—is close by my side.

Down the stairs. Across the hall. To the door.

I rip it open and see two things at once:

Kai is still running this way, not back to the woods.

The plane is nearly overhead.

There's a whistling noise in my ears, and I look up. Something is falling from the sky.

I was too slow. Too late.

I stand still; strangely calm, because there is nothing I can do, except hope that Kai is far enough away to survive. Fractions of seconds hang apart, like counting beads on a string, but no matter how much time seems to slow, there is still not enough of it to save me.

Callie—*Jenna*—embraces me and Chamberlain and flows all around—she is dark, cool, soothing.

Below us in the garden, maybe a hundred yards away, Kai's steps have stalled now too—*horror, fear, pain* wash through his aura in a kaleidoscope of sound and color.

And love.

I'm sorry, I project to Kai, and I am.

CHAPTER 19

KAI

SHAY'S MIND IS IN MINE, her heart open to me and mine to her. Then abruptly she breaks the connection so I can't share this, and she pushes me away.

Intense light fills my eyes.

Sound blasts into my skull—as if the earth is ripped apart and everything in it. I'm thrown backward, and my head hits the ground, hard.

"Shay! Shay!"

I know I'm screaming her name, but I can't hear it over the rush and roar. I scramble to turn, to see what I'm afraid to see, shielding my head with my arms as debris flies through the air.

The front of the house—where Shay stood in the door—is completely destroyed. A blaze of fire grows to consume it.

Shay!

CHAPTER 20

JENNA

IT WAS INSTINCT. I DIDN'T THINK ABOUT IT, I just *did*: threw myself at Shay as that thing was falling from the sky, forming a thin layer all around her—covering and protecting her and that huge cat in her arms.

Too thin.

Spread out like this, when the massive blast hits it burns, tears, begins to destroy me.

I scream in pain.

I could roll into a ball and get out of here, and save myself. But what about Shay?

No.

I've done so many things that are wrong.

Let this be the one right thing.

CHAPTER 21

SHAY

LIGHT.

SOUND.

Simple words aren't enough. It's like diving into the brightness of the sun with stars exploding all around us—as if we're caught in a smaller version of the big bang. A tiny part of me is detached enough to wonder what sort of bomb it is that behaves like this, while another, bigger part of me marvels that I can still wonder anything at all.

Callie? I mean, Jenna?

She doesn't answer. She's covering me, all over, every inch of me—and Chamberlain too.

But she's *screaming* in pain, horrible pain.

I have to get us out of here.

CHAPTER 22

KAI

THERE ARE PEOPLE RUNNING TOWARD ME. Freja, Alex, that young girl—the one who told me where Shay had gone.

Freja reaches me first, pulls me to my feet. She's saying something, but I can't hear her; she's trying to pull me away, back from the burning house.

There's a roar in the air. The plane that did this has circled and is coming back again.

The girl stands and stares at it in the sky.

The plane abruptly twists and plummets toward the earth on the other side of the house. Did she do *that*?

Where it hits, another explosion rivals the first.

The one that landed on Shay.

I shield my eyes, look up at the destruction.

Flames are growing, and I imagine Shay is standing there in their midst, swaying on her feet, walking toward us.

But then I hear the gasps of Freja and the others.

Something—someone?—*is* moving. A girl on fire walks through the inferno; she is a dark core enveloped in overwhelming brightness.

It is Shay, it must be, but not Shay too: a girl, but something much more at the same time. Girl and goddess? The light and waves of power that should have destroyed her are absorbed, blocked. A dark shimmer inside the light surrounds her, and then—for a fraction of a second only—it seems to have movement and life of its own, one that something inside me recognizes and answers to.

But then the dark shimmer lightens and starts to disintegrate.

CHAPTER 23

JENNA

I'M SORRY, SHAY. I TRIED. *I tried as hard as I could.*

Pain . . .

Burning . . .

Tearing . . .

Peace.

CHAPTER 24

SHAY

CALLIE/JENNA WAS HOLDING ME in a cool knot, but the knot is unraveling . . .

Undoing . . .

I run from the flames behind us.

Callie? Callie? Then, *Jenna?* I call her name again and again, but she doesn't answer.

She saved me, but she's not here.

She's not anywhere.

Somehow what happened has destroyed her; she knew it would, but she stayed with me anyway.

And now she's gone.

I want to fall to the ground, to rage, to scream—to grieve yet another loss—but then I look up and Kai is still there. Some part of me registers I have to move, to get away from heat still too intense and close behind me, and somehow I take a step, and another, and another, my eyes fixed on Kai, and my steps get faster until I'm running.

I stop when I get close: something is wrong. I see now that Beatriz and Elena are here too. A tall girl with bright hair is next to them—one I don't know. And the four of them are staring at me, a mixture of wonder and fear on their faces. Chamberlain squirms in my arms and I bend to put him down.

Alex stands off to the side. Could he *really* be Dr. 1, like Callie—Jenna—said?

I'll deal with him later.

I focus on Kai. His face is white, and there's a trickle of blood on the side of his head—has he been hurt, was he too close to that explosion?

I step toward Kai; he steps toward me. He is hesitant; there is confusion and fear in his eyes, and it tears into me inside to see it.

"Shay? Is it really you?" he whispers.

He reaches out his hands—they're shaking. I hold out mine and he takes them, slowly, carefully, like he's not sure what they are, but they're still my flesh and blood, and the touch seems to reassure him.

Or are they? Is this really happening? Maybe I died and I'm dreaming. If I did and death holds dreams of Kai, it's not such a bad thing.

Then all at once he pulls me to him. His arms wrap around me and hold me so tight that the feel of his body makes this finally real, makes *him* real.

I didn't die; I'm not dreaming: Kai is really here.

He's completely freaked out by what he saw, hurt, but he's holding me like he'll never let go. His aura may be confusion and fear, but it is also wonder, joy, and love.

CHAPTER 25

KAI

SHAY'S ALIVE. I DON'T UNDERSTAND HOW, but she's alive. I pull away from her a little to look at her again, to make sure it's truly her, living and breathing and all in one piece. And she's not the girl-goddess I saw before, enveloped in flame. It is only Shay, but I know she is so much more. Can I ever see her as I did before, without always knowing this? I can't *unsee* what just happened. She is bewildered, sad; scared too—of me?—no, that isn't it, not exactly. Emotions flit across her face so fast I can't follow.

But then I notice something else: there's dried blood on her arms, her neck, in her hair, and I'm running my hands over her, trying to find where she's hurt, but there are just some scratches, not enough for so much blood.

She shakes her head. "It's not mine," she says, and I know what she said, but I still can't hear the words out loud—my ears aren't right. From the blast? Then tears are spilling out of her eyes, and I draw her close again.

How did Shay survive? A bomb exploded where she stood; she was enveloped in fire. I saw her step through it and thought I was dreaming, imagining—and here she is.

Her mind touches mine lightly, and I don't pull away. I can feel she is doing what I did to her—checking to see if I'm hurt—but instead of running hands over my body, she's feeling inside me. And then all at once there's a warm rush on my head where I hit it when I fell, and in my ears; then the rustling, whistling noise is gone, and I can hear again.

Others are walking closer now too—the small girl who told me where Shay was is touching her as if she needed to do that as much as I did to know Shay is still alive.

Freja is here also, eyes wide. "Where's Callie?" she says.

Shay looks up from my chest and shakes her head. "She saved me," she whispers. "She saved me, and now she's gone."

Shay is crying again, not making sense, saying things I don't understand about Callie not being Callie. How can she be gone? And she's asking about the other men, the ones who were fighting the soldiers.

"They came with Alex," the girl says. "He brought them to save us. He wasn't here before because he went to get them."

Speaking of the devil, Alex comes up to us now. As he steps closer, Shay pulls away from me a little, straightens and meets his eye.

"How did you survive that blast?" Alex says. "There was something around you, shielding you. What was it?"

"It was Callie. She saved me. Or should I say . . . Jenna?"

"Ah. I wondered if she'd tell you," Alex says, and I'm looking between them, confused. Who's Jenna?

"Where is she now?" Alex asks.

"Nowhere," Shay says, and almost chokes on the word. "She saved me, and she's gone. The blast destroyed her."

And now that she's said it again and the words are taking shape inside me, I start to believe them. *Callie.* My sister. Is she really gone this time?

"Interesting," Alex says.

Interesting? My hands are fists and I would launch myself at him, flatten him, but for Shay's soft touch on my mind—asking me not to, not now, and I can't refuse her anything after what she's been through. Even that.

"Where were you when the soldiers came, Alex?" Shay says.

"A miscalculation. I knew we were at risk; I was arranging a safer place to move all of us. SAR got here much sooner than I thought they could."

"Someone was blocking us, and Spike died. Do you know anything about that?"

"SAR had a survivor working for them; he's dead now."

Shay stares back at Alex, then finally nods. "We've got some things to talk about."

"Yes. We have. But for now, I suggest we get as far away from here as we can. Some of the soldiers from SAR escaped, including Kirkland-Smith. More soldiers or another bomber may soon follow. We're parked about half a dozen miles from here; we need to get there as fast as we can and put some distance between us and this place."

There is something going on here, something more between Shay and Alex that is unsaid—or said silently—that I don't understand.

But Shay nods. "Yes. Let's go. But I'm not going anywhere until"—she swallows—"we take care of Spike." And there is such pain on her face as she says it that even as part of me reaches to hold her, to comfort her, another part demands to know—Spike? Who is Spike?

My friend, she whispers inside me. *He was my friend.*

CHAPTER 26

SHAY

WITH SO MANY HANDS TO HELP DIG SPIKE'S GRAVE, from this crowd of about twenty still living that Alex has brought along to save us, it doesn't take long. I ask Alex, what about the other bodies? Their own dead and the soldiers? But he says there's no time, and that their group—whoever they are—doesn't believe any part of the person remains once the spirit has left. They're just doing this one grave for me.

They place Spike's body inside. His face, untouched, seems strangely peaceful now; it's his back and chest that are a mess of blood.

I stand there, Beatriz and Elena by my side. Heads bowed. A minute of silence; that is all Alex said we could have.

Spike would still be alive if it weren't for me. If I hadn't got all squeamish about attacking those two soldiers, many more of them would be too; we could have gotten away before this battle was even needed.

It's my fault. All of this; my fault.

The first handful of dirt is mine. Shovelfuls follow, and soon Spike is gone from my eyes forever. Gone to the earth.

Then we run.

The sheer speed and physical need to fill my lungs and throw one foot down on the ground after another, again and again, numb the pain, but can never erase it.

CHAPTER 27

KAI

FREJA'S MIND TOUCHES MINE lightly as we run.

What the hell is going on? she says.

I've got no idea.

Could Shay be right—has Callie been destroyed?

She was already dead, already a ghost. How can you destroy a ghost?

But if she wasn't destroyed like Shay said . . . then where is she?

To that I have no answer.

I'm shaking inside, like I've lost Callie all over again. Right at the end, as Shay stood in the fire, I thought I could see something around her: was that my sister?

Shay said something crazy about Callie being somebody else, a girl named Jenna who pretended to be Callie. But I don't believe it. Callie always had the craziest imagination, and she often pretended to be her imaginary friends or characters in stories when she was little. Maybe everything that has happened to her pushed her back to that time.

But does that mean . . . that Callie is really gone? She saved Shay, and now she's gone? I choke on the pain, one I can't face; not now.

I watch Shay run at my side. All this seems unreal, impossible—but nothing would have sounded real or possible about how Shay survived if I hadn't seen it with my own eyes.

I never got to say goodbye to Callie—again. The pain of that is an agony, but it rests easier than it did before. Maybe now, after everything Callie's been through, she's finally at peace.

We run on. Everyone seemed to accept without comment that we should do as Alex said; for now at least. Given dead soldiers and potential bombers and the fact that Kirkland-Smith and some others got away, getting as far from there as fast and with as many people who can fight as possible seemed sensible.

Yet . . . this is Alex. Not somebody I want to follow anywhere.

Why? Freja says, reading my thought. *Tell me some more about this guy.*

You know he was my stepfather—Callie's dad. In so many ways, I hated him. I give her a quick summary—his manipulations, the way he treated us, my suspicion he was involved in Callie's disappearance. Though that seems less likely now: even *he* wouldn't have given his daughter over to be experimented on in Shetland, would he?

And he saved Shay from the trap, and again today; this I also know.

Do you think he can be trusted? Freja asks.

I give the mental equivalent of a snort. *I never will. But I will give him a teeny, tiny benefit of the doubt, just for now—for the first time ever. To really know, though, we need to know more about what is going on here. Who are these people with Alex? He said he brought them to rescue everyone, but from where?*

They haven't said much so far, but then there hasn't been much time for chitchat. Yet there is something about them that seems slightly . . . odd. It's hard to focus on just what that may be.

They do what Alex says without question. They seem to have been good at killing people—they won against the soldiers—but at the same time don't seem the type. I mean, they don't look like my idea of mercenaries, or soldiers, or anything like that; they don't look as though they'd get off on violence for its own sake. In another context I'd think they were Alex's professor friends at the university. But with more muscles and guns.

Has Shay told you what's been going on?

I glance at Shay again, still running by my other side. She seems remote, closed off. What has she been through?

Today—the bomb—she and that cat walked out of an inferno. The cat that I now realize one of Alex's followers is bringing along. It's being held tightly and looks really pissed off about it.

And Shay? Pale, slight—physically she doesn't look strong enough to keep up this pace much longer, yet I know she has reserves—and abilities—I can't begin to understand.

What has she become?

Ask her, Freja says, and I'm startled when I realize that she'd been listening to my thoughts still, that I'd forgotten to block them off. I do so now.

Shay? I try to project to her silently. She glances up at me, eyes wide, and her pace falters for a second, then rights itself.

Kai. She says my name inside, the touch of her mind that is her and only her, the same way that her hand in mine, her lips on mine, are her and only her.

Tell me. Tell me everything.

CHAPTER 28

SHAY

I DON'T KNOW WHERE TO START or what to say. So much has happened that it feels like a million years since Kai and I have been together—I feel remote, changed; and also completely drained and charged up, both at the same time. And now I'm remembering how freaked Kai had been when I killed that soldier who was going to shoot us in Killin. What would he think of what I've done to more—so many more—today?

He'd be repelled, repulsed. I am.

Then Alex projects: *We're nearly there.* I tell Kai, a way to delay answering him.

A moment later we've reached a barn. Inside it are a dozen cars, different makes and models.

Alex is directing us to one of them.

"Where are we going?" Kai asks.

"Do you want to stay and wait for the army?" Alex says. "I'm sure they're on the way."

"It's a reasonable question," I say to Alex. "Where are you taking us?"

"I can give you the coordinates, if you like: it's a remote airfield of ours in the Borders. A stepping-stone to our ultimate destination, but I won't tell you about that just yet. Let's get away from here to the airfield, then we'll talk. You can leave then, if you want to—I'll even give you a car or take you where you want to go. But for now let's just get out of here."

I'm expecting Kai to protest, to argue against going with Alex, so I'm surprised when he nods.

Kai and I get in the back of one of the cars as Alex directs, and Kai waves Freja over to sit in the front, but she shakes her head. She gets in another car with Alex instead.

The back door opens again, and Chamberlain is deposited on my knee by one of Alex's crowd; his hands are covered in scratches.

Meow, meow, meeeeeeeow . . . ! He's indignant, fur ruffled.

The man who put him in the back gets into the driver's seat in front of me, and Chamberlain hisses.

"Some cats just don't know how lucky they are to be rescued. I'm Aristotle," the man says, and starts the car.

"Hi. I'm Shay, this is Kai, and the lucky cat is Chamberlain. Thank you for bringing him." I'd refused to leave without him, but he's a big cat. I could never have kept up that pace if I'd been carrying him.

"No worries."

"How far is it to this airfield?" Kai asks.

"Over a hundred miles; it'll take hours on these minor roads. Get some sleep if you can."

"Then where do we fly to?" Kai says.

"You'll have to ask Xander."

"Xander?" I say.

"You know, the tall, silver-haired guy who orders us around." He grins, and I'm unsettled. They've just done some sort of SWAT team rescue where some of them have died—and a whole lot of the other side—and he seems completely unfazed by the whole thing.

And they know Alex—who is Alexander, I remember now—as *Xander*?

And Callie—I mean, Jenna—knew him as Dr. 1. Alex—Xander—Dr. 1: is he all three?

"Who is this *us*, exactly, that he orders around?" Kai says.

"You'll have to ask Xander."

Kai and I exchange a glance. I try a few more variations on our questions, even using some gentle mental persuasion, but get nowhere.

And I wonder: am I questioning Aristotle to avoid answering what Kai asked me earlier?

Tell me everything, he said. Not an unreasonable demand in the circumstances. And there are so many things I want—*need*—to know too: everywhere he has been, what has happened with him, how he found us. And who is this Freja? I sensed a closeness between them.

But it's all just too much—*way* too much—after everything else that has happened in this day that is now night.

I sigh, settle back against the seat, eyes closed. Chamberlain is crashed out now, half on my lap and half on the seat by the door, and his rumbling purr is reminding me how tired I am too.

Kai?

Yes?

There's a lot to talk about, I know there is, but I just can't right now. Can we just be, as we are? You and me. Together.

His arm slips around my shoulder a moment later. His hand strokes my hair, and my thoughts are jumping even though my exhaustion is complete—distressing visions and flashes of the day flit through my mind in random order until finally I slip into an uneasy sleep.

When I wake with a start, it's pouring, and there is a crash of thunder—it was probably the storm that woke me. We're still driving in the dark, still playing follow-the-leader with other cars that I can barely see through the driving rain.

It looks like Chamberlain has forgiven Aristotle; he's asleep on the front passenger seat now. Or maybe he just wanted space to stretch out.

The more I wake up, the more the pain from yesterday comes

back, throwing up images and emotions too strong to handle, one after another.

Spike saved me. Callie—*Jenna*—did too. Who was she? It's too late to ask her now. They're both gone. And Spike and his steady friendship meant more to me than I even realized; his loss has left me twisted up in knots of pain.

And although Kai is next to me, here, right now, where I've longed for him to be for so long, I can't believe it.

What is real, what isn't?

Callie isn't—wasn't—*Callie:* she wasn't Kai's sister. She was someone named Jenna, she said. She knew she was the one spreading the epidemic.

And she said that Alex—my *father*—is Dr. 1: the person behind everything on Shetland and Jenna's death too; the first time, when she was "cured" in fire.

Can this be true? I know Mum and Kai never trusted him. I know he hides things sometimes. But can this person that I know—one who saved my life, several times, and the lives of others—really be capable of such a thing?

My blood quickens when an implication hits me that hadn't really sunk in before: what about the real Callie? Where is Kai's sister? If Jenna took her identity, she must have known her—was the real Callie experimented on at Shetland too? By her own father?

But in the midst of all these questions that have no answers, there is one thing that must be real, and true, and now. I lean across and gently kiss Kai.

He stirs. Sleepy eyes open and hold mine.

There is much to say, but there is one way to say the most important thing of all—the best way.

I kiss him again and again, hoping Aristotle's eyes are firmly on the road ahead.

There is just Kai and me and now.

CHAPTER 29

KAI

THERE'S A THROAT-CLEARING SOUND in front of us and we spring apart.

"We'll be there soon," Aristotle says.

Shay's cheeks are flushed. I stare at her, drink her in, wonder that she is here, alive and warm at my side. I take her hand.

With all that has happened, all that I can't unsee and the things I need to know, how it feels to kiss her and then to hold her hand like I am, right at this moment, are the truths that matter the most. Yet there is one thing I must say *now*, before being close to her makes me forget it.

We need to talk, I say.

Yes, she says, but instead she kisses me again.

I kiss her back quickly, and then firmly hold her away. *That's not how you talk.*

It's one way. She smiles, and her eyes are on me like there is nothing else in the world to see.

You have to stop looking at me like that and just listen. This is serious.

Okay.

I was really angry with you when you left me at Shetland. I trusted you, and you put me to sleep, and when I woke up you were gone.

But do you understand why I did it?

I know you thought you were doing the right thing. But survivors aren't carriers—you were wrong.

I know that now. But at the time I thought I was a carrier; that it was my fault many people had died. I may have been wrong, but I truly thought I was spreading the disease—that I had to turn myself in. What good would it have done for both of us to have gone?

I don't want to argue with you about something that has already happened. But there is something you have to promise me.

What's that?

That you will never, ever disappear on me like that again—with no goodbye, no chance to discuss things. If you think you have to leave, you have to tell me to my face and explain why: there can be no more secrets between us.

You're right. I'm sorry. And I promise—no more secrets. And I won't pull a disappearing act again either. Tears are slipping out of her eyes and I want to kiss them from her face, but when I try to pull her close she holds her hands against me. *There are things I have to tell you too.*

Go on.

I tried to tell you before, but with everything that was happening after the bomb I'm not sure you took it in. It wasn't Callie who saved me from the blast. It wasn't her that was destroyed. The one we knew as Callie was never actually her from the beginning. It was a girl named Jenna. She took on Callie's identity.

I frown. *That's not possible. She knew all that stuff about me and home—stuff only Callie could know. And there's stuff I haven't told you about her that may explain this.*

What's that?

She had imaginary friends when she was younger and sometimes pretended to be one of them. I think with everything she's been through that she must have regressed back to that.

And Shay is thinking, considering what I said; but then she shakes her head. *I was completely joined with her, and I'm certain: it wasn't Callie. But there's more I have to tell you. She was the carrier.*

What? Are you serious?

Yes. I thought it was me, but she was there with us all along. And she was also in Shetland and Aberdeen. I worked it out a while ago, and she confirmed it; she admitted that she knew.

I stare back at Shay. All of this is too much—way too much—to take in.

To believe.

But the car is starting to slow, we must be nearly there, and there is something else I have to tell her that can't wait. I push all that aside to work out later.

Listen, there is one more thing I have to tell you: I'm sorry.

What for?

This—how we are talking together now, with your mind touching mine—I'm sorry I resisted it for so long. But now I understand why it upset me so much. It was because of Alex.

She half frowns, puzzlement in her thoughts. *Alex? I don't understand. What do you mean?*

I'm sure I told you how manipulative he was with us, but I didn't understand how or why, and why he always made me so angry. It's because he was like you—could do the things you can do, but didn't ask permission. He'd just dive into my head and tell me what to do, and back then I couldn't do anything but obey. I hated him.

She shakes her head. *Are you saying he was a survivor—years ago?*

Yes. Since I first knew him—before he married my mother, before Callie was born.

And it is clear and loud in her thoughts: she doesn't believe me.

It's not possible, Kai. Until it escaped from Shetland—just a few months ago—this disease didn't exist outside of a lab. You know that.

I know what I know: he was one of you, and he has been for years.

Kai, you're wrong. Maybe he was just really good at the usual psychological sort of manipulation?

Just because I'm not one of you doesn't mean I can't recognize the games you can play in people's minds. I know what I know. And between this and all the unbelievable things Shay has told me and expects me to accept without question, now I'm angry and getting angrier.

I push her out of my mind.

CHAPTER 30

SHAY

***KAI? KAI!* I TRY AGAIN,** but he's still ignoring me.

I fight back tears and peer out of the window. The last part of that conversation would have gone better out loud: when Kai is in my mind it's impossible to be tactful—he knew I didn't believe him.

Just like I knew he didn't believe me about Jenna.

But Kai *must* be mistaken. What he said is completely crazy. Isn't it? I frown, thinking. Even if Alex infected himself in his lab in Shetland and survived, it couldn't have been that many years ago. The technology used was developed at CERN; it didn't exist back then.

The car stops. It's still dark and hard to see anything in this heavy rain, but it looks like we're here.

Wherever *here* is.

Aristotle is gathering up Chamberlain, who is back to hissing.

"It's a short dash to the hangar, follow me!" he says, and opens his door and bolts.

I hurry after him, glad of the cold shock of the rain pelting down. I sense that Kai hesitates, then follows behind us.

We step through an open door just yards away, but I'm already soaked. The door catches in the wind and bangs loudly on the metal wall until somebody grabs hold of it again. Alex and Freja and some of the others are here already, and more come in behind us.

"This weather is bad news," Alex says. "We won't be able to take off until the wind dies down. But at least they won't be sending anyone after us by air either." He looks over at Kai, then at me. "Now it's time for us to talk."

He gestures us, Freja, Elena, and Beatriz to chairs and a table along a wall, kind of an open office. Alex is asking for tea and sandwiches to be brought. We're walking across to the chairs as a group, and I'm panicking inside.

This isn't the way to do this; I need to talk to Kai alone first. I try to hail him silently, but still he resists.

"Kai," I say, out loud now, voice low. "There are things we need to talk about, that I haven't had a chance to tell you." I hear the lie myself: isn't it more that I haven't been able to make myself? "I'm sorry."

Alex has reached us now. "Come; sit. We've got things to discuss."

CHAPTER 31

KAI

FREJA AND THE OTHER TWO SURVIVORS—Elena and Beatriz—sit down where Alex said.

"I'd rather stand," I say.

"As you will," Alex says.

Shay stays upright next to me, that cat by her feet. There are things she hasn't had a chance to tell me, she says; what more could there be?

"Alex—or should I say *Xander*?" Shay says. "Who are these people with you?"

"We are members of a group called Multiverse. I'm the leader."

Multiverse? I glance at Shay and can see the name means something to her.

"That's a commune, right?" Shay says. "With chapters all over the world? Something to do with worshipping truth."

His eyes are surprised. "Very good, and mostly true—not so much the worshipping part, but we are dedicated to the pursuit of true knowledge."

"Is that what you were doing on Shetland—pursuing knowledge?"

I frown. On Shetland? They were on Shetland?

"The girl we knew as Callie—though that isn't who she was really, is it, Alex?—she told me that you were the one behind it all. That you're Dr. 1: that it was you who created antimatter in an underground Shetland lab and caused the epidemic."

The others are exchanging glances, waves of shock across their faces. Did she *really* just say that *Alex* is Dr. 1?

No matter how I've always despised him, I'm still struggling with *this*—could he be the one who is responsible for so much death and misery? My sister's father, a man we lived with, who was married to my mother all those years?

And then I realize: he's not denying anything.

I'd always been sure he must have been involved in Callie's disappearance; just when I finally decided to give him the benefit of the doubt, now this?

Then I'm moving, flying to Alex, to *hurt* him like he hurt Callie. As if they were expecting this, some of this Multiverse crowd have leaped to grab me, hold me back, and there are three of them and it is all they can do to stop me.

Alex shakes his head. "Kai, you've always been so quick to judge without having all the facts."

"The facts?" Shay says. "How about these ones: you experimented on people, killed them; you unleashed an epidemic that has killed millions, and will likely kill many more."

"We had no way of knowing that would happen and regret it very much," Alex says. But does *sorry* mean anything when these are the consequences?

"Were you working with SAR? Developing a weapon?" Shay says.

"We had our own agenda, but yes: they thought we were working for them, at any rate. Now they're trying to bury their role in what happened by burying all of us."

"What was your agenda?"

"We were attempting to cure cancer—another killer of millions. Every single one of the subjects at Shetland had terminal cancer and had volunteered to take part. And it *worked*. We were so close to success when that accident happened."

"Callie was just a child!" I say. "Your child. She didn't have cancer. How could you?" I'm struggling against the arms that hold me but can't get away from them.

"That ghost girl you knew wasn't your sister, Kai. Hasn't Shay explained it all to you? She was a cancer patient; consent was given by her family. She was our success—when she survived the antimatter injections, her cancer was completely gone."

"Stop lying; you know who she was. And you 'cured' her in fire! She was burned alive—*you* did that."

He frowns. "What has she told you?" He shakes his head. "Sadly, she was mentally ill—likely a result of secondary brain cancer that she had before the treatment. She didn't even know who she was at the end. She died in the fires from the accident with the particle accelerator, the one that destroyed the facility and much of the island."

"I don't believe you. She *was* Callie; I know my own sister. She knew things only Callie could know."

Alex shakes his head. "As usual, Kai, you refuse to see the truth. Enough of this pointless discussion; time is short." His eyes lock on Shay, then on Freja, Beatriz, and Elena, in turn. "Join us. Join Multiverse. Together—as survivors—we have what it takes to find the answers that will save our planet."

They're *not* actually buying into what he is saying?

I struggle again. "Let me go!"

"In a moment. Listen to me, Kai. You've been having problems, ah, *adjusting* to Shay's abilities. You're looking for a reason for your unreasonable reactions to her, and you'd like to blame me—another one with the same abilities."

"*What?*"

"It's not my fault you can't handle Shay being different from you—being superior to you. It's not her fault either."

He's using that mild, reasonable tone—everything he says sounds so right when he says it, but I know he's just trying to mess around in my mind in another way now.

All I want to do is get away from him, from Shay; from all of *them.*

Alex nods and they release me. I head for the door. I'm getting the hell out of here.

CHAPTER 32

SHAY

I'M LOCKED IN XANDER'S GAZE: he is Xander now. Alex is someone I used to know, before all these other things about him came to light. Somehow it helps me to segment the two halves of him with his name.

Is he telling the truth?

With an effort of will, I pull my eyes away from his. *Kai: I haven't lost you; I can't.* But Freja has already gone after him; the door shuts with a clang behind them.

"I'm sorry," Alex says. And he truly is, of this I'm sure. "I know how much it hurts to be different. I know how much it hurts to lose somebody because of it." There are echoes of his own pain inside him and there is also something that tells me *who* he means—who he lost. I should run after Kai too, but I can't leave this alone.

"Who was it that you lost? Tell me about her."

He tilts his head to one side, considering my request—curious why I ask?—then nods to himself and answers. "She had long wavy dark hair; that glorious Scottish accent. Much younger than me." He looks at me again and half frowns. Can he read the signs, see them in my face, my hair? "She lived with her aunt near my house in Killin—correction, the house that my ex, Kai's mother, now owns."

"You're from Killin, aren't you, Shay?" Elena says.

And I almost see the moment it happens, when the blocks spin into place in Xander's mind: Killin. Mum. Me. And would he ever have made this leap if I hadn't asked him about her? Perhaps, perhaps not, yet I did it anyway. Despite my resolution to never tell him, maybe there is something inside me that needed him to know.

There is genuine shock in his eyes. "I could always tell there was something you were hiding when you considered me, but I couldn't work out what it could possibly be. You're Moyra's daughter? And . . . mine?"

Elena and Beatriz look between us, confused; realization coming slower.

"One day Moyra left me. She just up and disappeared, and it broke my heart. But I didn't know about you. I would have searched for her if I did."

"I know. She told me you never knew." She also told me she left him because he had a *wrongness* inside: what did she sense all that time ago? Then it hits me, and I'm filled with shock that I'm careful to hide from my face and my aura. Kai was right, wasn't he? Xander was a survivor even back then. How is that even *possible*? I don't know, but from what Mum said, what she showed me in her thoughts and memories before she died, I'm both certain that it's true and surprised I didn't realize it before.

I should have believed Kai when he told me, and I ache with knowing it too late.

"Did you always know I was your father, even that first time we met in Edinburgh?" Xander asks.

"No, not then. Mum told me just before she died."

"Ah, Moyra," he says, and there is real pain on his face, through his aura, to know she has died—even after so long. "But why didn't you tell me I'm your father before now?" he says.

Lots of reasons: Mum. Kai. Callie. The death of millions. But I don't get a chance to say any of it.

CHAPTER 33

KAI

A VOICE CALLS through the pounding rain behind me, and something lifts inside—is it Shay, has she followed me?

But it's Freja.

I keep walking through the trees, already soaked to the skin. The sky is just starting to lighten behind the clouds, some watered-down version of dawn that gives almost enough light to see the path at my feet.

She catches up. "Where are you going?"

"I don't know."

"That ex-stepfather of yours is a piece of work, isn't he?"

"Huh."

"Don't let him play you."

"What?"

"He deliberately made you angry so you'd leave, can't you see that? You're doing exactly what he wants you to do."

"But she believes him. Shay believes him!" And the fury and pain surge through me again.

"Does she? It looked to me like she was challenging him all the way, finding out what she could, but she never once said, 'Yes, Alex, you're right,' did she?"

"Maybe not, but why the hell didn't she tell me before that he was the one behind Shetland? It's kind of big. It didn't just slip her mind."

"Honestly, Kai, cut the girl some slack. She survived having a bomb dropped on her head yesterday. She might have made it look easy, but I'm guessing it wasn't. And two of her friends—Spike and Callie, or whoever she really was—died in front of her. She's been in shock."

I stop and turn to Freja. She's momentarily lit up by a flash of lightning—she's soaked now too, her short hair, half red and half blonde at the roots, is plastered to her skin. She's shivering and telling me what's what—stuff I should have been able to work out for myself.

I thunk my head with my hand. "Bloody hell. You're right."

"Of course I am."

"You're a good friend," I say. I almost go to hug her, but then my arms fall back, not sure if I should.

But if she notices that, she ignores it. She grins. "Yes. Yes, I am."

"Do I go back now with my tail between my legs to beg forgiveness from Shay and to try to take another swing at Alex?"

"Sounds like a plan. Come on."

She links her arm in mine, and we take a step in the right direction: toward Shay.

But then there is light—

Sound—

A massive blast fills the night.

We dive into the trees.

CHAPTER 34

SHAY

SOUND FILLS THE NIGHT, and it takes me back to the house, to the bomb, to Callie/Jenna, and I curl up in terror. It is a moment before I come back to myself enough to realize it isn't here—it's somewhere in the distance.

Elena's hand is on my shoulder, and she helps me to my feet.

Now Xander is in the center of a group of Multiverse, and everyone is talking at once. Their words start to penetrate:

"We have to get out of here *now*."

"Can we take off in this weather?"

"Without lights?"

"We can if we have to."

Then they are rushing, running, doing things to the small plane in the hangar.

Finally I manage to get Xander's attention. "What's happened?"

"We set an explosive device on the access road the way we came," Xander says. "It's been tripped. A remote camera confirms that it's

SAR. Somehow they've followed us; they're coming. That'll only slow them down."

"But where is Kai? Is he all right?"

"Kai and Freja are being watched by one of us. They're fine. They're on their way back here now."

The big hangar doors are opened, and we're pelted with wind and rain. The darkness isn't complete anymore; dawn is coming, but it is limp and weak.

Xander turns to me. "Decide *now*. Join us. Together, we can change the world."

I'm staring back at him. He's deluded to think I would want to change the world the way he does, or that I'd want anything to do with him after all that he's done, just because of an accident of parentage. But I hide my feelings down deep.

What about your other daughter? I ask him, silently. *Where is the real Callie?*

There is hesitation, uncertainty, in Xander's aura—something not often seen there. Finally he shakes his head. *We have to build trust between us for me to answer you. Come with us and find out.*

I have to go with him. Don't I? I'll never find Xander again if he doesn't want me to, and he's the only one who knows where Callie is. And Kai didn't believe me about Callie and Jenna. The only way I can show him the truth is to find her.

Alex holds out a hand and though I'd rather strike out, I reach out and take it. In the midst of the chaos around us, he smiles. Then he reaches into a pocket, and a necklace dangles from his fingers.

It's gold, with a model of an atom hanging from it: just like the one the real Callie was wearing when I saw her in the woods—the day she disappeared.

"Allow me?" he says, and I lean forward while he does up the catch. An atom slips cool against my skin.

CHAPTER 35

KAI

"CAN YOU SEE WHAT'S HAPPENING?" I say.

Freja unfocuses and is silent a moment, then comes back. "It's the road. There's been a blast a few miles from here, the way we came. I think it's SAR. They're pulling bits of trees and other debris out of the way and will be heading this way soon."

We run back through the trees to the hangar just as everyone is scrambling onto the small plane. Shay is almost up to the steps; she turns and sees us.

Alex is next to her, a hand on her shoulder.

"Ah, there you are, Kai," Alex says. "Are you coming with us? If not, you're just in time to say goodbye."

"Let her go!"

"My *daughter* is free to come or go as she chooses. She has decided to come with us."

"Your *what*?" I'm sure this is some trick of Alex's, but then I look at Shay, wait for her to tell me it's a lie, but she says nothing.

Her expressive face is all dismay, guilt.

"Shay? Is this true? Is he really your father?"

She shrugs helplessly. "Yes. He is."

"Is this something he's told you? Don't believe him."

But she's shaking her head. "No. Mum told me."

"*What?*" I stare at her in shock.

"She told me just before she died."

"You've known all this time, and you didn't tell me?"

She doesn't answer—what can she say? *No more secrets*—we agreed. Okay, there may have been some things she didn't have the chance to tell me, but she's known Alex was her father since her mother died. All that time we were alone together, traveling to Shetland, and there too. There were plenty of chances.

And that's not all. She stands there, about to leave with him, after she promised to never pull a disappearing act again.

This can't be true.

It *can't*.

But I see it there, in her eyes—confirmation. Eyes that are pleading for forgiveness; her mind reaches for mine, but I push her away.

"Are you going of your free will?" I say.

"Yes," she says. "I'm sorry." But along with regret her eyes are saying something *else*.

She tries again to reach me inside, and again I push her away. What is there to say when she's already decided to leave? With *Alex*. Her father.

"Then go," I say.

I turn my back to her and walk away.

CHAPTER 36

SHAY

KAI WON'T LET ME IN: I try again and again, even resort to attempting to force myself into his mind, but somehow he blocks me.

We're in the plane; Elena, Beatriz, and Chamberlain, too. We're leaving Kai and Freja behind to fend for themselves. Xander says they'll be fine, that they've got enough time to get away in the car he gave them—that SAR will assume all of us left on the plane. That they're racing away in the other direction from the airstrip even now. But I'm still scared for them.

I climb into a seat, feeling like the world has gone wrong, as if gravity has reversed. I'm in slow motion—stuck in thick syrup—each step a crime against nature, a betrayal. Each step is in the wrong direction: away from Kai.

Kai? I try again, unable to stop myself. They shouldn't be out of range yet, but still there is no answer.

Freja is with him. Can I reach her?

Freja?

Her mind is like ice.

Please listen to me.

Why should I? Do you have any idea how much you've hurt Kai?

I fight the tears that threaten. *You don't understand. I'm just pretending to join Xander and Multiverse. I'm going undercover to find Callie. Please tell Kai! I can't—he's blocking me. Tell him to come after me and his sister.*

Freja is uncertain. *Are you sure it wasn't Callie who was with us all along?*

Yes. It wasn't her; it was another girl, Jenna, who'd taken on Callie's identity. We were linked before she was destroyed: I know she told the truth.

And do you truly believe that the real Callie is still alive somewhere?

Yes. And that this is the only way to find her. Tell Kai. Please.

Freja is thinking, considering, keeping her thoughts locked away. Finally she comes back.

Okay. I hope you find her. Take care.

CHAPTER 37

KAI

I CAN'T STOP MYSELF. I slow down and look back just in time to watch the small plane disappear on the horizon.

I can't get my head around this. Alex is Shay's father? How could she have kept that from me for so long?

How could she leave with him?

After everything we were to each other. After everything I did to find her.

The pain is giving way to anger—anger is better. Anger is safer. But maybe not when I'm driving; I accelerate on the wet road more than I should and almost lose control.

"Kai? I'm so sorry." Freja is still here, forgotten, at my side, and I slow down to a safer speed.

"I don't understand how she could go with that man after all he's done," I say. "She tried to speak to me in my mind, but I blocked her. I was too angry to listen." *I should have listened.*

"I know—she told me."

"You spoke? Tell me what she said." Now there is hope inside that there is some reasonable explanation like the one Freja had for me earlier; one that will make everything all right again.

"I asked her if she knew how much she was hurting you. And . . ." Freja hesitates, and I glance at her. She's looking away from me now like she's afraid to say any more, and my hope slips away.

"Whatever it is, tell me."

"I'm sorry, Kai, but she said she needed to go to be with her father."

I grip the steering wheel so hard my hands ache and my knuckles go white. "How could she trust him? Not just because he caused the epidemic. I've told her about him; things he's done to me, my family."

"I don't know. Maybe it's because she lost her mother that she needs to try to build a relationship with her dad. No matter who he is, he is still her family."

Alex is her family. I'm not, not in any sense of the word; not anymore. She's made that clear. She's made this choice, and there is nothing I can do about it.

"That's not all," Freja says. "I know you know Alex and what he is capable of. How he somehow twists things to make everything happen the way he wants. And he sold it to her, Kai. The whole superiority complex; that survivors can change the world and make it better. That they don't belong with ordinary people. Like you."

"That just doesn't sound like Shay."

Yet how well did I really know her? She knew Alex was her father and never told me. *How* could she do that? She knows how I feel about Alex.

Maybe . . . that's why.

The anger is bleeding away, and I fight to get it back; I need it. But I still can't believe that Shay is really gone. It feels like something is missing from all of this, some reason that will make everything make sense, make the Shay I knew be the same girl who has left me now.

The same girl who has left me *again*.

But Freja is here; she hasn't left. She's only here at all because she was trying to help me find Shay, and I let her. I knew it wasn't right, but I took advantage of her feelings for me—feelings that I wasn't returning.

Even though I wanted her. Being alone with her when Shay was so far away—well, it wasn't always easy to remember that Freja was just my friend.

And here she is still, trying to help me understand what can't be understood.

She doesn't deserve how I've treated her.

"Thank you," I say, leaving *for what* unsaid. There is too much to say.

"It's okay," she says.

We drive on in silence. The sky is starting to clear, the sun peeking through.

I don't know where we're going, beyond getting as far away from SAR as we can. As to what comes next, this now goes way beyond just getting the truth out about the cause of the epidemic: I want—*need*—to tell everyone what Alex has done. Expose him to the world for what he truly is.

Beyond that I can't think past what has happened—Shay keeping secrets from me, telling me these crazy things about Callie; Shay leaving with Alex. It's like I'm standing on a line drawn by my feet, and on one side there is before this happened, and on the other is after. The two aren't connected in any way that makes sense.

Before, everything was about finding Shay. Saving her.

Loving her.

And after? What now?

There are too many questions I can't answer.

I'm here, Kai. I'll help you, Freja whispers in my mind, and her hand touches mine.

CHAPTER 38

SHAY

I GRIP THE ARMS OF THE SEAT as the plane lurches again, then drops. As if we've fallen through a trapdoor to another world, we fall and fall; my stomach drops along with my body, then slams back in place as we jerk back up again. The turbulence from the storm matches the fear and pain inside me—fear that has nothing to do with falling out of the sky.

Can I trust Freja to be in my corner? I didn't know her for long, but I know she helped Kai find me, that she's his friend. All I can do is hope that Kai listens to her, that he understands why I had to leave.

That he sees I'm doing this for him, to find his sister.

Where is Xander taking us? Will Callie be there?

I go back in my mind to the moment that brought Kai and me together—that chance sighting of Callie in the woods in Killin, in a world that has changed beyond imagining since then. Just like I have.

I see her in my memory: a living, breathing girl, walking up the steep hill in the woods. Her long dark hair; blue eyes that widened with alarm when she heard my voice, then calmed when she saw me. I wish again, *so much,* that I could travel in time; that I could stop her from walking to the road and getting into that car, never to be seen again.

I can't go back and change what happened. But I will her to be alive, and well, as she was then—as if me wanting something enough can make it happen.

I *will* make Xander trust me, and I'll never let him see what I plan to do. I *will* find Callie, and take her back to her mother and Kai.

It somehow seems right that the girl who brought Kai and me together in the first place should do it again now.

Callie, wherever you are, whatever has happened to you: hang in there. I'm coming.